Morning Noon & Night
CAN'T GET ENOUGH

Edited by

Nancey Flowers

This is a work of fiction. The author's have invented the characters. Any resemblance to actual persons, living or dead, is purely coincidental.

Morning, Noon & Night: Can't Get Enough
"Bus Route 69" copyright © 2006 by Goldie Banks
"Sweet Dreams" copyright © 2006 by William Fredrick Cooper
"More & More" copyright © 2006 by William Fredrick Cooper
"Picked Up" copyright © 2006 by E. Geoffrey Depp
"The Lesson" copyright © 2006 by Penelope Flynn
"Pulse" copyright © 2006 by Anna J.
"Raw" copyright © 2006 by Kenji Jasper
"Enough" copyright © 2006 by Natosha Gale Lewis
"Sweet Surrender" copyright © 2006 by Scottie Lowe
"Mariah's Gotta Have It" copyright © 2006 by Marissa Monteilh
"Put Ya Tongue In It" copyright © 2006 by Maryann Reid
"Know Your Role" copyright © 2006 by Jamez Williams
"Thug Bar" copyright © 2006 by Winslow Wong

Cover design by Anika Sabree
Cover Photograph: © BananaStock
Interior Design by Nancey Flowers

First Flowers in Bloom trade paperback printing 2006

For more information, send correspondence to:
Flowers in Bloom Publishing, Inc.
P.O. Box 473106
Brooklyn, New York 11247
www.flowersinbloompublishing.com

Library of Congress Cataloging-in-Publication Data
Flowers, Nancey
Morning, Noon & Night: Can't Get Enough/ Editor–Nancey Flowers, 1st ed.
Library of Congress Control Number: 2006921238

ISBN: 0-9708191-4-5
Printed in Canada

Contents

Morning
Noon & Night
CAN'T GET ENOUGH

Edited by

Nancey Flowers

Introduction

My computer crashed at my job today. The *IT Guy* that came by to fix my workstation was sexy. Before he left my office, the computer wasn't the only thing he fixed. *IT Guy* knew how to stroke every key just right and made my *Pulse* race.

When he went down to taste my snatch, I told him to *Put Ya Tongue In It,* and he slid that snake into my pussy, causing my sweet sap to dribble down his chin. My thick cum filled his mouth twice, and I couldn't get *Enough* as I moaned a *Sweet Surrender* in his ear. Then he removed his beautiful cock from his trousers, and I wanted him to do me *Raw.* I swiped the office supplies and papers to the floor and lay spread eagle across my desk and waited for him to insert his love stick into my overflowing canal. *IT Guy* had other things in mind and yanked me from my military position and flipped me doggy style. He said, *"Know Your Role"* and slapped my plump ass.

He teased me and partially entered his rod into my honey well. He ordered me to say, *"Mariah's Gotta Have It"* and made me repeat it over and over. With each pump I felt the swell of his cock. Several times he removed his dick and spanked me with it, which aroused me even more. I put one of my breasts in my mouth and placed his hand on the other. He fondled my pillowy areolas until my nipples swelled.

His movements began to increase, and I knew he was about to cum. I quickly pulled away and fell to my knees. I gently took him into my mouth and commenced to sucking him off. I licked my sweetness off his cock and circled the head with my tongue. He begged for *More and More* as I used my mouth on his tip, jerked his shaft with one hand and pressed my fingers near his asshole with the other. This oral stimulation was better known as *The Lesson,* and *IT Guy* was a quick study as he convulsed hard, sending a torrent of hot liquid into my throat.

IT Guy was a nice morning snack, but I wanted dinner, too, and decided to take *Bus Route 69* to *Thug Bar.* This joint was the place to get *Picked Up* by some of the finest men in Brooklyn, and they knew how to lay the pipe with no strings attached.

No sooner than I walked into the lounge did I spot Big G, one of my regular lovers. We made eye contact immediately, and within minutes we were heading to my place. I was definitely going to have a good night and thanks to Big G and *IT Guy,* I would rest peacefully and have *Sweet Dreams.*

Sweet Dreams

by

William Fredrick Cooper

Why the frown, baby? Dreading another cold, lonely night? No need to fret, my precious. It doesn't have to be. Open the doors to your mind tonight, and allow me to invade your dreams. Am I invited in to fulfill all your fantasies? The choice is yours.

So your answer is yes, I see. Good. If you're good at taking orders, then follow me down the corridors of passion. Here is where I will turn sensuous dreams into sexual realities. Just use your imaginative key and open the door to your delight.

I see door number one is your first choice. Let's enter into this erotic dimension:

We're in a bungalow, far from the places we're supposed to be, situated upon a mountaintop amid a wicked snowstorm. Whistling, whipping winds beat against the log cabin door, swirling the snow outside into blizzardlike conditions. A crackling fireplace extends its warmth to us, but I think it wants something in return. Adhering to its call to find our zone, we lounge unclothed on oversized pillows. The yellow-orange flame blazes its heat onto us, but it's about to get hotter.

If I ever wanted to be snowed in with someone, it would be you, my queen. You are like a goddess from Greek mythology, and I wouldn't mind showing you what I learned from our oral history lesson. Like Floetry, you "Say Yes," and I'll proceed. Slowly crawling to you with glass in hand, red wine trickles onto your nudeness as our tongues affectionately mingle by firelight. Pulling back ever so slightly to recover lost senses, my erected protrusion leaves you trembling in anticipation.

But it's not time for that treat, sweetie. Daddy's kind of famished. No food in the cabin, you say? Oh, yes there is. Your clit is thick and throbbing and begging to be stretched under the steamy suction of my lips. And you know I love the taste of your love box. No need to say yes, baby; I'm ready to feast.

Lowering myself to your generous opening while laying you back onto the bear rug underneath, you spread your legs wide for me as my brim circles around an aroused jewel. Listening intently for your body's response, the purring sighs and moans give good indication that I'm licking and loving your pussy right. Seductively stroking your smooth slit, Picasso is creating a new work of art with his paintbrush. My appetite is intensified by your eager, squirming hole, so I spread your lips with my fingers, exposing the inside of your tunnel. Seeing the juices building tells me that my kitty is begging for anything—my fingers, fist, or tongue— inside of her.

Bringing my mouth to your paradise, you meet me halfway by shoving yourself against my face as I slip a finger between your cheeks and probe elsewhere. Opening wide, I cover you completely while dining. Ferociously flicking the pink interior of your triangle with my oral me, you push yourself harder and harder against my mouth while bucking yourself up and down on my finger.

Mmm, you taste so good, honey. Your cries, once fantastically frantic, are loud and hoarse as they echo off the cabin walls. Your body is beginning to spasm, and I can't wait for your geyser to gush the juices that I love so much. Mmm, here it comes: a gorgeous, gigantic orgasm…Damn, Mommy, I'm drowning from the faucet flow streaming from you, but I'm glad you oblige to my oral stimulation of you. As you slump back in satisfaction, I smear your love potion all over my bald head and clean face.

Where'd the rest go? I drank it, baby.

Honey, each moment with you in our shared dreamland is simply wonderful, but you can't go to sleep yet, my love. We have all night. Use the next key. Bypass door number two and venture to door number three.

I hear the roar of the ocean, smell its purity, but am unable to see it. We're out past midnight, on a beach with friends, gathered around a small fire. Sipping on champagne, I sense your anxiousness, your need for us to be alone. It is confirmed by the sensuous exchange.

"Daddy, do you want to get out of here?"

"I was thinking the same thing. I'm kind of horny."

"You need some of Mommy's loving?"

"That would be nice."

Seeing your mischievous grin hardens my groin immediately, something I pray will go unnoticed as I rise. Gently taking your hand and leading you way down the sandy beach along the shore, we share a loving gaze while watching ebony waves softly smooth the sand. Basking in the essence of serenity as we stroll, we approach several large boulders. Exchanging a smile, we both know what's about to happen next.

"Mmm, I can't wait to taste you."

As moonlight glistens over the lake below, you sink to your knees. Removing my swimming trunks, initially you seem content with just stroking it. Jerking me firmly, the evolution from a semi-erect statue to a vision of veins has you flowing like a waterfall. As the precum from my lollipop top meanders down the thickness of me, making it slick and difficult to hold on to, your demands change midstream.

"Oh, God, I want you in my mouth."

Damn, you know what hearing that does to me. Loving the talent of your titillating tongue, to hear the mistress of her craft yearn to make a nice, sloppy mess of things downtown has me begging for insulation into her hungry brim.

"Go crazy, Daddy," you say before insertion. The watery-warm sensation that follows has my eyes rolling to the top of my head. With no trouble whatsoever, you take all of me inside all of your oral you. Moving maddeningly with magical motions, you drive me crazy by varying the tempo of your strokes in the sexiest manner possible. Bobbing back and forth along my stiffness, sliding and sucking me in a frantic, furious fervor, I caress your head tenderly while losing control of my body.

"Shit, baby," I say, groaning. Filling the air with shrieks and shrills of delight as you work my tool like a vacuum, I know you feel the pulsing sensation of me along your oral cavity and the back of your throat. My pelvic area synchronizes with the movements of your mouth as my rigid rod goes into overdrive. Shaking and shimmering, you know the joy I receive when watching you drink my salty, steamy satisfaction. Shaking violently, I spurt uncontrollably as a hurricane of my seed pumps from me into your orifice. You smile deviously as you swallow all of me and lick your lips as if you want more in your oral pouch.

"Mmm. Mommy's so greedy."

"Damn, baby." I breathe, then kneel to lick a morsel of my creamy overspill off your chin. You see, the freak in you brings out the freak in me, my dear.

I'm almost wiped out, but we can't stop now. Wait. You're already opening door number two.

That's a good choice, my pleasure pet. We're in broad daylight, having a country picnic in my garden of love. The heat of summer shines on our seclusion, and the moment seems perfect. Birds serenade us with a familiar melody of love, and I notice a seductive gleam in your eyes. (Damn, why are you always starting shit? Are you a student of Zane or Mary Morrison, or just a horny Scorpio?) I know exactly what you want, so I politely place the food back in our picnic basket, save the whipped cream and cherries.

Stripping those Daisy Dukes from you, Daddy decides that he wants a sundae. Laying you back in my tenderness and spraying your already clenching love nest with the flavored foam, the maraschino ornaments are a perfect topping as I set out to devour and destroy my creation with an active, oral instrument.

Turning my head slightly sideways, I inhale to savor the aroma of your deliciously drenched, dessert-dressed honey hole. Slick juices ooze from you, causing the whipped cream to run along your thighs. Navigating the musky mixture with my tongue, low guttural moans escape you as my fingertips then aroused brim meet your heart-shaped outer lips.

"Mommy's tangy treasure needs your mouth, right now," you announce.

"Your wish is my command."

Separating your velvet folds, I place a cherry into my mouth before diving into your delightful, desirable, delectable entrance. Licking the bottom of your inner sanctuary, my mouth and nose probe deeper as munching sounds leave me. Damn, baby, you have no idea how good you taste. Flattening my tongue while pleasurably pleasing your dairy-tasting perineum, I feel you writhe and groan while pumping your hips into me. Damn, I love it when you do that.

Never neglecting to nibble on your ruby pearl, I place a cherry on your hard bead then suction it off with my lips. The coolness of my action causes you to squirm and squeal. Mmm, Daddy likes that shit.

Wrapping myself around your clit, I suck voraciously while working up and down with a creative critter. Flittering and fluttering on the knob of your furnace, I feel your body bucking wildly as I trace the letters of the alphabet over your bead. You didn't make it to Z today, honey. Swaying like the Leaning Tower of Pisa, stiffening, then shuddering, I feel your body arching in preparation for release. I can't wait for the mother of all waterfalls to drown me. I wanna soak up all of your affection. Ecstatically exploding, your drenched channel pulsates in my face as an overflow of liquid squirts out. Sucking every drop of climax from your intimate tunnel, I bring myself to your face; nose covered in whipped cream, appetite satisfied.

"Taste that," I announce.

Kissing my lips, you oblige.

"That's all of you on my face." We smile, and while sharing a French kiss, you extract the cherry from my mouth and eat it. Seeing the impish grin on my face, you become worried.

"What's wrong, sugar?"

"You think we're done, huh?"

I love it when I see your eyes widen in curiosity. Soon, the look turns to amazement as I break out the blindfold.

"I want you to guess what I'm placing in your mouth, honey."

You play along as first a grape, next a shrimp, then crackers and cheese satisfy your hunger. Testing your lips with red wine, then teasing them with chocolate-covered strawberries, I silently undo my zipper and place an abnormally large sausage in your hand.

"I've been waiting for this piece of meat." Eagerly taking my still-growing flesh, you enjoy the smooth feel of its purple bulb against your lips. The hot air of affection you blow on me brings me to my full length. Fat and veiny, chocolate and shiny, my love organ yearns to stretch the confines of your throat with its texture.

Aggressively, you wrap your palm around me and stroke my arousal. Varying the speed of your stimulation, a bubble of white sauce escapes me, and you capture it with that long lizard between lusciously loving lips that make me diamond-hard.

"Taste it," I say, moaning.

You oblige. Parting your oral pleasure as wide as you can manage and taking my manhood, you scratch your fingernails ever so tenderly on my sac of seeds. Slathering circles around my tip with dripping saliva, my pole is seductively slick as you glide your tongue over every inch.

"Nice and sloppy," you say.

Damn, my lady is so nasty. And I love it. Each time your brim clutches me, I thrust forward a bit more to meet your greedy bobbing. Sucking and slurping, the motions of you have me pushing me deeper and deeper in. Grinding against your jaw with it, then gripping the back of your head, I feel the pressure building as I increase the tempo of delight. Pumping my hips in pleasure, your sensational skills match my arousal stroke for stroke.

"Every thrust brings me closer, Mommy; Daddy wants to let it all go," I say, moaning.

Grunting softly, a generous lotion of lust leaves me. Gulping frantically at my release while using your fingers to catch some overflow, my copious stream spills onto your chin and breasts. Smiling contentedly, you meet my heated gaze with a nod of your head.

"I need you now," you beg.

"Don't worry, Mommy. I want to show how a real man takes care of his queen."

As we make out like new lovers, my fingers probe your triangular pleasure chest. Mmm, messy, sloppy wet, just the way I like it. I feel like Christopher Columbus exploring the new world once again.

"Write your name in this pussy," you say.

"That's what it's made for, baby."

The incredible feeling when teasing you and torturing me as I let my tip rest against your entry is indescribable. Finally succumbing to sensations, my love spike slips up, slips in, and…amen. Lost in a familiar sauce, I drape your legs over my arms and take the Nestea plunge. With slow yet tender strokes, the slurping sounds your channel make as I impale you have us grunting and groaning in unison.

"So good. So deep. Keep going, Daddy."

Encouraged by your greedy wantonness, as I thrust deeper and deeper, I slide a finger elsewhere, sending you spiraling into uncharted realms of physical bliss. Our bodies mesh into one, your hips flex wildly as you take me in to the hilt. Lovingly pumping and longingly pleasing you, the view of you tossing and turning beneath me has me breathing faster while working to satisfy you. Our bodies are fusing into a heap of sweaty flesh.

Continuing with measured, methodical motion, my masculinity massages your G-spot slowly, then swiftly. You placed your fingertips along my backside, then part my buttocks as you place one finger in. Stroking and strumming my anus as I generously gyrate inside you, I feel you stiffen, shudder, and shake as you always do when nearing a body-tingling, mind-blowing orgasm.

"Don't come yet," I command. "Let's do it together, Mommy. Together."

Seductively swiveling my hips in a circular motion, I slow the tempo of my dance to ensure the prolonging of our passion. Our tongues meet attentively and affectionately as we savor the exchange of deep, passionate kisses. I can tell you want to milk every last ounce of love from my masculinity.

"Mmm, feed Mommy," you rasp.

Feeling myself swell while moaning savagely, there is no point holding back my spurts of gratitude after watching your comfortable, content convulsions. Sharing our synchronized orgasms, we elevate to another dimension and level of pleasure as simultaneous moans are heard throughout my garden. Drifting into an exhausted existence, the heated communal is matched only by the humid skies above....

You have to go now. For the moments of passion we shared throughout the night are broken by sunlight and the distant sound of an alarm ringing. Don't look so sad, my precious. There's always tonight, and I'll be waiting.

Put Ya Tongue In It

by

Maryann Reid

You want me to go where?"

"Come on, Nicole. It's in Las Vegas, not Amsterdam. It's just a small sex convention, very professional, very HBO *Real Sex*."

"Small, meaning like two hundred thousand people," Nicole said as she jotted down some notes on her pad. "Hotel and air?"

"As always, but you'll have to pay your everyday expenses. I'll make sure you get it back when you return. It's only for the weekend."

"You know Shawn is not going to be happy about all this. He already thinks I have a wandering eye. And now I'm supposed to tell him I'm going to a sex convention?"

"For work. It's for work!" Adam said, raising his hands above his head. "Hey, you may learn some new tricks."

Nicole playfully waved her pen at him. "I want two dollars a word for this."

"A dollar fifty."

"Deal," she said, leaning forward in her chair and shaking Adam's hand.

He started typing away on his computer. In less than a minute, he printed out a small agreement.

Laughing, Nicole snatched the paper from him, accepting the story.

"You better pray I come back from Las Vegas with enough tricks to get me a damn engagement ring," she said, pointing at him.

Nicole couldn't believe what she had signed up for. Most of her stories had to do with business and entrepreneurship. Now she had to take on a new kind of business, one that reminded her where she was lacking. Lately, her sex life with her man, Shawn, had been as dry as badly cooked fried chicken. A part of her was looking at her new assignment as an opportunity. She needed a break to release her pent-up sexual energy somehow. Her attraction for Shawn was getting weaker. He had been unemployed for six months and gaining weight while he slept all day. He had no money left in his savings, either. The assignment might save their relationship, she thought. She might even come across some new gadget to help Shawn last more than few minutes, or even something with which she could get off on her own.

She loved Shawn, but their eight-year relationship was the same ole, same ole to Nicole. But she took part of the blame. Since he'd been downsized from his lucrative computer job, she had had sex with three different men. Having sex with men she'd met provided that extra excitement she needed in her life, something Shawn used to fulfill with his surprise romantic getaways and lavascious appetite for taping everything from their sex acts to her showers alone.

When she walked in their apartment, Shawn was asleep on the couch with a dried-up bowl of corn flakes and dirty socks on the floor. Nothing new. But he was her man.

"What's up, big head. Did you go on that interview?" she asked after waking him.

He moaned and turned over on his side, playfully reaching for her legs. "Nah. It was too cold."

She stepped back. "It's only like sixty-five degrees. When the summer comes, it's gonna be too hot to wear a suit," Nicole said, picking up his dingy socks. She flung them at him. "I need help. Either you get a job soon, or you need to move back in with your momma."

He wiped the sleep from his eye. "When I did that the last time, you called me to come back that same week. You need to make up your damn mind," he muttered.

"I will, I will," she said, walking to the bedroom. She hated the thought of living alone, and he knew that. She didn't want him to leave, but she didn't want him to stay.

"I fried some chicken this morning, and I made a salad. It's in the fridge," Shawn said as he sat up and flicked the remote.

Nicole smiled as she undressed and slipped on a pink silk robe. That was one thing Shawn was good at, throwing down in the kitchen, she thought. A man who could cook was her weakness. Well, second weakness. A man with a tireless tongue and a wicked dick was her first.

Shawn walked in on Nicole examining herself in the mirror. She was getting thick, she thought. Finally, her lanky frame was getting a shape.

"I think I may need a bushwhacker the next time I go down there," Shawn said as he laughed at her posing in the mirror. She hadn't shaved in months and was seriously considered a Brazilian wax.

"When will that be?" she asked, tying her robe and shooting him a nasty look.

He sat on the edge of the wooden sleigh bed. "Come on, baby. You know how much I like hunting in the forest," he said, smiling.

She playfully rolled her eyes at him through the mirror. His dark skin looked like syrupy molasses, but his once chiseled features were now rounded. She wanted her old Shawn back, the ruggedly handsome, tall, business suit–clad man who used to dig her pussy out like she had diamonds in it.

"Shawn, do you still love me?" She sat on her vanity chair.

"I do," he said, smirking. "I know I ain't the man I used to be, but you're still the woman I fell in love with."

Nicole wrapped her long hair around her head with the comb to prevent it from getting wet in the shower.

"You love me?" His deep, smooth voice sounded fragile.

"Yeah." Nicole laughed nervously as she tied her head with a scarf. She wasn't in love with him. She hadn't been for the last three years. She walked over to him. "Why don't you fuck me like you used to any-more?"

"What? We have sex, but I'm used to you. That's not a bad thing, is it?" he asked, scratching his head. "I'm just depressed, Nicole, but it ain't got nothing to do with you."

"I know we make love, but I said 'fuck.' " I want you to fuck me like we did when we met—anywhere, anyhow. Remember that time you ate me out in my momma's bathroom and my uncle Johnny walked in and nearly caught a heart attack?" Nicole laughed.

Shawn shook his head. "Yeah, but we're older now. That shit wasn't cool. We not even allowed back in your momma's bathroom."

"Well, not the one in her bedroom anyway," Nicole said, grinning. She massaged Shawn's broad shoulders, but he grew tense.

He took her French-manicured hand and bought it down to his pants. "Can you give me some head?"

Nicole snatched her hand back. "Hell no," she said, flying out of the room. "You haven't even smelled my pussy in months. I'm tired of giving you head and getting three-minute sessions whenever you're in the mood."

Shawn followed her down the hall. "Come here," he said, grabbing her by the arm. "You fuckin' somebody?"

"Somebody has to," she spat back. "Get off me." She pulled out of his grip.

"What?" Shawn's dark skin turned purplish red in contempt.

"I think we need some time apart," Nicole said as they sat in the kitchen. "I have an assignment in Las Vegas for a few days."

"For what?"

"I'm covering a sex convention. It's a business article."

"For how long?"

"A week."

"When do we leave? I think we need to get away," he said, suddenly in a much better mood.

"I have to go alone. It's work." Nicole didn't like where this was going. She wanted Shawn to miss her and perhaps, when she returned, she'd have missed him too.

"You ain't going alone," he said, raising his voice.

"Shawn, it's business. Don't fucking start." Nicole got up and took the chicken out of the fridge.

"Oh, I see," he said, raising his hands. "Until I get a job, you ain't gonna listen to shit I gotta say."

"Basically," Nicole mumbled and put the chicken in the microwave. "This is money we both need, Shawn. I got a job, unlike some people."

Shawn stared at her in disbelief. Her disrespect for him was outright, but he couldn't fight back. It was true. He didn't have a job, and they did need the money she earned.

Nicole turned around to face his solemn expression. *Man up,* she thought. But then she realized they were both tired and battered, taking cheap shots at each other's self-esteem. It had boiled down to this. She kept a straight face, though she wanted to scream out her frustration. "I don't want no drama about this. I'm going."

Shawn shrugged.

There was a time she used to listen and do anything he asked. *Wash my clothes.* Done. *Fried fish on Fridays.* Done. *Stop going to your momma's house so much.* Done. *Don't wear too much makeup.* Done.

Shawn finally looked up and said, "So it's some sex story?"

"Yes."

"About?"

"Fetishes. Sex business. Stuff like that."

"Interesting," he said, rolling his eyes. "I probably won't hear back from your ass if you meet a nigga with one of those nasty fetishes like sucking toes or some shit."

"Or a nigga who got a fetish for work," she shot back.

"That's a good one." He smiled. "Promise me one thing?"

"What?" She took the chicken out of the microwave and placed it on a plastic plate with some salad.

"That if you find a woman who has a fetish for cooking and cleaning, call me."

"Shit, if she's got a job, you may have to get in line," Nicole said, sinking her teeth into a juicy, crispy leg.

Shawn bent his head back in disgust. "You just get crazier the older you get."

"It ain't no fun if your homey can't get none," Nicole said, laughing. Shawn was aware of her bisexual tendencies, but it wasn't anything they discussed openly.

"Yo, whatever," he said. "Just be in that room when I call you at night. If I have to come to Las Vegas—"

"You ain't going nowhere," Nicole said, rolling her eyes at him, "but I promise to call every night."

Their eyes locked, and neither of them wanted to say the unspoken. But neither of them knew what to really expect.

A few days later, Nicole was at the MGM Grand Hotel room in Las Vegas. The hotel was the designated place for the Gallagher Lifestyles Convention, and everything catered to the participants, even the food named Fries 69, Tantalizing T-Bone Steak, Doggy-Style Country Biscuits, and drinks with names like Lick My Lips. It seemed like the whole city was reveling in this soup du jour of lust, and Nicole couldn't wait to take a sip.

She walked up and down the aisles with names like Rub My Dickie, Tickle My Nipple, and Spermies Candy. It was still early, around 2:00 P.M., and the convention center was bustling with activity. Men and women, single or coupled, crowded the tables for a touch and sometimes taste of the latest gadgets and toys.

"What's this?" Nicole asked as she picked up an item shaped like a puppy.

"It's a little dog," said the chubby purveyor of goods who looked to be about seventy.

"Oh." Nicole checked out the miniature pink dog from side to side to see what was so special about it.

"It vibrates on your pussy. Watch this," he blurted and took the toy from Nicole's hands.

Nicole's eyes widened as the dog flicked its tongue out on the man's palms.

"Feel this," he summoned.

Nicole opened her palms up for the dog's long, vibrating tongue. It felt ticklish, but surprisingly good.

"See, you just keep it pressed against ya, like this," he said, pressing the dog against her hand.

Rhythmic, massagelike movements spread up to Nicole's fingers. The little pink dog was cute, she thought, and if she liked the way her hand felt, she only imagined what else it could do.

"But why a dog?" she asked, still holding the toy.

"Everybody needs something a little different every now and then. People can get a little monotonous. Know what I mean?" the old man said, laughing.

"Well, anything that involves an animal in real life is just wrong, in my humble opinion," she said, rolling her eyes. She handed the dog back to the man and kept walking.

"Here, try this nightstick dildo," he said, waving it in the air.

She began to wonder whether she was going to relate to these people at all. When she looked around and saw the bevy of activity of thousands of feet marching to the next exhibit, she realized she had to connect with someone. This was her assignment. It mattered that she talked to the right people and get the right story. She passed by neat booths with brightly colored signage that lined the rows of the crowded space. She stopped at a booth that was attended by a tall brother with midnight skin and bedroom eyes. He had a neat goatee and was dressed in a gray business suit and lavender tie. His eyes fixated on her about the same time she saw him. He was one of the few black people there and didn't look like anything Nicole was expecting.

"Looking for anything special?" he asked as Nicole stood just a few feet away from him. There was a throng of potential customers at his booth filling out forms and checking out the toys on display. Nicole watched him ordering some of his attendants to collect all the customers' surveys. He was the man in the charge, she thought, which piqued her interest.

Nicole shook her head. "No." She didn't want tell him that she was a reporter on a story. It would kill the spontaneity of what she was trying to do—fit in. She also didn't want anyone giving her a sales pitch; she wanted the real thing.

Nicole picked up a device as small as the tip of her thumb that was displayed on his table.

"You like your pussy eaten?" he asked in a clinical manner, but with a sly, sexy smile.

Nicole tried to act like she was asked that question all the time. "Umm, yeah. What woman doesn't love that?"

"Size is everything these days. People are looking for toys that are convenient and can be carried around discreetly," he said, stepping around the table.

Nicole liked how businesslike he sounded. She thought he was about to put the moves on her. "What is it used for? It's as small as a quarter."

"Well," he said, picking up the device, "it's for when your husband is eating your pussy. He can keep this under your ass. It sends these unimaginable sensations to your clit when it vibrates."

"I'm not married," Nicole corrected him, not sure why she did.

"Well, your man, your girl, or whoever can use it. Check this out." He eagerly pointed out another treat. "This is my most popular item."

Nicole took the red packet that reminded her of a condom wrapper. "Is it an aphrodisiac powder that you put in someone's drink or food? I read about these," she said, wanting to take it home with her.

"Nah. It's a cream. Do you have one of those hooded clits?"

Nicole covered smile with her hand. "It's deep down, embedded in my skin. You need a flashlight to try to find that thing," she said, laughing.

But the man looked at her pitifully. Then said in his deep, throaty voice, "You take some of this and spread it on top of your pussy, the most sensitive area, and watch it swell. You won't be able to close your legs without cumming."

Nicole had never heard of such a thing.

"It's on me," he said, putting his hands over her clasped one, which held the packet.

"Okay," she said, shrugging as she slipped it in her green, fringed pocket book.

"I'm Darnell," he said, extending his large, brown hand to shake hers. "Nicole."

"You don't come to these things often, do you?"

"This is nothing." She waved, trying to play it off, but she couldn't stop herself from laughing.

Darnell laughed too. "I bet I know more about your pussy in five minutes than any man you've met." He just stood there gazing at her.

"You were just doing your job, I'm sure," she said, blushing.

At that time a few customers gathered around him with questions. Nicole waited. She had to know what was really up with him.

When he was done, he turned and asked her, "Can we meet tonight for drinks?"

Nicole didn't hesitate to accept. "When and where?"

"At the hotel lobby, about seven?"

"See you there," she said as he watched her walk away. And just like that, Darnell went back to what he did best, talking about pussy.

A little after seven, Nicole met Darnell at the hotel bar near the lobby. He was dressed casually this time in loose-fitting jeans, a black Guayabera shirt, and black shoes. When he saw Nicole approach him at the bar, he stood at attention.

"You look good enough to eat." He smiled as he complimented her short jean skirt, gold heels, and red short-sleeved ruffled top. She wanted to look and feel sexy for him. This was her time to escape from her worries and explore to what this unique meeting with Darnell could lead. It could be more than a just a story, she hoped.

In a gentlemanly fashion, he took her hand as they walked to a more discreet booth at the end of the restaurant. She liked his style. He seemed to be a man who knew what he wanted, when and where.

"So, what really brings you to this convention? I don't get the vibe this is your everyday thing. This is my life," he said as he examined the menu.

"I'll have a martini, no ice," Nicole said as the attractive, red-haired waitress took their drink orders.

"Henny, straight. Thanks," Darnell said. Once the waitress turned her back, he asked, "Well?"

"I might as well tell you. I'm doing a story. I'm a reporter for *Fast Pace,* a business magazine, and I'm doing a short profile on the convention. But, please," she said, reaching over to touch his hand, "don't treat me like a writer. I want the real experience of this place."

Darnell smiled, showing off his pearly-white teeth and dimples. "The real experience? What's that?"

Nicole averted her eyes to the ceiling for a clue. "I don't know. Anything that people do when they get here. I want to find out what kind of people come here."

"People like you," he said plainly. "People like me."

"Who are you?" Nicole asked, intrigued by his mystery. She felt there was more to this man than pussy gadgets.

He rubbed his goatee and leaned back in his chair. His eyes narrowed in on her. "I'm many things. But to keep it simple, I was an investment banker for ten years, working in Manhattan, quit, and opened up this business last year after I turned thirty-five. I wanted to do something I loved."

The waitress returned with their drinks and placed the luscious concoctions before them before taking their order. Nicole hurriedly sipped hers while Darnell swirled his.

"And that is?"

"Pussy. I love it in a way that can interfere with my normal daily routine."

Nicole stayed quiet. She didn't want to interrupt his train of thought, something she learned in journalism school.

Darnell sipped his drink then said, "I have a fetish for eating pussy. My ex-girlfriend had it hard. I was down there morning, noon, and night. I'd pop up at her job. I made her do some crazy shit just to get me off."

Nicole squeezed her thighs together and wanted more, but she was confused. "See, most men say they like it, but once they get you, the chase is over. That's over too. They don't do it as often, and it becomes boring. My man, right now, I swear he doesn't like it, but he tells me he does. Bullshit."

"Maybe he does really like it," Darnell said, laughing. "Think about it. Everybody eats pussy now, even women. Everybody likes it for a reason."

"Hmmm," Nicole said, nursing her drink. She licked the salt off the side of the glass. "I tried it a few times with a girlfriend of mine who's now married. We did it out of curiosity, and I loved it. I loved eating it and being eaten by a man or woman. However, I'm straight, bisexual every now and then."

They both laughed. Just then, the waitress laid down their order of shrimp cocktail, and they dug right in, talking about his fetish.

"So I started this business because I needed to make money doing what I loved. I come out here every year, clear about twenty-five thousand in sales and pre-orders and the rest of the year, I gross over a million on internet orders through my site—"

Nicole jotted down some notes because she had a hunch that later there would be little time for talking.

At midnight, Nicole and Darnell headed to the Deluxe, a club just down the street from the hotel. Nicole was on a buzz, and she loved it. She couldn't tell when she had partied with a man like this. She felt safe with him. Darnell was a free spirit like her, and she was ready to soar.

The club was jam-packed with people on the first level, with red strobe lights dancing around the room, and brown and white bodies pumping to the latest beats. They were playing rap, R & B, and lots of Prince. This was her type of party, and she couldn't wait to get out on the floor.

As soon as they found a spot, she and Darnell began grooving to a hot reggae hit. Darnell was a good dancer, she noticed, firmly holding her body against his. She was impressed by the bulge in his pants. It felt like a knot of large marbles. Just pressing against it made her pussy throb in sync with the beat.

"Listen," he said, his lips grazing the side of her ear, "there's a little room in the back. Wanna chill in there and relax?"

"Tired, already?" Nicole teased as she wound her hips on him. "Can't handle this?" She turned around and backed up her voluptuous rounded ass against him.

"Come on," he said, guiding her to the upstairs room.

Nicole was no fool. She knew what time it was, but she liked playing along.

The room was small with smooth, red velvet sofas, a big-screen TV that showed porn-rated hip-hop videos and had a glass window where you could see the club below but no one could see in. A waiter came in and placed a bottle of Dom and a small silver case down on a tray.

Nicole was still dancing as hard as she was downstairs as Darnell popped their bottle. She spun around so hard one time, she ended up on her ass.

Darnell cracked up at her and poured two glasses of champagne. Nicole was on the floor rolling in laughter at her silliness. Something had to be in her drink, she thought. She hadn't acted so ditzy in a while. This was the real her. Free to be.

She crawled over to Darnell who held both of their glasses. He helped her up and set her on his lap.

"Take a little of this," he said, giving her some champagne. "I don't need you getting sober any time soon."

"Darnell, I'm drunk, but I do what I do because I want to. Anything that happens tonight is because I made it happen," she said, kissing his lips.

Darnell opened his mouth as they both teased and sucked on each other's tongues. He ran his hands up her thighs, playing with the edge of her panties. Nicole spread her legs more while Darnell explored the inside of her pussy with his thumb. He sucked her juices off the tip. He gently slid her off him and placed her on her back on the sofa. Slipping off her panties, Nicole closed her eyes, ready to see how a man with a pussy-eating fetish really got down.

"Here," he said and gave her a small pill. He took one too.

"X," Nicole said, swallowing the pill. "Excellent." She spread her legs and arched her back. Darnell was still fully clothed. She noticed something cool trickle down on her pussy to her ass. Her mouth parted and her eyes rolled back when she saw Darnell pour champagne down her pussy. He sucked it off and turned his tongue into a feather, lapping her up from her ass to her clit. Then he stopped.

Nicole was whimsical. Every nerve on her body responded to Darnell's slightest touch. It was all about her. He knew he had a lot to prove with all that talking he did earlier. "Let's dance," he said, helping her stand.

Nicole pulled down her skirt, which was still halfway up her ass. She stumbled and giggled as they moved nice and slow. He stood against the glass, unbuttoned her blouse, and viciously sucked on her titties. Then Nicole felt another hand. It pulled up her skirt to her ass. A tongue slipped up and down her ass all the way to her pussy.

Nicole panted as Darnell sucked on her nipples like a newborn and someone else ate her pussy from the back. She felt completely out of control and didn't want this moment to end. She bent over and got on her knees, rolling her ass all over the floor. Darnell sat on the couch and watched. He sipped his champagne as a strange man feasted on Nicole's pussy like a sweet watermelon.

"Bring her over here," Darnell ordered as he sat with his arms waiting. Nicole finally saw who this man was eating her out. He was a twin, Darnell's exact opposite.

With her wet juices still on his chin, the man led Nicole back to Darnell. "This bitch is a wild one," the guy said with a mean, stern expression. Nicole wondered if he was gonna stay.

She climbed onto Darnell's lap. Her pussy felt like it had just been to the spa, but she still hadn't come. "Make me come, Darnell, please," she begged. He raised her body up until his mouth met her pussy. He leaned his head back and positioned Nicole to sit on his face, her favorite position. Darnell cupped her ass as she rocked back and forth. The other man watched from across the room, jerking his dick. Nicole couldn't wait to come so she could get some of that dick inside her.

Darnell sucked on her pussy like it was a Blow-Pop. It was like he was talking to it and it was singing back. He found her spot and sucked on it as he made of his own sounds of pleasure. He couldn't get enough of it moaning and groaning as much as Nicole. She dripped her cum all over his mouth, and he licked it up and went back for more. Nicole came again, her second multiple orgasm in ten years.

Her body was limp. It was almost like she had a full sex session, but the party was just starting. The other man got behind her and rammed his dick in her pussy.

"Yeah, give it to me. Fuck me like a dog," she said, squealing. But nothing excited her more than when she saw Darnell's pants drop to the ground. She didn't even give him a chance to pull it out. While he sat on the couch, she stuffed his freed dick in her mouth. Deep throat was her specialty, and Darnell was uncircumcised, making it even better. Nicole loved to play with the extra meat.

As the man slapped her sweat-drenched ass and danced his dick in her wet pussy, Nicole's mouth was full of Darnell. She gave him the ultimate spit shine, deep-throating him until he called out her name.

"Damn, Nicole," he said, playing in her ear. "You look good with my dick in your mouth. I can get used to this."

Nicole didn't answer. She felt taken over by something that just wanted to swallow her whole. Her pussy was being pumped so well, she had to return the good vibes she was feeling. She licked the sides of his dick, slipping his head in and out of her mouth. Spit slid down the sides of his dick, and she slurped it right up. Darnell had to be a good twelve inches, and it was enough meat to keep her busy for a while. Thoughts of her getting fucked by two men blew her mind. This wasn't something she could tell anyone.

"I'ma come. Hold on," Darnell said, sweat trickling down his forehead. Nicole popped his dick out of her mouth. "I got to get some of that pussy," he told the man behind her.

Without further ado, Nicole sat on Darnell's dick and rode him like a thoroughbred. She could feel him inside her enlarging as she struggled to fit him all in. He proved that he was more than good at licking the kitty. She bent over on him, and a dick was in her ass. All three of their voices yelled out as they all exploded in their own state of ecstasy. Completely spent, Nicole looked around at the two men spread out naked across the room, exhausted. She was, too, but smiling. The night was more than a fantasy turned reality, and it was her very own little secret.

The next morning, Nicole found herself back in her hotel room. She didn't know how she got there, but she was in her nightgown and tucked carefully in the bed. No one was around but her. She immediately called Shawn.

"Hi, baby," she said, blocking out what happened. She felt horrible, though.

"I called you ten times last night. At three A.M., you was still working on your story?"

Nicole searched for what to say. "I was probably sleep."

"With who?"

"Stop it, Shawn. I'm tired. I was interviewing people all day. Something you should do—"

Then the phone clicked off.

Back to reality, she thought, but she wasn't ready to go back.

She dialed Darnell.

"Who was that man?" she asked as soon as he picked up.

He laughed. "Who do you think? My twin brother."

"So you guys do that all the time?"

"Do what?"

"What happened between all three of us last night."

"I don't know what you're talking about. We had dinner, and I took you back to the room—alone."

Nicole quieted. She knew damn well they all fucked, but she respected Darnell for letting her keep her respect. If the previous night was to remain as liberated and as beautiful as it was, she knew it couldn't be brought up again. She had to respect the fantasy. "Yeah, that's right," she finally said.

"Hey, why don't you meet me for breakfast in about an hour?" he said.

"I will." Then she hung up. One thing she noticed was that she felt free for the first time in years.

Nicole never did meet Darnell for breakfast. She spent the day talking to convention administrators and interviewing more people. By Sunday night, she filed her story and was on the next plane home. That week, she broke up with Shawn and finally found for what she had been looking—the sense of being free and getting exactly what she needed.

Enough

by

Natosha Gale Lewis

I'd been working a little too hard lately. The things that I should have been paying attention to the most, I seemed to be constantly neglecting. Working these twelve-hour back-to-back shifts in this telephone-sex industry is definitely getting in the way of my social life.

When Cinnamon finally relieved me on Friday morning, I should have been exhausted, but I was pumped up and ready to go.

I'd been working at Morning, Noon, and Night, Inc., a place where one just can't get enough, for the past six months. I originally took this job because my bills were starting to pile up, and I didn't want to have to dance for a few dollars or sell my ass on the avenue, so this was the next best thing. Not that there's anything wrong with doing what you've gotta do to make that cheddar, but I enjoy sex, and I would've probably been giving my pussy away instead of making money at the other jobs. I heard about Morning, Noon, and Night, Inc., from a girl who lives in my co-op building, and the rest as they say is history.

At Morning, Noon, and Night, Inc., it's supposed to strictly be about business. However, I emphasize the word *supposed* to be about business. Big Sexy owns the place, and the asshole is so cheap that he would never think to hire a night manager because he fears someone might rip him off. He's extremely generous when it comes to me. He just loves the taste of my pussy and can never get enough.

The real secret to how I make so much money is my ability to get people to call in around the clock. I really can't take too much credit for this because the entire time that I'm getting my callers off, Big Sexy is usually getting me off. He's actually taking the liberty, allowing me to make calls in the security of his office. This provides us with the utmost privacy. While I'm riding his ten-inch dick or he's licking the juices from my ever-flowing, raspberry-tasting pussy, we seem to be the perfect combination in getting those clients to call in. Now, how he makes sure that the other girls and guys are making their calls and not cutting side deals is news to me. The calls are recorded, so I'm assuming that Big Sexy replays each one after I leave. However, during the twelve hours that I'm there, I swear that we're going at it for practically my entire shift. You would think that would get old after a while, but Big Sexy is the best at what he does, which in turn, makes me his number one phone sex operator.

One day was a little different. Big Sexy kept inquiring about my after-work affairs, asking me where I was going.

"I'm going to Ling's, damn. You act like I'm your woman or something," I replied.

"You need to be my woman. I don't want you giving that good-tasting raspberry pussy to nobody else. That needs to be mine. Can't nobody do you better than I can," Big Sexy said, knowing he was speaking the gospel.

I decided that I was going to do something that I wanted to do: pamper myself silly. Now, after the night that I had with Big Sexy, my ass should have been tired, but again, I was pumped and ready to go.

When I got off work, I called and made my appointment. I decided to get a pedicure and manicure, have my eyebrows and a Brazilian wax and a much-needed massage to top it off. I went to my girl Ling's Full-Service Nail Salon and Spa because girlfriend knows how to hook a sistah up. Ling is a pretty young girl from the Philippines.

"Tia, are you ready?" the soft voice whispered through the closed door.

"Yes. I'm ready," I responded just as quietly.

The door opened and closed slowly. I was lying on my back, eyes closed, with a huge, soft terry-cloth towel draped over me.

"Ma'am, I'm Shawn, and I'll be servicing you today. I have a few questions before I begin," he continued, still in a soft, but deep whisper. "Is there a chance you could be pregnant?"

My eyes shot open. "No. Not at all..." That's when I saw him. Shawn was the most beautiful creature I'd ever laid eyes on. His muscles rippled on his six-three frame, his jet-black, curly hair was cut just above his shoulders. His eyes were the most perfectly shaped orbs I'd ever seen on a man. My guess was that he was Black and Filipino. "Damn." I allowed the word to slip from my lips.

"Ma'am?"

"Huh?" I replied.

"I was asking you if there's an area you needed me to concentrate on today."

"Yes, as a matter fact I do. I'm completely stressed out all over. Just do me all over."

"With pleasure," he stated with a sexy grin forming on his luscious lips.

"I mean—"

"I know what you meant. Just relax, close your eyes. I'm going to begin by putting some warm oil on you then working from your shoulders to your feet."

"Oh no, I'm very ticklish. Please don't touch my feet," I stated.

"Sure. Anything you want or desire."

Shawn began, just as he promised, by massaging my shoulders, which were taut and definitely needed special attention. He kneaded and kneaded until a soft moan escaped my lips.

"You like that, huh?"

"Yes, yes," I whispered softly.

"You have beautiful skin. So soft and delicate. I bet your pussy is just as soft."

"Yes, yes." I was rather caught up and didn't realize what Shawn had just said.

"Did I startle you?" Shawn asked.

"I don't startle easily, Shawn," I said, unwrapping myself from the towel, allowing Shawn a full view of what I was offering.

There was no need to say anything else. Shawn began slowly tracing my ears with his tongue. It was warm, and just the feeling of it sent electrifying tingles up and down my spine. He then began, sucking and licking on my neck, in small then large circles. He began to play with my pussy, first inserting one, then two fingers in and out, until a slurping sound could be heard. I reached for his penis and was rather shocked when he moved my hands. "You always please others. Today is the day you are pleased. I want you to feel how you make me feel."

Suddenly, I opened my eyes, recognizing his voice.

"Yes, baby, it's me. I'm one of your clients. Don't worry. I'm going to take very good care of you and trust me, you won't be disappointed."

Part of me wanted to run. Was this a crazed and deranged client? The way Shawn made me feel, if he were a masked murderer, he was definitely killing me softly with the wet kisses he was placing around my navel. He then opened up my pussy, and my cup of wetness exploded in his hands. He placed his soft, hot, wet tongue on my pussy, and it surely felt as if this were the first time that anyone had ever kissed my clit so delicately yet so passionately. Big Sexy was great, but Shawn was a master at sucking all of the juices that flowed from within me.

"I want you to cum in my mouth. Do it now, baby," Shawn commanded.

As if on cue, my body began shaking uncontrollably, and although I just knew I had experienced every ounce of ecstasy in the world, nothing compared to what I was feeling as I flowed in Shawn's mouth.

I lay limp on the massage table, not able to get up.

"I'm not done with you just yet. Would you like a happy ending?" Shawn asked.

I didn't say a word, but then again, I didn't need to. Shawn went over to a small dresser and pulled out a condom. As he began to open the package, I slid off the table. I took the package from him then attempted to put the condom on him. I wanted to feel his enormous-sized penis. I took his dick in my hands and began stroking him ever so gently on the tip.

"Damn," he said. He grabbed my breasts and squeezed tightly, taking a fully erect nipple in his mouth.

He flicked and licked as I screamed out, "Damn the titties, stick your dick in my wet pussy."

Shawn backed me up to a wall, grabbed my leg, and placed it around my foot on the massage table as he put his rock-hard dick in the warmth of my pussy, its wetness causing a river to flow down my legs. He thrust and thrust then pulled his dick out of me and dropped to his knees to taste my pussy again.

"Damn, your pussy tastes like raspberries." Big Sexy always said that, perhaps it's true. Shawn licked and licked then pulled up the top of my box again so that he could taste all of my clit in his mouth. Faster, faster, faster, his tongue went as I thrust my hips so that my clit could be all in his mouth, then I came a second time.

"You want a real happy ending?" Shawn asked.

"How happy can I get?" I asked.

"Turn over on your stomach, face down, but don't ask anymore questions. We're about to turn this up another notch."

I figured this was a dream come true, and the loving was great, so to hell with any inhibitions. I was going full throttle, whatever the hell that meant. I lay on the table as Shawn continued to massage my back. I was just getting it good when I noticed the door open. Although I couldn't see a face, I could see a set of men's feet—or rather a woman with a pair of rough-looking feet. As Shawn continued to massage and knead my neck, I felt a pair of hands knead my ass. One finger, then two entered me, and a soft moan escaped my mouth. One of the unknown person's foot straddled the table then stepped up on the side of the table. I felt a large dick prying to get into my tight space. My pussy was so worn out, and it hurt so good to feel this unknown, yet very familiar, great-feeling dick in me. The unknown person pounded and pounded, and I was able to back that thing up and proud to say that I took that beating like a true champion. The whole time, Shawn continued massaging me, even sucking on my toes. I climaxed for the third time, and suddenly, for the first time ever, I was officially worn out and couldn't—or didn't want to—see another dick again, no matter how big or small. I looked down again and noticed Big Sexy's ugly toes. I thought I had it bad.

I suddenly turned around. "What the hell are you doing here?" I asked.

"I just couldn't let you give that pussy away to nobody else and not let me get in on the action. You ready for the next round? My boy Shawn here is down for whatever and will service you any way you like. We've got the parlor for the rest of the afternoon."

I grabbed my dress, quickly threw it on, and left the room. Hell, my stuff was hurting. Big Sexy was officially on a diet from this great-tasting pussy.

I arrived home and suddenly felt sleepy. I thought of the great massage Shawn had given me, and thoughts of him running his muscular hands all over my body, slipping his fingers in and out of my wetness, caused me to get moist again. There was no way I could be getting excited again. I pushed the thoughts to the back of my mind.

I went upstairs and decided to run a warm bath to unwind and relax. I had been up for fifteen hours straight, and I was slowly beginning to feel the effects of the morning, noon, and night. I climbed into the tub, and the warm water felt so good that my eyes instantly began to get heavy. The warmness of the bath drained every ounce of life from me, and I quickly washed and just wanted the comfort of my down pillows to nestle my sleepy head.

I dried off with my favorite thick blue terry-cloth towel and began to lotion my body with my favorite raspberry fragrance. I placed my leg high up on the side of my bed and applied lotion to my legs, my thighs, and my ass. I suddenly found myself slipping a finger into my moist cave. I began slowly removing my finger and opted for my plastic lover to service me. Abdul was already at the ready on my nightstand.

I would be caught dead in an alley before I ran out of C batteries. I made that fatal mistake once before and trust me, it wasn't good. The only way that I can truly fall asleep is just after a toe-curling climax.

I lay on the bed and cranked up the vibrator to the highest setting the control had to offer. Within two minutes flat, I was cumming all over again. I drifted off to a peaceful sleep.

I awakened six hours later to the sun going down and Abdul still cushioned between my thighs. I began laughing when I realized the noise I was hearing was someone ringing my doorbell. I thought of not answering, but it was obvious that whoever it was wasn't going away. I got up and looked through the peephole. It was Ling from the nail salon.

Ling and I have been friends and neighbors for about three years, and even though she's bisexual, she's never, ever crossed the line, but I know she's got a thing for me. I can tell by the way she looks at me and rubs my feet whenever she gives me my pedicures.

I opened the door, still halfway asleep. "Hey, Ling. What brings you over?" I asked.

"I wanted to see if you wanted to grab a drink or something later. I saw you briefly at the shop today, but you left once you got your massage. Did you forget I was supposed to give you a manicure and pedicure?" she asked.

"Girl, why didn't you ever tell me about Shawn? I got so wrapped up in his massage and services, I left before I could see you," I said.

"Yeah, Shawn and Big Sexy got to have all of the fun. I guess you would never give a girl like me a chance, huh?" Ling asked.

"Ling, you know I'm not into women."

"Let me show you what you're missing," she said.

I didn't know if I should curse her out or take her up on her offer. I had always heard that women were better lovers than men. Just as I was going to decline her offer, my doorbell rang again.

"Now who is it? Good thing I got a few hours of sleep," I said, heading for the door. I peeped through the peephole, and low and behold, it was Big Sexy and Shawn.

I opened the door to two smiling men.

"I gave you enough time to sleep. Now it's time to party. We're about to kick things up a notch," Big Sexy said, pushing past me. Shawn kissed me on the lips then squeezed my breasts, causing my nipples to get erect instantly. I left the three of them in the living room then headed to the bathroom to get a quick wash and at least brush my teeth. You only live once right? I figured, *Fuck it, I ain't married and I ain't hurting nobody. It is what it is.*

I came out of the bathroom butt naked, and Big Sexy was on his knees with Ling pinned up against the wall with his head deep in her pussy. Shawn was sitting on the couch, massaging his shaft.

"What about me? I can't get any service over here?" I asked.

Shawn motioned for me to come to him. He looked so damn sexy with his erotic grin, and although he hadn't penetrated me earlier, something told me that I was in for the ride of a lifetime. I walked over to him and commenced to suck the life out of his penis. I slowly, yet passionately gave him my full deep-throating skills. I was on my knees, and by the throb of his penis, I could tell he was about to cum in my mouth. The more excited I got him, the more passion I put into my skillful technique. I suddenly felt the warmest, softest, yet most satisfying tongue begin to ever so delicately eat my pussy.

"Damn," I murmured as I climaxed immediately. This caused Shawn to fill my mouth with his juices while I also experienced an indescribable feeling down below. It turned me on and sent me to a sexual height I had never known before. I turned around to command Big Sexy to begin hitting that ass from the back, because the sensation was unexplainable, and that's when I realized that it was Ling who had provided such heightened pleasure. Ling flipped me over and began eating me again. I must have come about four more times.

Shawn was sucking Ling's breasts, his huge penis was back in my mouth while Big Sexy was pounding the life out of Ling. It was one huge fuck fest, and I was loving it. There was just one problem: I still hadn't experienced what it was like to have Shawn's big dick inside of me. I stood and turned around. I backed my ass right up in Shawn's face and guided his dick inside of me. Big Sexy was still pounding Ling and surprisingly, I began playing with her pussy as she screamed in utter delight. Three hours later, we were all exhausted, and no one could move.

I must have fallen asleep because when I awakened I was back in my bed and I didn't even remember getting up, letting everyone out, and going back in my bed. I must have been exhausted. I couldn't even remember fucking so many times in one weekend, but hell, I'm thirty-two, and it's believed that a woman is just entering her sexual peak during this time, so if I didn't have any hang-ups about my lifestyle, I damn sure didn't expect anyone else to have any.

I walked into the living room, and Ling was the only one in there. She was lying on the couch watching TV. "Oh, I see you're finally up," she said.

"Where are Big Sexy and Shawn?" I asked.

"They went to get some wine and something to eat. They've only been gone for about an hour. I know you're tired. Have we worn out our welcome?" Ling asked.

"Naw, you guys are cool," I said, thinking it was getting pretty awkward with just the two of us there, especially after what we did. I didn't think of myself as bisexual, but I did actually enjoy Ling's touch.

Ling turned off the television and went to the front door. She came back with her foot tub and pedicure equipment. "I never did give you your pedicure," she said.

"You don't have to do that right now. I can come to the shop some other time."

"I want to. You have such beautiful feet. I love to touch you. You don't see how I give you special attention?" Ling asked.

"Ling, I think you should know I'm not gay."

"Please don't insult me. I know you're not gay, but why don't you just live for the moment and not try to label yourself? Close your eyes. If you like the feel, no matter who's touching you, than I'd say relish in those feelings and go with the flow."

I thought about it, and Ling was right. She ran tepid water in the foot massager, and I lay back and allowed Ling's touch to take me away. She massaged my feet until I thought I was going to have another orgasm right then and there. I looked down at her on the floor and was instantly aroused—partly because she was beautiful and partly because of the longing in her eyes to satisfy me. I closed my eyes again then felt Ling's hands trace the softness of my thighs. She massaged up and down my legs then slowly, yet gently, she opened the mouth of my cave and allowed the water from the foot massager to run over my wetness. Ling then began licking very delicately until I spread my legs wider and wider, climaxing harder than I ever had before.

Ling placed a finger inside of me, slowly pulling it in and out as she slipped a finger inside of my ass. Again, I climaxed, causing my body to jerk and twist in utter bliss.

By the time Saturday rolled around, I was truly on cloud nine. I had gotten plenty of rest, and I was finally comfortable with the experiences that I had over the weekend. I came—literally and figuratively—I saw, and I conquered any and every fear that I had ever had about sex. At the end of the proverbial day, I could honestly say that although Ling and I shared those intimate moments, I was definitely not into women. I needed a big dick any day of the week. Surprisingly, even Big Sexy was starting to get old to me. I needed some new dick.

Don't get me wrong. Big Sexy had it going on, but you know when two people lay down unattached, one of them is going to eventually get up with feelings, and I didn't want that kind of drama. Shawn was cool, too, but again, I needed some new experiences, and none of the people from my weekend tryst were going to cut it that night. Since I was in an adventuresome mood, I was going to hook up with this new guy I had met on the internet a few months ago. Since he lived all the way in Piscataway, New Jersey and I lived in Philly, it was hard for us to hook up, but this was going to be the night.

We had agreed to meet at the Borgada in Atlantic City, New Jersey, and I was so looking forward to meeting him. We had met on

HappyFucking.com, which is an internet site where a person can post their most desirable fantasies. Since I had always wanted to be with two men and had actually done that plus more during the past weekend with Ling, Big Sexy, and Shawn, I didn't know what to expect from David, my internet date.

I saw David, although he didn't see me since he was checking into the hotel room. I stood off to the side, just to make sure his ass wasn't crazy and to also make sure that I was attracted to him sexually. I knew that he was going to make all of my fantasies come true. I could just tell by the way he was built—strong arms, beautiful smile, and eyes that told me that he would be down for whatever, however, and that he was probably not going to have the largest dick in the world, but hey, those are ones who are usually the best lovers. They have to compensate in other ways.

I told David to bring some surprises with him and to meet me on the beach under the boardwalk, just in front of the club. We'd get to the hotel room later. I had on a white sundress and was completely naked underneath. I had already instructed David to walk up behind me, without turning me around, and lift up my sundress. I wanted him to stick his strong fingers in my pussy before he ever got a look at me. I felt David approaching. I could feel his warm breath on my neck, and I was almost forced to turn around just so I could rip off his clothes. I was horny, but I was going to drag this fantasy out, and we didn't have to get to the hotel any time soon.

David kissed me on the back of my neck and my earlobes and ran his tongue down the middle of my back. He cupped my breasts and slowly began massaging each nipple through the flimsy material. I reached back and began untying his cargo pants. I reached inside and found his not-so-big dick, but it would definitely do. Size truly doesn't matter. David pulled up my dress and began kissing my ass. He stuck his tongue between my cheeks as I held open my ass so that he could taste all of me. David inserted his finger, slowly and methodically. I climaxed, then he stood, ripped open a condom, quickly fumbled to put it on, and put his penis inside of me. I lay down, knees in the sand, ass up in the air. David straddled me and thrust his dick in and out, and his warmness made his shaft feel like home to me. He slipped his dick out of me, and I took him in my mouth, licking all of my juices off him. David came almost instantly, and I made sure that I didn't waste any of his juices as I swallowed each and every last drop.

"Nice to meet you, Tia. I'm David. Are you ready for your surprise?" he asked.

"That wasn't it?" I questioned.

"I hope you're not tired, because it's going to be a long night."

We walked back to the hotel, hand in hand, laughing as if we had been friends and lovers for years. I felt comfortable with David and was pleased that we had finally been able to connect in such a way. We had checked each other's background to make sure that we weren't disease infected or crazy lunatics. I loved to live on the wild side, but hey, only fools gamble twice.

By the time David and I got back to the hotel, a chilled bottle of Dom Perignon was on ice and a box of exquisite chocolates was laid on the bed.

"I want you to take a shower with me," David said. He began slowly undressing me and marveled at the sight of my breasts. He delicately removed my dress, and as I stepped out of it, David's warm mouth was there to greet each of my nipples. He slowly and gently flicked his tongue over my erect buds, and I thought I was going to scream. David stopped long enough to pour champagne in each of our flutes and quickly took a gulp of the bubbly. He lay me down on the bed, and with his mouth still full of the champagne, he sucked the sweetness off my breasts with the sweet-tasting liquid.

"Do you have any more condoms?" I asked.

"Naw, baby, we don't need any more of those," David said.

"Like hell we don't. I know it's corny but, no glove, no love," I said.

"Fuck. I only had that one," he said.

"Call the front desk and see what time the store closes," I suggested.

David called the front desk, and the store was closed. "Yo, you guys have any condoms down there at the front desk?...Word? How much?...Alright, send somebody up," he said to the person on the other end of the line. David jumped up, still naked, and ran to the bathroom.

There was a soft knock on the door. I debated calling David, but heard him taking a quick shower. Now, why the hell he did that was unknown to me. I ran to the door, looked through the peephole, and saw a fine-ass white boy in the hallway. I slowly cracked opened the door. "How much are they?" I asked.

"One for three dollars," he said.

"Wait right here." I pushed the door, not shutting it completely and walked over to David's pants pockets to look for some money. I grabbed a five-dollar bill and turned, and there was the white dude standing there gawking at me in all of my nakedness. He wore this seductive smile, and the way in which he was lusting at me, just staring at my breasts, caused me to get excited. I figured I'd fuck with him a little, just to have some fun.

I walked up to him and began rubbing my breasts in his face. I asked him, "You ever fucked a black chick?"

"My girl is black," he said.

"What you know about really fucking a black woman? You any good at your game?" I asked. He grabbed me by the waist and began sucking my breasts. He slid his hand down to my growing-wet pussy then instantly dropped to his knees. I placed one foot on the side of the bed so that he could taste my throbbing clitoris. This white dude had it going on. I pushed the back of his head, deeper, deeper, and came all over his face. His lips looked like two glazed doughnuts.

The bathroom door was flung open, and David came out, drying himself with a towel, not realizing that the white dude was still on his knees, my leg still cocked up on the bed.

"What the fuck is this? Get the fuck outta here before I kick your fucking ass," David said as the white dude scrambled to his feet, dropping the condom and running out the door.

"Now why did you go and do that? I bet if I walked out of that bathroom and some white chick was deep-throating that dick, you wouldn't have allowed me to kick her ass out," I said.

"That was foul. How you gonna let some guy you don't even know lick your pussy, just like that?" David asked.

"You mean just like you, a guy I don't know who just licked my pussy? Because I can, and guys do it all of the time. Now, you wanna keep acting like a little bitch, or are we gonna fuck?" I asked.

"You acting really mannish right about now," David whined.

"Man up and let's fuck."

David sat down and snatched me by the waist. He grabbed my hair and pulled tightly, kissing me roughly on the lips. It turned me on. David stopped kissing me. "I want this to be a memorable experience for us. I'm straight trippin'. We did agree that it is what it is, but damn, you straight went for yours."

"You talk too much." I stood and went to pick up the condom. I knew my pussy was straight in David's face. I tossed him the condom and said, "Here. Put that on. I'll be right back." I jumped in the shower to quickly wash the white dude's saliva off me. When I exited the bathroom, David was masturbating and looked as if he needed some help. I squirted a generous amount of lotion into my hand and spread equal amounts on both hands. I slowly began rubbing the thick lotion up and down David's dick, from the base to the tip. I placed his shaft between my ample-sized breasts and David began thrusting his hips harder and harder. The lotion was practically gone when David squirted profusely on my chest.

I lay down for a few moments, and David asked me to stand. He lay down first on the bed then positioned me so that my pussy was sitting on his face. I pride myself on my strong legs, and I began slowly bouncing up and down so that I could control the amount of pressure David's tongue applied to my clit. I creamed all of my juices on him almost instantly. David and I must have sexed each other for hours, until he finally passed out across the bed. I should have been tired, but I was still pumped and ready to go. So, that's what I did. I quickly dressed and headed back to Philly. I never wanted to lay eyes on David again. Not that the loving wasn't good, but he served his purpose, and I was on to my next adventure. Besides, he was definitely the type to catch feelings, and I wasn't built for that at the moment. It was all about how many times a day, week, or month I could get pleasured.

The sun was coming up, and I mafe it back to Philly in record time. I headed for Yvette, my twin sister's place in Cherry Hill, New Jersey, to check on her house while she and her husband were out of town. I was actually supposed to check on her house all week, but a sistah was kind of tied up, literally and figuratively speaking.

My sister is a true diva. She's beautiful, smart, funny, but definitely pretentious. We're obviously very different from each other. Where I walk on the wild side, Yvette has matured and is so different from me. My brother-in-law is an extremely handsome man. He's about five-eleven, nicely built, dark as midnight, and he's also very intelligent. They truly make a great couple, but I can tell their bedroom life is probably very stiff. More than likely it's my sister's fault. She needs a good lesson in how a woman can display her sexiness without being a hoe.

By the time I arrived to my sister's home, it was about 9:00 A.M. I grabbed the mail, placed it in the study, then checked all of the windows and doors to make sure they were locked. The poor cat was probably dead, but knowing my sister, she had some type of contraption so that he received fresh water and food each day. I looked into the pantry where the cat slept, and sure enough, he was doing just fine. He had clean water and fresh food, just like I knew there would be. It made no sense that my sister asked me to come check on her house, just like usual. I didn't know why she needed me to baby-sit her home, hell, she lived in a mini mansion, and her security alarm was probably better than the White House's system. Yvette wasn't due in from her business trip until 9:00 P.M. and Marcus was supposed to arrive from his fraternity conclave around 7:30 P.M.

Since I had the whole day ahead of me, I decided to take a nice, hot, and relaxing bubble bath in their huge whirlpool. I turned on the internal wall radio system, and the snazzy sounds of The Gap Band filled the air. I thought about throwing some Will Downing up in there, but I had already decided that I was going to stay the entire day there, so I had plenty of time to check out the five-thousand CD collection.

I was taking my deep soak in the bathroom when my hand innocently grazed my nipple. This caused me to instantly get horny. I gently squeezed my nipple then slid my other hand between my legs and began lightly pinching my clit. I was dumbfounded. After all of the attention David had given me the night prior, why was I still so horny? Was I turning into a nymphomaniac for real? Or is it true that when women hit their peak, there's nothing that can keep them sexually satisfied? Who knows and who cares? As long as I could get my freak on, up, in, and out, I didn't need the questions answered. Hell, I'm a grown-ass woman, and I'm not hurting anybody.

I continued playing with my pussy then sat on the side of the whirl-pool so that I could open my legs even wider and get my fingers nice and wet from the juices that were squirting out of me. I had my hand so far up in my pussy that I almost fell over the side when I felt someone began massaging my breasts from behind. It could only be one person: Marcus.

He rubbed his warm body against my back. I could feel him, rock hard, poking me. I turned around and began sucking his huge dick, deep-throating the hell out of him. He smelled so good and tasted even better. I have always wanted to fuck my brother-in-law, if only to teach him how to really fuck my sister. There was one thing that my sister never had to worry about and that was me trying to take her man. For me, it was simply about the teaching, and if I could show him how to get her to release that freak in her, it was all worth the effort. I know that my brother-in-law is a good man, but he probably had a chick on the side anyway, so the way that I looked at it, I was keeping it in the family. Yvette and I were practically the same person anyway. Hell, we're twins. As long as I was able to get my needs fulfilled, nobody had to get hurt.

I felt Marcus tensing up, and I looked up at his face, and it was all contorted. He grabbed me by the back of the neck, pushing my head, causing his the tip of his dick to hit my tonsils. He began squirting in my mouth, and I swallowed each and every last drop. His huge dick limped pitifully as it dangled in the air.

He picked me up and set me on the vanity. He spread my legs open wide then dropped to his knees where he feasted in my offerings. He licked my pussy like a true champion. He nibbled lightly on my clit, and I jerked back and hit my head on the mirror. I slid on my back and placed my feet on his back. I wanted him to taste all of me. He spread the mouth of my pussy open even more and dug his tongue way up inside of me, igniting a fire that I've never known before. I was about to cum all over his face, head, and neck when my sister walked in, butt naked.

"You don't eat me like that," she said.

"Omigod," I screamed. I wasn't sure how she would react to me sleeping with her husband. I mean I know men cheat and women experiment, but would my sister see it that way?

My sister said nothing as she got down on fours, turned so that she was positioned directly under Marcus and began sucking his balls and his dick. His once limp dick was back to erect again. Marcus dove his tongue deeper inside of my pussy, but it was hard for me to concentrate because as I looked down, my sister was going to town, sucking her husband's dick better than anything I've ever seen—or done for that matter. It was obvious that my sister wasn't the innocent little nerd I thought she was.

I couldn't concentrate on her technique for much longer. I had a nut to bust. No sooner than I thought that, Marcus pulled his tongue out of my saturated pussy, stuck his middle finger in my wetness then inserted his finger into my ass, causing me to lose control. I began bucking, and I swear my eyes rolled into the back of my head. Marcus then began trembling and shaking. It was apparent that my sister had brought him to his own climax.

Marcus pulled me from the vanity; bent me over, face down, ass up; and plunged his large dick into my ass as I spread my cheeks wide to accept him. I had only had anal pleasure once in my lifetime, and that was with Big Sexy, but the pain was intense, yet the feeling of Marcus slowly gliding in and out of my anal cavity, sent electrifying shockwaves throughout my ass. I wanted to scream, so I did. "You black bastard. You son o' bitch. Oh yeah, fuck me. Fuck me," I demanded. Marcus gave it to me harder, and I was loving it.

Yvette left the bathroom, which made me a little more at ease, but she returned a few moments later and took a seat on the side of the whirl-pool, looking quite bored. I closed my eyes tight and held on to the vanity. I was about to explode, and I almost lost my mind. The orgasm that I was experiencing was bigger, better, more outrageous than any-thing I'd ever experienced. I was simply losing my mind. Marcus tightly grabbed hold of my shoulders, as if he were going to fall over. He took one final thrust, and we exploded together, each gasping for breath.

"Get in the shower. Both of you," Yvette command.

I climbed in, and Marcus followed. I began scrubbing away the sweat and sex, and Marcus followed suit. After we each bathed thor-oughly, Marcus took the washcloth and began lathering my breasts, caus-ing my nipples to get erect, yet again.

I don't know how long we stayed in the shower, but, needless to say, Marcus picked me up, lay me on my back, my feet in the air, and began pounding the hell out of my pussy as the water cascaded all around us. I was screaming in delight as I thrust harder and harder, hoping to reach yet another orgasm. Although the climax that I had was small, it was still enough to cause me to be on a natural high, chasing another plateau that I wasn't sure existed. I was at the height of my sexual arousal.

When we climbed out of the shower, there were two huge white towels on the rack. Marcus took one and began drying me off slowly.

"You're beautiful," he said.

I didn't know what to say, so I opted to say nothing.

Yvette came back into the bathroom. "Go to our bedroom, baby.

Tia, I have a surprise for you," Yvette stated with a smile and walked back out.

I used the lotion in their cabinet to smooth all over my body. I didn't know what to expect. Yvette and I had shared men in the past, but never her husband. I didn't know if I could expect this kind of activity in the future or if this was just a one-stop shop.

I came out of the room and walked slowly down the hall to Yvette and Marcus' room. I heard laughter and soft whispers coming from behind the wall. I slowly opened the door and noticed that there was a man whose face I couldn't see since his back was turned to me. Before the man's familiar body registered, I heard his voice. All eyes were on me as I stepped into the room. Slowly, he turned around with a smile, and there was Big Sexy.

"Tia, I hope you don't mind that I invited Big Sexy," Yvette stated. "I thought we could have a little more fun before the day is over."

I wanted to collapse right then and there on the floor. Didn't these people know that I had been on what seemed like a citywide fucking spree for the past week and I was exhausted? A person, no matter how big or strong, could only take so much. I faked a weak smile but they caught on to my apprehension.

"What's the matter, baby?" Big Sexy asked.

"Nothing. Nothing's wrong," I lied.

"If you're tired, how about we take our little party on home and we can always catch up with these guys at another time?" Big Sexy said. "I just thought that you were down for whatever. You were the one who said that you were at some sexual peak and you needed to be satisfied."

My twin yelled out, "You too? Girl, I thought something was wrong with me. Morning, noon, and night. I just can't get enough."

Big Sexy walked up to my sister, spread her legs, and began slurping her wetness, which instantly creamed his face. Marcus began sucking on her breasts, and my sister looked as if she were in utter bliss. My sexual beast began awakening, yet again.

Marcus looked up. "Come over here and get with this party, girl."

I headed into the bathroom and grabbed my dress, quickly putting it on. I walked back into the bedroom, and Marcus and Big Sexy looked up as Yvette opened her legs even wider.

"Where the hell are you going?" they said in unison.

"I've officially had enough, and I don't want to see any of you in any type of sexual way any time soon. I had some great sex morning, noon, and night, and I have officially had enough."

Picked Up
by
E. Geoffrey Depp

As Monica sat on her couch she, thought, sooner or later she would have to tell him. She couldn't hide it from Geoff forever. But how? How could she let him know that she no longer desired men—at least not at the moment? Her first affair against him was with a woman who had stolen her, mind, body, and soul.

She never thought of being with another woman—until the evening she went out alone. The night Geoff left her to go on a business trip. She sat in the house and decided she would dress and go out for a drink or two. It was the first time she had been out without him since they met, but it would only be for an hour or two she told herself, not all night. Monica had gone into the bedroom and began to get dressed. After showering, she had looked at herself in the full-length mirror.

Girl, you are gorgeous, she had thought. She had lifted one of her 40DD breasts and admired it in the mirror before turning sideways and admiring her round ass. Not bad for a thirty-something woman with two children. After putting on her black mini-dress, high-heeled boots, and leather jacket, off she had gone to the club, not knowing her life was about to change.

Denise was on the prowl, looking for her next love, the next woman she would convert to her side of life. Her style was smooth: she would find the woman she wanted then like a tiger tracking and claiming her prey, she would pounce. Her game was tighter than any man could ever hope to have. She knew she could have any woman who crossed her path. She had a caramel complexion, almond-shaped light brown eyes that could burn right down to your core, short curly reddish-brown hair, and was thick in all the right places. Dressed to seduce, she was definitely on the prowl that night when she spotted Monica standing at the bar. Denise had to have her that night. She had to make her move before the male vultures had started to circle swooped on the big, beautiful vision of a woman.

As one guy had clumsily tried to pick up the woman, Denise had laughed to herself, walked in between them, and began a conversation like she had been waiting for her all night. "Hey, girl. Where you been? I been waiting on you for almost half an hour."

When the guy had walked away rejected. Monica had thanked her new friend for rescuing her. They introduced themselves, and Denise had offered to buy Monica a drink. Small talk and laughter at the men who had tried to pick them up filled almost an hour before Denise had decided to make her next move. She had said she needed to use the restroom and had asked if Monica wanted to come with her. When they had entered the ladies' room, Denise had pulled out a small vial of cocaine and asked Monica if she would like to try some.

"Fire and Desire" had started playing on the speakers in the ladies' room. Denise had moved closer to Monica, sensing that she would not pull away. Monica had not backed up. She had accepted the cocaine and Denise's closeness. They had both felt good to her. The 'caine had eased her nerves of being out alone, and Denise had somehow seemed to know what she was feeling.

They had finished in the bathroom and returned to the bar. Monica's favorite old-school jam was still playing, and she wanted to dance. Denise had asked and she had accepted. She had never danced with a woman before. Somehow it felt right, a familiar body against hers. Monica had started feeling moisture between her thighs, the type she only felt when her fiancé danced with her. She was confused but it felt good.

Denise had decided it was time to take the next step. She had leaned in and kissed Monica on the neck slow and tender, just barely touching her lips to her soft skin. Monica had moaned, signaling to Denise it was time. Denise had led her off the dance floor and back to their barstools. The conversation had turned to Monica's relationship status. Denise had asked if she had a man and where he was that night. Monica had told Denise she was engaged but her fiancé was gone on a weekend business trip.

With this new information Denise had put the rest of her plan into motion. She knew this was the woman she would take home. This was her new lover. She would mold her into the woman she wanted her to be. She would take her from her man. They had laughed and talked for a little while longer. Denise had asked Monica if she would like to get out of the loud club and go somewhere quieter where they could talk and get to know each other better. She had accepted. Not knowing what to expect, she had followed Denise's car to Denise's home.

Her home was elegantly furnished, everything in chrome and white. When they had entered the living room, Monica had immediately felt the need to take off her boots, not wanting to soil the white shag carpet. It had felt good to her bare feet, and it had relaxed her nerves quickly. She had to admit to herself that she was a little nervous, more than she should have been with another woman. But something was different with Denise, almost like she had been picked up.

Denise had come back in the living room with two glasses of white wine and offered one to Monica before sitting on the plush white couch next to her. She had reached on the coffee table and picked up a remote, pointed it at the fireplace, and pushed a button, causing the gas fireplace to come to life. She had picked up another remote, and Prince's "Adore" filled the air. They had both sipped wine and moved their head to the music. Seeing the look on Monica's face, Denise had set her glass on the coffee table, taken Monica's glass, and set it down as well. She had grabbed Monica's hand and led her to the middle of the floor, placed her arms around Monica's ample waist, and started a slow dance. Moving her hands up and down Monica's back, gently rubbing her rear end as she passed it, Denise had began to feel the tension leaving her body. She knew she had her.

Monica had moaned as Denise massaged her round ass while slowly raising her dress to reveal a matching thong and bra set. Denise was pleased to see that Monica did not resist her advances. She had began kissing her gently on the neck and shoulders, moving slowly to her juicy red lips. She had given her more passionate kisses and began to get moist herself when she realized the kisses were being returned with equal passion. Denise had broken their embrace and stepped back, pulling Monica's dress over her head then guiding her down to lay on the shag carpet. Removing her own clothing, she had lay next to her.

They had lay there in a full-body embrace. Denise had began kissing, sucking, and licking all over Monica's body. Her hands and lips had moved with the ease of the most experienced male. Even better, she knew exactly which buttons to push and exactly where they were. She had kissed and sucked on Monica's neck while one hand had alternated between massaging each breast and the other had made tiny circles on Monica's clit through her soaked panties.

Denise had felt her wetness and knew her desire had risen to new heights. She knew she had her trophy. She had begun licking and kissing slowly and deliberately down Monica's body, moving ever closer to her destination. Once she had reached Monica's center, she had began to lick up and down Monica's soaked silk panties, savoring the aroma and taste of the moisture there. She could taste the orgasm that was building inside of Monica. Slowly she had began to remove the panties to reveal her prize: Monica's secret button. Monica had raised her hips to ease the removal. The moans and groans that were coming out as Denise had began a full assault on Monica's clit could have wakened the dead, but Denise didn't care. Her house was far enough from her neighbors to muffle any noise they might hear. Monica was all hers and hers alone that night.

After Monica's first orgasm, Denise had paused momentarily to glance at her. She had looked so lovely laying there on that white carpet totally nude. Could it be that one woman had finally captured her heart? Was the hunter being caught by the prey? She had vowed from the day a woman stole her first true love from her, that she would never love again, especially not a man. She would only hunt, capture, and release. But this woman lying before her was the most beautiful she had ever seen. Denise suddenly wanted to love her not possess her. Caught up by these new feelings, she had taken her hand and led her to the bedroom to the oversize king sleigh bed to deliver Monica's first experience the right way, the only way.

She had laid Monica on the bed and reached in her nightstand to retrieve her eight-inch vibrator. Lying next to Monica, she had started massaging her breasts while rubbing the vibrator up and down her slit. Monica had moaned loudly as Denise had performed her magic on her. Denise had seen to it that Monica quickly reached her climax, and she had switched her movements.

After about forty-five minutes of taking her to the edge and bringing her back, Denise finally let Monica have her orgasm, to which she had been coming close for so long. She had inserted the vibrator into Monica and pistoned it with the force of the most powerful engine. Monica had come more forcefully than she ever had in her life. She could not wait to return the experience and favor to Denise that she had given to her.

She had switched the arrangement and had begun doing to Denise what she had done to her. She had proven to be a quick learner as Denise had began to wiggle and squirm at Monica's touch. Denise was amazed at how quickly Monica brought her to climax and so skillfully eased off as to not let her cum too fast. She had worked her. Her tongue had moved over her nipples as her fingers so agilely manipulated her clit and pocket. Monica was in complete control, like she had been doing this for years. They had slept in each other's arms for the rest of the night before separating the following morning, promising to make something of this new relationship.

As Monica sat in her living room reliving that night, just thinking about it made her wet. She debated on what to tell Geoff. She finally decided that she couldn't totally give up men because she loved the feeling Geoff gave her so much. Maybe, she thought, there was a way to combine both of them. Maybe she could have Denise and Geoff. If they could make her feel that good separately, what could they make her feel together? Maybe she could have her cake and eat it too.

Geoff walked in the door and interrupted her thoughts. Monica simply asked him to have a seat. She needed to talk to him about something. Maybe they could live happily ever after.

Mariah's Gotta Have It
by
Marissa Monteilh

If You Don't Know Me by Now

"When am I gonna be able to make love to you, Mariah?"

"When I'm sure," I replied to Malik from my jeweled Blackberry just before boarding the plane to see him at his new place in Baltimore.

He spoke through his mobile speakerphone while a L'il Kim CD cut blasted in the background. "With all we've been through, if you don't know me by now, you will never know me."

"It'll be right when we're committed."

"We're way past that."

"I mean, when we set a date."

"A date for what?"

I stood behind a woman who I could just feel overheard my every word as I tried to keep it down. I explained. "To get married. We've talked about it."

"Oh, so now you're telling me that you're gonna be some born-again virgin until you become a wife?" Sarcasm was not Malik's normal flavor.

I readjusted the strap to my oversized canvas purse, turned to my right side, looking down at the pale blue carpet. "No. Just until we set a date."

"Mariah, I love you."

"And I love you."

A Nelly song now played. "This wasn't the deal when we first started talking. You said just until you felt we were committed."

Proceeding at a snail's pace in the single-file line, I spoke my words through my teeth. "I know, but sex is very powerful, and to have to come back from what I know would be a very strong connection, I'm just not sure I'd be able to take that."

"What makes you think you'd have to come back from it?" The background music ceased.

"I'm just protecting myself." I'm sure I really didn't sound so sure of myself any longer.

"You know what? I'm just pulling up, and I'm running late." I heard the chirp of his Escalade alarm. "They're calling us. I'll pick you up at the airport after practice."

"I can't wait. See you then." He hung up seconds before I did. I gave the agent my ticket and headed down the ramp to the awaiting airplane door, headed to see this man who'd been playing by my rules. But I was starting to feel that if I didn't watch myself in my effort to protect my own heart, somebody else was going to satisfy the very intimate needs I was apparently neglecting.

Your Love Is King

Malik is young enough to be my son, and he's in the daggoned NFL. That's another reason why I'd been so cautious. But damn, what a man. We had been through a lot of major drama together: folks who thought I was too old for him, that he was too young for me, conflict over my trust issues after shaking my ex-Mr. Wrong, our issues with our estranged fathers, being that mine died right after I tried to get closer, and then Malik's father showed up for moral support after many years of abandoning him. See Malik got in a little trouble after a young white girl made false accusations once he reported to training camp in Baltimore. We got it all straightened out, but it showed me a whole other side of him that I really needed to see. It showed me that Malik could be trusted. Not to mention the fact that my three kids adored him. And the brownie points he earned by hanging tough when my father died weighed extremely heavily upon my decision to keep him in my life, in spite of our May-December age difference.

We were like day and night really in some ways and alike in others. In spite of me being forty and him being twenty-one, I was kind of classy conservative and he was kind of hip. But I liked his style and could hang with it. He liked my style at times even more than I did. And he'd been on his own since he was fifteen, so in many ways he was more mature than most forty-year-old grown-ass men I knew.

One of my challenges had been that I'd been trying to get past my nymphomania stage. I was physically addicted to a man for seven long years. Took all I could do to not lose my mind from that disconnection. It was like coming down from drugs because I was majorly addicted. His dick was like crack cocaine. Thank God Malik was right there to at least distract me. I could credit my success at "de-bonding" to the many weekly relationship classes I had attended that were taught by the love doctor, Dr. Singer. One thing I'd learned was that you must have the three C's in every relationship—chemistry, compatibility, and communication.

Malik and I were fairly compatible. We liked the same music, enjoyed bowling and cooking, and watching old *Martin* and *In Living Color* reruns, and he was into family like I am.

And we communicated very well. We talked on the phone all the time. He listened and then replied. I listened and then responded. He didn't judge me for my opinions, I didn't get all in his ass for his thoughts, and I respected him. The biggest thing he did, which no one else had ever done before, was that he cherished my feelings. That was a major turn-on for me. And he let me set the tone of the relationship, as in our need to talk and get to know each other before touching.

And chemistry? Hell, I knew there was chemistry when I first saw his sexy Michael Jordan baldhead when he was interning at that movie studio in Hollywood. My wetter than wet, hotter than hot pussy felt like it could have detached itself from me and landed straight on his dick all on its own.

So with all that said, and after all this time, I'd say we are definitely in a strong relationship. He'd been everything to me other than all up in me. And even though we were in different states, it was working. Aside from all of the sleeping-together allowances, the "Just don't let him in" rules, I'd say it was time to . . . fuck. Because even though I'd been trying to tame the hot side of me, the sex machine side of me, and ignore the fact I could have the dick up inside me 24/7 and never complain, it was time that Malik knew that Mariah's gotta have it too. And I mean now, as in today.

All I Do Is Think of You

I guess we'd been way past the talking and deep into the touching part. Thus far, boyfriend had been able to get it on in a major way when it came to bedroom romancing. I mean, it was like he was twice his age. He could stick his long tongue deep into my ear and make the downtown juices drip like percolating coffee. He could suck and flick my nipple like it was a clit. He could fist me with his whole hand, first with his index and middle fingers, then the knuckles and then the rest, one by one, like a porno pro, and Lord knows I could take it like the freak that I was—or am. And he could grind that long stiff one along the pubic area of my pussy like he was stripping at The Right Track while I placed folded dollars in the crack of his muscular ass. Not to mention that he could go down on my hairy mound in a way that no man had ever done in my entire life.

And Malik didn't just get to it. He approached it, he located it like it had been lost and found, and he teased it like he was reading a pussy's mind. The trail he took was always different, sometimes traveling down the right side of my stomach, fooling around near my hipbone, then proceeding downward to my upper thigh. Oh but no, it would be too easy to simply head over to the left and hit the spot, no he had to make a path down my thigh, dashing inward and upward until he hit my knee, sucking it and biting it and kissing it for just a moment, and then just like clockwork, my anxious hips would start urging his mouth along, hoping his X-rated face would come back up to the mound that secreted syrupy juices as a thankful result of this tempting torture. Having mercy for a moment on my pathetic weak flesh, he would head uptown and zigzag to my inner thigh, lightly flicking only the outer skin of my blood-swollen meat. I would quiver and moan and scoot and then my hand would politely encourage the back of his head to continue. But he would proceed to the other thigh and flick his wet point along my butterscotch skin as though it tasted the same as its color.

And then suddenly, he would proceed upward again and point his tongue to separate my labia, licking up and down with short, swizzling motions. It was unbearable pleasure. He would move his arms upward and scoot upward as well, placing his elbows along my knees to make sure my legs stayed straight as a board so that the ultimate rush of blood could flow from my booty to my clit to my flexed quads and down to the curve of my calves and on to the tips of my flexed toes. How else would he want me to explode but full force?

And of course my burst was going to be grand, like it was the last nut I'd ever bust in life because no one did it like Malik who approached the pussy. He kissed it with full lips as if he loved it. He traced the fullness of my waiting lips with his tongue, and he moaned along with me. The vibration of his moan permeated my hot skin. He would press his face closer and kiss me harder, reaching under me to grip my butt cheeks, lifting my hips so that my rock-hard clit was secured directly, deep between his lips.

Licking it was never enough for Malik. It might be for some, but was never enough for my stud. Malik would move his face back and forth along my skin, finding the exact spot to bury himself, scooting his face downward to find my erect clit, directly sucking it with an expert moustache ride as quick as a butterfly's wings. I would feel my hardness stiffen even more, growing as he sucked it gently within his mouth. The sensation was erotic and nasty, and it made my fantasies run wild.

I envisioned him in the backseat of a limousine on his knees, sucking off that conservative-ass woman who owned his team. He was on his knees, she was butt naked with a lace thong around her ankles, and he was turning her out. I was driving the limo, and through the rearview mirror, the vision turned me on so intensely, that I could feel the buildup from my ass to my pussy. My legs were parted, and with one hand I rubbed my mound through my panties.

As I fantasized, Malik paused just so he could insert the length of two fingers inside of me before he went back to pussy eating 101. And as he probed deep inside my liquid-sugar vagina, he lip smacked and sucked me up again, telling me, "Give me that sweet cum. I know you want to give it all to me."

With my eyes shut I responded, "Uh-huh," while I resumed my visual, this time with his boss about to bust a wet wave right in his face.

"Malik, I had no idea you could work it like this," she said loudly, looking down at him with an amazed lust.

His dark black skin, her milky white skin, her skinny ass getting turned out, his big muscular body with his fine baldhead buried between her long legs.

"Malik, I'm, I'm, awwwahhhh," I screamed as I pulsated deep into his awaiting mouth.

He kept his head steady as I released then he swallowed, planting a kiss as he backed away. "It throbs so hard," he said while coming up from his hard work, aiming for my face as he gave me the tongue action of my life.

Malik then lay upon his back, and it was my turn to take over.

From underneath my midnight-blue lap blanket, I removed my busy fingers from the front of my soaking-wet scarlet panties just as I heard the startling sound of a female voice.

"Ladies and gentlemen, the captain has turned on the fasten seat belt sign. Please return to your seats, as we'll be arriving at our destination shortly. Please be sure your seat backs are brought to an upright position and that your tray tables are secured firmly. The current temperature in Baltimore is seventy-eight degrees. From all of us here at Delta airlines, we want to thank you for flying this afternoon and wish you safe travels while you're here in Baltimore."

This was one time when sitting alone in the last row up against the window was definitely a good thing.

So Amazing

His molasses ass was standing at the baggage claim area, looking like the star he was in his Ravens baseball cap and black-and-purple team sweat suit. He looked like that mocha-smooth-skinned running back, Terrell Davis. Damn, Malik was one fine nigga.

As soon as he saw me, his pleased brown eyes spoke just before his words. "Hey, baby. It's so good to see you."

I quickly ran up to him with wide-open arms. He immediately picked me up, planting a kiss on my lips with his full, chiseled mouth. He smelled of Vera Wang for men.

As he lowered me, I could feel his hard-ass dick up against my belly. I was truly blessed.

"It's good to see you, too, Malik. I've been waiting for this for too long."

I hugged him around his neck, and he hugged me right up against my behind, taking a minute to grab two handfuls of soft ass before slapping me on my bottom right in front of everyone.

I didn't even glance around to see who noticed. "You look really good, Malik. The NFL agrees with you," I said as we walked toward the parking lot under the afternoon sun. He pulled my leopard luggage behind him with his protective arm around my waist.

"Having you here agrees with me," he said as though sincere.

Oh hell, yeah. It was on for sure—this afternoon, this evening, and in the morning too.

Love Has Found Its Way

We sauntered through some of the designer stores downtown and then into Sears where he had an account. He ended up choosing a trendy store called Classic Urban Interiors. He wrote a check for the total of about four rooms' worth of furniture.

I strolled along next to him wearing my short red knit skirt, sheer ruffled blouse, and copper-and-silver peep-toe pumps. My feet were killing me, but Malik held on tight and kept checking me out from behind so I endured the pain of looking sexy for my man.

Hours passed before we headed home. Malik had his hand on my lap, holding my hand as he drove. He played a Jeffrey Osborne CD, replaying the "You Should be Mine" cut over and over, singing every word. "Can you woo, woo, woo?" he belted out as if he had a microphone.

He bobbed his head while turning the corner to his Beverly Hills–like, Rose Creek subdivision. My chin dropped at the sight of the palatial ranch-style homes.

A new white Dodge Charger that was all detailed and pimped out in chrome pulled up as Malik pressed the garage door opener, waiting to pull in.

As the tinted gray driver-side window slowly rolled down, a pretty face stared over at both of us. "Hey, Malik," she said with a friendly smile. My chin dropped farther.

"Hey," he said as he pulled his black truck right up into the three-car garage, only looking over for a quick second, then making sure the garage door lowered behind him. Yeah, he was a damn vulva magnet that's for sure.

I only inquired, "Who's that?"

"That's Amanda who lives next door."

"Amanda?" We both got out and closed the car doors.

"Mariah, she's got a boyfriend, and I'm not interested in her in the least. I would have opened the door for you."

"Oh, no problem. She looks mighty young."

"I don't care."

"Yeah, well I do."

He made sure to change the subject as we headed into the house through the door that led from the garage to the kitchen, "What do you want to eat?" He tossed his keys onto the small kitchen desk.

"Whatever you want." I told myself, *Mariah, don't start any shit.*

He opened the side-by-side refrigerator and perused the contents. I stood behind him, looking in as well as he opened the freezer. "I don't have a damn thing in here. Don't even have any frozen chicken breasts to make on my Foreman grill."

I stepped away, admiring the grand kitchen. "Then that'll be our next stop tomorrow, the grocery store."

"You can go and drop me off. I've got a meeting at nine in the morning."

I looked over at Malik as I heard his doorbell ring.

"Who's that?" I asked.

He handed me a stack of menus. "I don't know." He continued to speak as he walked toward the front door. "I say we order something like pizza or Chinese."

I glanced through the menus then placed them on the dinette. "Chinese sounds good."

"Hey, and would you mind also going to like Linens and Things or somewhere like that to get the guestroom bedding and anything else like, well you know, statues and plants and things that'll give it a woman's touch?"

"I will. That'll be fun." I watched him as he turned the brass door-knob.

"Hi, Malik. Sorry to bother you." A girlie voice was all I heard.

"Hey, what's up?"

I walked closer to the door then stopped within ten feet of Malik. Girlfriend looked like a freakin' sex symbol. She wore a dark green pair of tight shorts and a low-cut yellow top with yellow-and-green tennis shoes. Her tan was as brown as mine.

She told Malik, "Gary told me to stop by, that he left his keys in your truck. He said he left word for you."

"Oh yeah, he did. I've been busy shopping with my lady. Come on in. Mariah, this is Becky. She's my teammate, Gary Ferguson's wife. They live right around the corner." Malik walked into the kitchen to get the set of keys.

"Nice to meet you."

"You too," I told her as she stepped past the threshold.

"So, are you from here?" she asked.

I crossed my arms. "No, I'm from L.A."

"I see." She gave me a long once-over. "Nice shoes."

"Thanks."

Malik walked back toward her as he spoke, handing her the key ring. "Becky, Mariah's the one I told you guys about."

"Thanks. Oh, okay. I remember Gary saying something. Well, it's nice to meet you. Sorry to bother you."

Malik replied, holding the door open with his right hand, "No problem."

"Nice meeting you too," I expressed.

She told me, "I'll see you soon. We'll have to have you two over for dinner one night."

"Sounds like a plan."

She headed out the door and turned for a second, twirling the ends of her long blond hair as she said, "Good-bye Malik. Good-bye, ahh, what was your name again? I'm sorry." she asked me.

Malik answered for me. "Mariah."

"Oh, okay. Bye, Mariah."

He closed the door and took my hand, leading me back toward the kitchen.

"Malik, are all of the girls around here white?"

"Mariah, I don't care about that. You're not trippin' off that again. Besides, that's not what I want or need to have."

"More than anything, she looked eighteen."

He turned to face me, placing his hands on my upper arms. "Mariah, you're with me. You'll meet more of the team wives soon enough. And they're all different races. Most are black. You'll see." He stepped away from me. "Did you find a place we can call and order food?"

"I did." I walked back to the menus and handed him the one on top. "Let's try this one." I sat at the kitchen table in deep thought while he dialed. What was I getting myself into?

I took a minute to look around his massive palace. After my baby made the cut, he signed a three-million-dollar deal for five years, and shit, he wasted no time in buying the six-thousand-square-foot lakeview home that we'd narrowed it down to over the Internet. This one was even more beautiful than I'd ever thought it could have been. It was spacious and new and done up in off white and black, with a little brown sprinkled throughout. He already had appliances, a flat-screen television, a bright red leather sectional in the living room, a pool table in his game room, and a huge king-size poster bed in the middle of his master suite. That day we bought him a beech wood bedroom set, laminated coffee tables, a formal walnut dining room set, an Italian bedroom set for one of his guest rooms, two huge sable-and-mocha lounge chairs and ottomans, and major pecan-and-bone furniture for his office.

I imagined how the new furniture would look, particularly the glass tables in his living room. And as I looked over at the enormous encased jersey hanging over the fireplace and all of his trophies and awards along the ledge, smack dab in the middle was a silver framed, eight-by-ten smiling photo of my jealous ass.

Sweet Sticky Thing

"That was good," I told Malik after I took my last bite. His surround-sound stereo serenaded us through our shrimp fried rice, cashew string beans, and tangerine chicken dinner. "Are you done?"

"Yes, baby." I stood and took his plate. "Thanks," he said kindly.

I heard him sing the words to Musiq's song, "Love." He looked at me with bedroom eyes even though we were in the kitchen. I headed toward the sink in my bare feet to rinse our plates from our Chinese food, bending over, opening the black dishwasher. Malik sat at the kitchen table, watching me with his grown and sexy butt, sipping on a black wineglass filled with chilled Muscato. He commented, "So domesticated looking at times but so damn sexy."

"Oh really? I'm not sure I like that word *domesticated*."

"But you like the word *sexy*, don't you?"

"At my age, I'll take it."

"Mariah, in your case, age is just a number because you look better than anyone's girlfriend or wife I know, and that's the truth."

"That's nice of you to say. I'll have to see that with my own eyes."

He leaned back, sitting with his legs open. "Come here."

"I'm putting away the dishes." He picked up his wineglass, rose to his feet, and took slow paced steps in my direction, bringing his wide-receiver frame within an inch of my face, setting his glass on the counter. "Malik, let me just . . ." Right away, he took my upper arm into his hand then took my other arm, turning me to face him. "What?" I asked.

He still had seduction in his eyes. "Thank you for flying out here and helping me figure out what to put in this place. I know how you feel about flying."

"I slept most of the way." And participated in mile-high masturbation. "And I had fun today."

"This place already seems more homey just having you here."

"Thanks, but anyone would be glad to help you do that. This house is like a mansion compared to my apartment. And it's probably cheaper than what I pay in expensive L.A."

He chuckled. "Probably so. Maybe you won't have to worry about rent anymore if you move here with me."

"Malik." I heard him loud and clear but pointed to the dishes. "You know I'm enjoying my new anchor job in L.A. And the kids are . . ."

He turned my chin toward him with his index finger and kissed me mid-sentence, pulling me close with a tight embrace that was powerful yet tender all at once. I felt my nipples begin to harden. He broke away from our lip-lock. "Where's your wine, baby?"

I exhaled loudly. "Mine's been gone."

"You want some more?" he asked like he was ready to get me juiced up.

I gave him a close-up stare. Now see if he'd just left me alone. "Actually after that kiss, what I want is for you to kiss me again."

He placed his lips on mine and slyly reached down to unbutton my blouse, unsnapping the hook of my bra from behind by touch, exposing my bare chest. I moved my own hands up to my breasts and began rubbing them, squeezing with a horny grip, then grabbing his hands and moving them along the hemline of my skirt. I raised the fabric up toward my waistline, finding my panty line and placing his hand inside.

He slipped his hand down to my brown-sugar lips while backing me up, step by step, against the large oak island. The coldness of the black-and-tan speckled granite countertop hit the small of my back as I was sandwiched between the island and the hardness of his crotch area. He turned his head to take my tongue into his mouth again while slowly fingering my split. He pressed one finger then another up into my vagina, giving me a soft finger ride with his index and middle fingers, pressing his hand upward and rubbing my clit area with his thumb. He repeatedly stuck his fingers in and out as I surrendered to the erotic movement.

He spoke into my ear. "Damn, this cunt is soaking wet."

"It's wet just for you. See what you do to me." I kissed his massive dark neck.

He circled my clit, sliding and rubbing the greasy wetness between my pussy hole to my cherry, over and over.

He spoke quietly. "Look at you, so juicy and so damn hot. That pussy is ready."

If he only knew. "Baby, hey, hold on a minute." A brainstorm rolled through my kinky mind. Something I'd been fantasizing about showing him.

"What?"

"Wait a second."

The X-rated instructor in me stepped toward the refrigerator after he removed his hand. He picked up his wineglass, finishing off the rest in one big gulp, and leaned back against the counter, watching me intently. I opened the freezer door and reached into a box I'd seen earlier.

"What's that?"

"This is what you're going to use to play with me."

I raised the frozen dessert toward his face. The size of his romantic eyes doubled.

"A Fudgesicle?"

"I guarantee you it's going to be gone in about three minutes."

Malik shook his head. "That's my girl. I'm glad I bought those bad boys now."

He lifted me up by my waist and propped me upon the counter, straightening my legs as she reached for my red silk panties, pulling them down all the way to my ankles and off each foot, tossing them onto the kitchen floor. He bent my legs back as I leaned back on my elbows while he took the frozen chocolate out of the package and then into his mouth. He sucked the Popsicle himself while looking into my eyes, then lowered it down to my hairy pussy, which awaited him.

"Pretty."

"Thanks, baby. Now please fuck me with it."

Malik leaned up to kiss my mouth as I tasted the chocolate from his icy tongue, then he looked down as he placed the Fudgesicle at the exact spot of my pussy, lightly using the tip to trace the design and shape of my swollen lips while he held on to the wooden stick.

"Oohhhh." I tightened my turned-on pussy muscles, feeling my vagina contract and jump.

"Is it too cold?"

"No, baby."

He moved it lower and found my hole, lightly inserting it into my tightness while the heat of my pussy walls sent the frozen stick swelling and dripping, leaving traces of dripped brown cream along the way.

"Deeper," I begged, watching his every move.

He pushed it inside farther. The thrill of the coldness combined with the visual of his hand pressing it inside, his muscular bicep flexing, his strong forearm moving along with his hand, and the feeling of the juices so wet inside of me, sent me into a sensual grind. It was a chocolate screw, and my pussy was enjoying every tantalizing turn.

In no time, what was an inch or more of width of a Popsicle was a wooden stick with barely a glimmer of Fudgesicle left. The remnants dripped along the counter and between my ass cheeks and the depth of my sloppy-wet pussy lips.

Lustfully, he looked up at me just as I leaned my head to the side, and he bent downward to bury his gorgeous face between my sweet, sticky thighs.

Whimpers of ecstasy escaped my lips.

My wetness increased as he took over, replacing the stick with his hot tongue. With his other hand, he fingered my clit while kissing every inch of my soaked skin. My pussy was dripping cream and chocolate, and he slurped every drop.

His tongue slid in and out as he tasted me and licked me and savored the sweetness of my milk-chocolate cunt. He sucked the fullness of my lips. It was sweet torture, and it had me beaten. While I looked down at his chocolate head bringing me pleasure so well, my mind raced, and I pumped my legs forward, feeling the throb approaching my middle. I felt a sudden strong spasm of pleasure. My orgasm exploded between my legs and onto his fine-ass face. He held tight to my thighs as I pressed my cum into his mouth. He licked my secretions with a firm tongue and then I heard him gulp just before he lightly kissed my pussy through the final seconds of my vaginal burst.

"Malik, aaah, that it so fucking good. Damnit."

Sexual Healing

Malik removed his clothes and stepped into his huge crimson-tiled shower behind me just after I stepped in with my shaver and bottle of Glo by J. Lo.

"Get your fine ass in here," I told him as I rubbed the scented body wash all over my skin.

He inspected my every curve with his eyes. "You're the one. You have the body of life."

He rubbed his dark body up against my ass. His dick was poking me at the very split of my generous ass. I reached for the pink shaver, placing it near my pussy.

"Baby, it looks so good. Why are you doing that?"

"Every now and then I just get rid of it. It's just easier than trimming it all up."

"Here, baby, let me do it for you."

I paused like surely he didn't want that job. "If you want to."

"I want to."

He took the Lady Shick from me as I placed my left foot onto the shower step. He got on his knees while the water ran down from my shoulders to the front of my body and down toward his hand. He placed the shaver at my hairline and gently shaved downward.

"Like this?" he asked.

I looked down at my giving man. "Yes. Just like you'd shave that pretty baldhead of yours."

Again he kept shaving with soft downward motions, moving my skin slightly so he could get a clean stroke, rinsing the shaver, even lifting my leg a little to the side so he could get all into the crevices and back near my ass.

"This is a pretty-ass pussy, baby."

"Thank you." I closed my eyes, feeling his fingertips upon my skin.

"It's like it was chiseled to look like this. It's the prettiest thing I've ever seen."

I moaned in reply and smiled.

He allowed the water to rinse me as I leaned back, brushing my short, wet hair back away from my face with my hand. He lightly placed a peck on my bare mound and stood. I let out a long breath while he hugged me. I rubbed my bareness against his thighs, bending slightly to allow his thigh to rub against my clit. I grinded toward him and pressed my groin harder as he hugged me while we stood beneath the warm spray of pulsating water.

The water actually soothed our heat as he reached down to finger my clit while I came in his hand.

"Malik, you love me so good," I said as I released every bit of my spasm against him.

After a long hug and final rinsing off our bodies, Malik stepped out first and took my hand to help me exit. This generous man, far from a little boy, handed me a large ebony towel and turned me around to dry my back, my butt, and my legs, and moved around to my front to dry my neck, chest, and between my legs. Our bodies glistened among the gold night-light as I checked us out in the floor-to-ceiling beveled mirror.

He reached for his glass of wine from the toffee-tiled bathroom sink. Upon my neck and wrists, I sprayed some of the perfume from the rainbow bottle of Pleasure he'd bought me from the Estee Lauder store earlier that day.

"Come with me." He took me by the hand. I followed. I grabbed my baby lotion with my other hand.

Feel the Fire

With maple syrup–scented roman candles burning inside of his glass fireplace, Malik laid my naked body upon his massive pillow-top mattress, enveloped in black-and-white wool cashmere bedding.

He stood over me butt naked and held his wineglass over my body. He dripped just enough droplets of wine upon my skin, filling my belly button then lowering himself to stick his tongue into the hollow of my belly as he slurped, pressing his tongue against my skin, pointing the tip inside then backing away. He poured drops along my hard nipples then up to my mouth where he dribbled the liquid grapes along my lips as I opened my mouth and allowed each drop to fall inside. He brought his mouth to mine and tasted me tongue to tongue. His teeth lightly teased my lower lip, and I squirmed.

My clit was erect as he lay upon me.

He gently bit my nipple then swirled his tongue, moving along to the other nipple, which was standing at attention. The hairs on my arms rose, my ass muscles tightened, my heart raced, knowing what Malik didn't know for sure that he was going to be digging inside of my body with his dick within ten minutes.

I touched him on his shoulder and sat up, leaning my upper body over toward him while he turned to his back. I sat up across his midsection, saddling him where he lay.

I bathed him with my tongue, starting with his toes, his knees, his inner thighs, then I took his largeness into my hand. Inch by inch, his thick veins pulsated as he grew within my grasp. His width was too wide for my complete grip.

I brought my pouty lips to his stiff cockhead and stuck my tongue out, pointing it slightly. As I grasped his penis, he grinded intently as though in serious anticipation of my deep-throat action. I cupped his balls, using the other hand to stroke his length, adding drooling spit to ease the long, slippery stroke. I ran my tongue over his swollen head as trickles of precum escaped his opening. I licked each drop and stuck the tip of my tongue into his tiny tip split, surrounding the opening with my hot mouth and wet tongue. My tongue made circles around his head. I brought his dick to my face and swabbed my skin with his stiffness, rubbing his cocoa smoothness up against my chin, neck, collarbone, cheeks, ears, forehead, and eyes then down to my soft round bosom. I found his hand with mine and took his two middle fingers into my mouth, looking up at him as he leaned his head back, surrendering to my motions. I resumed sucking his penis with a firm grip, so deep into my mouth that another inch and I'd be choking on dick. I bobbed up and down passionately.

"Mariah, that's it." His toes were curling.

I moved downward to his scrotum then to his full, beautiful balls. I flicked my tongue back up to his head and down to his balls, taking one into my mouth and then the other, swirling them both about, making sure to give slippery ease with my saliva. He breathed deeper, and I looked up at him as I saw nothing but lust in his eyes. He watched my every move.

I ran my fingernails around the area of his asshole then followed the spot with my mouth, kissing his asshole and poking my stiff tongue inside as far as it would go, squinting my eyes and grabbing his ass cheeks.

"Fuck, that feels good. Damn you know what you're doing."

Yes, I do, Malik, I said to myself. To him I just said, "Uh-huh."

"You're a great lover, Mariah."

"You make me want to, baby. Here, you do it for me," I told him as I found his right hand and put it on his own perfect dick.

"Huh?"

"You do it. Show me how you do it when you're thinking about me and I'm not here."

He moved his hand away, and I moved it back.

"Let me watch you jack yourself off, baby. I'll help you."

I reached over to his headboard shelf and grabbed the bottle of baby lotion, pouring a generous handful onto my left hand, reaching over to place all of it on the tip of his dick.

"Here, you stroke it for me."

He closed his eyes as I lay on his left side. I grinded against his hip and sucked his stiff left nipple, lightly squeezing the right nipple with my left hand.

He sucked air through his teeth. "Oh fuck." He stroked to the sound of sloshing lotion.

"You like that?" I spoke close to his chest.

"Uh-huh," he responded, giving himself a full up-and-down hand job.

"Stroke that dick like you do when you're imagining screwing me in the shower. Do you pretend to be fucking me from behind?"

His eyes were shut tight. "Yes."

"Do you bend down so you can get in past my ass cheeks and pump away, grabbing your big hard dick and pretending your hand is my deep yellow pussy?"

"Yes."

I sucked his nipple like mad, twisting his other one with my saliva-soaked fingers. "Do you come good for me, babe, shooting all over the shower wall?"

"Yes."

"Do you squeeze that cum out of your long dick, pretending to be fucking me in the ass?"

"Yes."

"Show me, Malik. Show me how you come when I'm not here. Show me how you'd come if my fat pussy were sitting on that dick right now. Show me how you'd shoot that hot cum all inside of this pretty pussy, baby. Show me how."

"Like this?" he asked, grunting and tossing his head from left to right, stroking himself wildly, smearing every bit of lotion from the base of his dick to the head, maneuvering his thumb over his tip.

"Yeah, give it long stokes. Is that how you like it stroked? That's how you like to cum?"

"Yes, Mariah, that's how I cum. Just like this."

While I sucked his bulletlike nipple as if I were sucking his dick, he propelled forceful squirts that jetted up and over onto his stomach, running down his hands as he still gripped himself tightly.

I spoke down toward his sperm. "That's my baby. That's my baby."

He ceased his stroke and looked down at himself. "Damn, girl. That felt so good, I can't even tell you."

"I'm sure it did."

"I'll be right back," he said, breathing at a fast pace.

Malik went into the bathroom, and all I heard was the sound of running water. I lay there knowing that pretty dick was going to be fucking me in just a matter of minutes, after all this time. And yes, he's a nipple and an ass man all right.

Lady

He hummed along with his stereo and approached the bed as he prepared to lie on top of me. I scooted to the edge of the bed and lay back, placing my feet flat on the floor.

"Get on your knees and watch me now," I told him with lust.

"Watch you what?"

"Watch me cum."

He prepared to put his mouth on my juiced-up pussy.

"No. No touching and no tasting. Just watch."

He sat on his knees as I pushed my mound within two inches of his face.

"Smell it."

He inhaled deeply through his nose.

"What does it smell like?"

"It smells like heaven."

"What does it look like?"

He spoke as if my clit was my ear. "It looks like the finest, most perfect pussy meat I've ever imagined in my entire life. It's like a fresh peach, and it's plump and fucking beautiful."

"Do you love it?"

"Yes."

"Do you want to see me rub it?"

"Yes."

"Like this?" I stuck one finger inside. With the other hand I pulled back the moist, red-clay skin of my hood to fully expose my large, pink bare fleshy clit standing at attention.

"Yes."

"Is that a pretty clit?"

"It's huge and pretty. Damnit."

I took my middle finger and rubbed my clit, bringing my finger to my mouth for saliva lubrication as I rubbed my clit again, then inserting three fingers inside of myself.

Malik's hand was moving fast along his shaft. I knew he was giving me his full attention, but I had to ask. "Are you watching?"

"Yes."

"Are you stroking your dick to this?"

"Yes."

"Are you hard again?"

"Yes."

"Do you want me to cum?"

"Yes."

"Tell me you love this pussy."

"I love this pussy."

I just had to try to take him to my old stomping grounds, Pussy University. Just had to make sure I secured my place. "Tell me this is the only pussy you'll ever need."

"This is the only pussy I'll ever need."

"Now kiss it lightly. And I want to hear you kiss it."

His face was in the right place. He gave a big wet smack. The sound was nasty, and it was working.

"Kiss it like you love it."

He kissed it again.

"I'm about to nut in your face, Malik."

"Give it to me," he told me with anticipation.

"Let me hear you. I need to hear you," I damn near yelled. He slobbered the sound of a big fat smack right at the position of my throbbing insides, and I fucked myself with my hand with speed and friction, enough to send me into the wild spasm of my pulsating orgasm. "Uuuh, yes, you love this pussy, Malik?"

"I love you, Mariah."

"Fuck," I yelled as I shuddered from his words.

Love's Holiday

Before I could even release the last bit of wetness that oozed from my inside tunnel, Malik lifted me from under my arms, backing me up toward the headboard. He placed my head on the down pillow and lay upon me.

"Mariah, can I cum inside of you?"

I said it, finally. "Yes, Malik."

With those two words, he parted my legs with his knee and extended my legs to rest upon his shoulders. He guided my pussy to his dick by grabbing my ass. It had been a long time since I'd had a dick inside of me. The anticipation was burning me into a heated sweat. I lay missionary, ready.

I tensed up in anticipation as he grabbed his dick and used his knuckles to check for the exact location of my opening. He then parted my swollen, smiling lips with his stiff cock. He rubbed the head of his wide penis up and down the length of my golden pussy and slowly began to push himself inside for the first time, slowly stretching his way in, all the while looking dead into my eyes as I returned the same expectant glance. Penetrating my walls with each gradual pump, Malik's cock was finally inside of my welcoming cunt. It was like a reunion of two long-lost strangers.

Wet like I'd never been before, I was ready in more ways than one. He moved slowly with purpose. I trembled with my arms around his neck.

"Are you okay?" he asked as he was just beginning to get about halfway in.

I replied with a bracing moan. "Yes."

It was as though I was having sex for the first time. The sensation was nasty and sweet and erotic and orgasmic and sensual and X-rated. I felt like I'd never known a dick before, other than the way this one felt as it entered me. He grinded in deeper, and all I could think was that I was full of my man's dick. I grinded my mound against him as he slipped his hard-on deeper inside. It was like he was growing and growing more and more the deeper he got. And it was a perfect fit.

As he pumped into my bald vagina, he brushed his nipples against mine. I reached down to put my own nipple into my mouth, sucking on it as I felt him throb. He leaned down and took my other nipple into his mouth as we both sucked each one together. He brought his mouth to mine and kissed me firmly yet softly.

"I've been waiting for this for so long," he told me, staring all through me.

"Me too." I was drunk with passion for this man.

He held my hands out at my sides, interlocking fingers as he grinded and pumped. His entire shaft engulfed my pussy.

He glanced down at me with passion. "Your body is so beautiful. It's like an hourglass, and your breasts, your legs, your waist... Mariah, you're perfect."

He fondled me and enjoyed me, which turned me on even more. He watched me as I breathed short, rapid breaths, more excited than I ever thought I'd be. I heard his words but what I felt was speaking a whole lot louder. I'd imagined this head for so long, masturbated to the thought of this very dick deep inside of my body, bringing me pleasure like this, exploring me as we made love.

I concentrated on his dick in my bare pussycat, as though a porno-flick camera were down there. I imagined what it would look like up close, coming out greasy, traveling back inside with the milky wetness surrounding his hardness, dripping along his balls. I massaged my nipple as his erection strengthened. He jerked.

He was deep inside me.

"So this is what it feels like, huh? This is the pussy that drove that nigga Kareem so crazy?"

I rubbed my snatch closer to him in reply, and he rubbed back. He was sweaty.

Suddenly our fucking felt wilder and nastier. He gripped me tightly as our bodies entwined. I wrapped my long, thick legs around his waist more firmly. Dr. Singer was right. Making love is much better than just having sex.

You Sure Love to Ball

He pulled back only to drive forward into me with one deep stoke after another, over and over, pounding harder and harder into my throbbing meat. I dug my frosted fingernails into his back and clamped down on him as he dove in. He sped up as my cries grew louder. He then shifted himself.

"What are you doing?" I asked as he pulled his length out of me.

"Turn over."

"Doggie style?" I sounded like I'd won the lottery.

"Yes." He jerked me up by my slim waist as I got up on all fours with my bodacious ass poked up high in buck-wild anticipation. Just as I thought I was going to get some dick from the back, he put his mouth on my wide-open, awaiting pussy, pressing his face deep against my hot sweaty skin, poking his heated tongue deep inside, reaching up under me to play with my erect nipples.

The words came out in a moan. "Baby, that feels so good."

"This pussy smells good."

"Fuck it some more," I begged.

"I don't want to cum yet, baby."

"Malik, we'll have plenty of time for that. Cum again and again if you want."

He instructed me, "Baby, turn over again. I want to look you in the eyes."

For the Lover in You

Malik suddenly reached over under the bed and turned me on my back, again finding my pussy with his finger. He carefully slipped his twenty-one-year-old dick into my forty-year-old pussy again, savoring the penetration, inch by inch, dick even harder than before, pussy even wetter than before. My walls felt even more swollen, even tighter as I gripped him welcomingly, surrounding his dick with my juicy grip.

"Baby, that's nice as shit."

I purred, "I've never felt like this in my entire life."

"Baby, there's something I want you to know."

"Uh-huh." I grooved to his grind with my eyes closed.

"I'm never leaving you."

My eyes opened spontaneously.

He continued, speaking nose to nose. "We're going to make this work. First of all, I would never hurt you. Mariah, this is heaven. You are heaven. I feel complete." He continued to dig in.

"Malik, I feel it too. I've been waiting for you to fuck me from the first moment I met you."

"I've loved you and I've wanted to express it like this, feeling you on the inside, feeling your heat, your depth, your walls, your muscles gripping me, and then look into your eyes at the same time." He was grinding hard while running it down.

"Aaah, damn that is go fucking good." The movement of my shaky legs caused my voice to quiver.

"You are so fucking good. So good, Mariah, that . . ."

He grabbed my left hand and then met my face again with his, opening his mouth to kiss me hard and deep. I moaned as he kissed me, and then I felt him slip something along my finger. He made my eyes meet his. "Baby, will you marry me?"

Fuck, what did he just ask me?

"What?"

"I said, will you marry me?"

My eyes flashed question marks. "Malik, are you sure?"

He still penetrated me with the strength of his cock. "Feel this. Feel what we have and then answer for yourself."

He inserted himself to the left and then to the right and pressed down to delve all the way inside, still looking me dead in my eyes.

I sighed my reply. "Yes."

I looked over, and even with the only light in the room being the flickering candlelight from the fireplace, I could see it. It was platinum, and bright, the diamond was square and huge.

"Malik, what did you do?"

"You wanted to set a date, so we'll set one."

"I can't believe you did this."

"I did this because I want you to know that I'm serious. I keep telling you I've found the woman for me, and it's you."

"I was going to give it to you anyway, Malik," I sort of joked just to shake me from the sure joke he must have been playing on my old ass.

He was serious. "Mariah, you were gonna get this ring anyway."

"Malik, you are so good to me. Hell yes, I'll be your wife." I held on tight.

"Damn, Mariah. Fuck, this pussy is so good."

I found myself clinching the sheets as he worked his penetration, almost as if sensing my need for him to again hit the very back of my depth. My fiancé was fucking the shit out of me.

For You

All I could hear in the air was Kenny Lattimore's voice serenading our union. It was as though our bodies were melting into the bed like hot wax. Malik reached down to grab the sides of my plump ass with each stroke as I squeezed my pussy muscles to the sensation. I didn't know how he was keeping himself from cumming.

"Damn, it's so tight," he spoke with volume.

My pussy was so soaking wet I could hear my own juices sloshing. He shoved himself into my flesh and leaned down onto my chest as I felt his hot breath along my neck. My legs shook involuntarily.

I could hear him panting as he lunged in and out of me, his balls slapping against my ass. He placed his hand behind my head, running his fingers though my brown nappy hair. Suddenly he shook, and I shook, and he pushed, and I pushed, and we moved quicker and quicker with urgency.

Immediately I knew something was up. He hit something deep inside, way back, again and again and again. This slick youngster had a few tricks up his sleeve himself. I felt greedy for wanting more but a deep tingling from my ass to my belly was growing, and I was no longer teaching him a damn thing. A hot flare repeated itself in a hurry, again and again, and he pumped in a rhythm that was pounding and rough. I revved like a Ferrari, and he took me into fifth gear in a hurry. It made me fucking dizzy and it made me high and it made me wetter and it made me hotter and it made me love him even more. Oxytocin like a motherfucker.

"You are fucking insatiable, aren't you?" he asked me in my ear, sounding like he was losing control too.

"Not right about now."

His voice grew deeper. "You're letting me knock the back out of it. Oh fuck, Mariah. This is it."

He moved the handfuls of ass up and back. Somebody's fucking phone rang major loud. If it was my kids, they'd better call back. If it was any of Malik's female admirers, I was about to let him bust a nut so strong he'd want to change his phone number quick.

I closed my eyes, almost afraid that I was going to pass out. I wanted to milk him, draining every drop of cum from his probing dick.

I talked him through it. "I don't want you to ever need another lover."

"Never." He used sweet, driving motions.

I looked down at our bodies, his fudge skin against my vanilla frame. It was as though we were born to end up intertwined like this, as though our souls were one in the same.

He kissed my smoky eyelids then buried his face into the hollow of my neck.

"Oh God," he said against my skin as he bucked.

His grind was fierce and erotic and full and slippery and fast. My body clenched, and I arched my back to move upward into his thrusting. My pussy gripped him tighter. As the pleasure increased, so did my pace.

"That'll do it. Mariah, I'm cumming. I'm cumming, baby." My thighs quivered. He lifted his head. His eyes spelled out loss of control. He kissed me ravenously then broke away as his face contorted. "Are you cumming?" he asked, jerking his head back.

"Yes, Malik. I'm cumming too."

"Cum with me, baby."

He let out a raunchy yell, draining himself while spurting.

I felt a dizziness that was paralyzing. A long explosion, like a hot damn burst of dynamite pulsated one after the other as the melding of our orgasms burned. The force of the ripples of pleasure rolled like thunder. He shot his creamy load inside of me. The tingling of the warmth of his juices made me boil. I panted, and he gritted his teeth. He panted, and I gritted my teeth. I continued to grind enough to drain every drop he secreted in my name. We were drenched with lust from an intense physical expression of overdue love. It was incredible. We slowed and kissed, and I felt the pulse of his final spurt. I smiled as I heard his moan. His body went limp. I heard him inhale. I exhaled.

He kissed my damp hair on the top of my head and looked down to blow my moist body dry. My fast-paced panting from trying to catch my breath showed my age. Hell, I'd almost lost my damn mind. But he was cool.

He settled on me and momentarily buried his face in my neck. He reached down to remove himself. The dripping of his sperm trickled between my legs. Our hot juices mingled. He turned onto his back and placed his baldhead on the sweaty pillow next to me as I turned toward him, resting my left arm around his defined, glistening chest.

I told him, "I must be dreaming." I still had the shakes from my forceful explosion.

"No, you're not. And thanks for making us wait." He breathed normally.

"Thanks for waiting."

I put one leg over his, hugged his waist, put my head on his shoulder, and drifted off to sleep along with Malik among the sensation of the afterglow. This was a perfect celebration of our love.

Save the Best for Last

Sunlight took over the room as his movement under the sheets awakened me. I guess he thought I hadn't had enough of his mouth on me—and he was right. I felt the cool breeze from the open window upon my face and the heat from his hot breath up against my morning pussy. I looked to the side and again eyed my chocolate diamond solitaire ring. Since I woke up to a new day I guess it really wasn't a dream.

I felt my man's skills, hitting the spot of that damn clit that he knew so well. His wet mouth was at work. I glanced down only to see his head under the bright white cotton sheet, going to town. A slow and steady sucking motion made me tense up, feeling a thrill of a sensation that was building, and it was coming fast. I placed my ring-fingered left hand over Malik's head and grinded my wide hips right along with him, pushing his face closer to me with the shimmer of the diamond glaring at me while feeling an emotion that was mixed with happiness and eroticism. I moaned.

I closed my eyes for one long second, and as I opened them, slow-rolling tears traced down each side of my content face, tears that symbolized the relief, the satisfaction, the long overdue change in my life, the best for last, my ability to now love a man completely. After forty years of having to have it, of craving sex and choosing men for all the wrong reasons, Mariah finally had it. Mariah finally had the love of a good man.

"I- I- I . . . I love you. Aaaaahhhhhh. I love you, Malik."

The Lesson

by

Penelope Flynn

Tracey Kelly watched as Maurice Pendergast spoke to the room-ful of guests visiting at the 1920s ten-bedroom mansion he had leased during his three-year contract at the university. He spoke in that deep, resonant voice that always made her tingle. He had been a lecturer then adjunct professor and this little get-together was to celebrate his receiving tenure as a full professor. Tracey hadn't been invited specifically, but there was an open invitation to the small faculty of which she was a member.

Dr. Pendergast didn't look like your average college professor. At six-four with a body seemingly chiseled from onyx that would have made the angels weep, he looked more like an athlete than a well-known author and lecturer in the area of metaphysics. His head was shaved bald. His dark brown eyes were focused and clear. His thirty-six-year-old features were sharp and angular except for his full, almost pouting lips. His neatly trimmed beard gave him a sophisticated and erudite air. Tracey found him to be extraordinarily attractive, as much for his genius as for his beauty.

The wine flowed throughout Dr. Pendergast's expansive study where he presided as a quiet but definite presence in the room. The twenty-seven or so guests had all made themselves comfortable, enjoying the informality of the large floor cushions provided by their host. As the evening wore on, the conversation turned from music to literature to popular culture to more personal things, and Tracey, like almost every other female in the room, wanted to get a little more personal with Dr. Pendergast.

Tracey was a little ashamed of herself for the way she reacted to Dr. Pendergast. After all, they were learned professionals, people who made their livings with their minds, not their bodies. However, as she watched him move through the room, so confident and self-assured, she could feel the heat rising from between her thighs as though a furnace was being stoked there.

Stop. Not nice, she chided herself, and certainly the thoughts she had about the beautiful Dr. Pendergast were not nice, not nice at all. They were naughty, sinful, and downright nasty. She imagined those big hands, which were the perfect size for cupping her large healthy breasts, roaming all over her body. She fantasized that those lips—those lips that were made to suck and to be sucked—were latched onto her nipples, making her scream for mercy. She imagined those same lips drawing a roadmap down her body to the indentation of her navel right before sliding down to the tops of her thighs and then moving on to quench the fire that was raging in her out-of-control furnace, those lips nestled between her thighs and feasting on her liquid heat. She imagined her legs locked around those fine black thighs and the weight of his six-four frame pressing down on her, possessing her.

But she also knew she wasn't the only one with those thoughts. Hers was a shared fantasy. In the study, the eyes of the women were locked on him, all waiting, hoping for the attention he had yet to bestow on any one of them. Even Dr. Blake, the disaffected literature professor who despised routine assemblies such as this one, managed to make her way out to the countryside, flaunting her body as much as any of the others. But Tracey couldn't throw stones. She was just as guilty as the rest, vying to be the one who would catch Dr. Pendergast's eye.

"Now that you're tenured, are you going to settle down here?" Dr. Phelps, head of the department, asked.

"If by settling down you mean finally buying this place, then yes," Dr. Pendergast replied.

"No, that's not what he means," Dr. Blake said as she shifted her frame that still retained its dancer's form after fifty-five years. "What he means is…is there a Mrs. Dr. Maurice Pendergast lurking somewhere ready to make her debut?"

Dr. Pendergast, a Ghanaian national who grew up in London, frowned a little then replied, "It is unlikely that I would find a suitable woman here in the states."

"What's that supposed to mean?" Tracey asked, drawing unintended attention to herself as she sat in her button-down blouse with her brown dreadlocks flowing down to the hem of her miniskirt, which barely reached her firm brown thighs in the position she was sitting.

"What I mean," he replied, without making eye contact, "is that I was raised to expect women to be demure. American women are a little too sexually overt for my tastes," he said while giving a sidelong glance toward Tracey. "They lack the restraint that a woman should have."

Dr. Pendergast's statement brought a thunderstorm of comments and criticism from the guests that lasted more than an hour. But throughout the discussion, Tracey was dumbstruck. She knew that Dr. Pendergast was a bit straitlaced, but she never dreamed he was that rigid. Since he arrived at the university three years prior, Tracey had been attracted to the statuesque giant. They had spoken a few times when she invited him out to lunch where she flirted with him shamelessly. She thought she recognized a spark, but he never followed up. Now she realized that there was a reason. To his way of thinking, she was promiscuous and unsuitable.

Tracey was no nymphomaniac, but she was no sexual shrinking violet, either. She had been with two men on the faculty, and they both quietly sang her praises. She had to admit, she had mad skills and had had every intention of employing all of them with Dr. Pendergast—well, at least she had before his little revelation.

The rest of the evening went smoothly, but the wine began to have its effect, and Tracey and several others took their leave then piled into the waiting cars and cabs to their various destinations. Tracey slipped into a cab with Elaine Richards, an art professor. Elaine was a sultry brunette with a slim build that contrasted with Tracey's more rounded voluptuous figure.

"Now what do you think of that?" Elaine asked Tracey as the cab headed toward the west side where they both lived. "I mean he looked directly at you when he said it."

"I think he's an ass," Tracey said sullenly.

"You're such a liar," Elaine said, laughing. "You've had a crush on him for three years and you're just itching to fuck him."

"Shut up, Elaine," Tracey groused. "He's made it pretty clear he's not interested."

"Maybe he's gay," Elaine offered in an attempt to console. "You know a lot of men who're built up like that are looking for another man."

"You could be right," Tracy replied, knowing that the sour-grapes rationale couldn't be further from the truth. She reached for her purse to check her phone messages and came upon a grim discovery. "Uh Elaine," she asked, "is my purse over there?"

"No," Elaine answered as she scoured her side of the cab. "It's not over here."

"Shit. I must have left it at Pendergast's place. I've got to go back."

"We can't go back," Elaine objected. "It took us half an hour to get this far, and you know I've got my flight to the conference early in the morning. I've just got to get some sleep."

"But I don't have my house keys. I don't even have my wallet to pay for a cab."

"No problem," Elaine said, smiling. "When we get to my place, just take my truck." She handed her cell phone to Tracey. "Call Pendergast and let him know that you'll be coming back."

Tracey dialed the phone number that came up in Elaine's address book. The phone rang a few times then the sound of Dr. Pendergast's voice sang through the receiver informing callers that he was unavailable. Tracey left a message saying that she was returning as soon as possible to reclaim her lost purse.

When the cab arrived at Elaine's, she handed Tracey the keys to her truck. Tracey immediately sped back toward the mansion. When she arrived, she parked in the circular driveway then walked to the large front door. The lights were still on, so she turned the knob and walked in.

"Helloooo," she called out from the foyer, but no one responded. She checked the study where the gathering took place, but her purse was not there. She called out again, "Helloooo. Dr. Pendergast?" But again there was no response. She looked up the large stairway toward the second floor then began to slowly ascend.

As she walked the hallway, she saw a flickering light and followed it to a room at the end of the hall. The door was partially open, and the ambient lighting bathed the room in a soft glow. She could see a dresser topped off by a large mirror. From the door she could see the reflection of the bed. As she prepared to step into the room, Dr. Pendergast crossed into view from an adjoining room with a bath towel wrapped loosely around his hips.

Tracey's breath stuck in her throat as Dr. Pendergast's lean, muscled frame moved silently through the room. His body was black, smooth, virtually hairless—at least what she could see of it. She felt her nipples tighten and the hum of her clit vibrating through her. He was as glorious as she had imagined he would be. His cobblestoned abs were perfectly symmetrical, his hipbones were pronounced above his shielded groin. Dark tiny nipples adorned his broad chest. His shoulders and back rippled with taut muscles. His delicious ass was muscular, and sadly significantly covered by the towel.

He stopped at the large-screen TV conveniently set across from his bed. He retrieved the remote then began searching a cabinet located underneath the screen. He pulled out a DVD from a shelf of many and popped it into the player. As he stepped away from the TV and toward the bed, the title Roun'-the-Way Girl appeared on the screen. Tracey grinned as she viewed the hokey title. Probably some B-rated film based on the LL Cool J song from back in the eighties.

From the mirror she could see Dr. Pendergast sitting on the edge of the bed, still with the towel wrapped around his waist. As she made her plans to sneak back downstairs, a BMW appeared on the TV screen and rolled down a street in Brooklyn before pulling up to a bus stop. A well-dressed bald black man leaned out and asked a young black woman with a head full of long, thick dreadlocks for directions. The twenty-something vixen with red lipstick and full lips was sucking seductively on a round red lollipop. Her thin shirt and miniskirt left very little to the imagination. The man examined her from head to toe while listening to the very convoluted directions. He finally asked if she could guide him to the address for which he was looking.

The girl hopped into the passenger's side of the car and took off with the stranger. The scenery sped by as the two engaged in a conversation filled with double entendres and suggestive poses.

The scene immediately cut to the man standing in a hotel room, his pants at his ankles, a long black cock jutting upward from his hairy groin. The girl was stripped to her waist and sporting the most beautiful round café-au-lait tits Tracey had ever seen. The man took a moment to squeeze and pinch the girl's brown pebble-sized nipples then guided her downward onto her knees to a spot in front of him. She began slurping copiously on the throbbing rod. The man moaned as he gripped her hair and guided his thick member farther down her throat. The blatant similarities between the actors and the two current occupants of the mansion was not lost on Tracey.

Soft groans became audible in the room. Tracey's eyes rose to the mirror, and she involuntarily covered her mouth with her hand to stifle her response. Maurice Pendergast lay on the bed, his eyes glued to the screen, the towel discarded. Both his large hands slowly stroked the most beautiful cock she had ever seen. The ten-inch anaconda was perfectly black, revealing only a teasing of pink at the seed-spewing slit. The erect gland was as thick as her wrist. Tracey's mouth watered as she watched him stroke in time with the movement of the girl's mouth on the screen. His thumb and forefinger encircled the head of his swollen cock. He moaned loudly as he squeezed thick droplets of precum from the slit and slathered the head and shaft. His eyes closed intermittently as his hand stroked faster, continuing to mimic the action on the screen.

Tracey was transfixed watching the movement of his hand on the Mt. Everest of dicks. Her hand moved almost as if of its own volition to massage the creamy wet spot that had spread in her panties. She bent her knees slightly, opening her thighs to accommodate her fingers, which slipped past the cum-slicked material and into her leaking pussy. Her eyes moved as if hypnotized between the scene on the screen and the frantically stroking Dr. Pendergast. Her fingers pumped her pussy with wild abandon, rubbing against her spot, sending waves of pleasure shooting from inside her as she milked her twat in time with the girl's sucking lips, in time with Dr. Pendergast's stroking hands.

The man on the screen moaned, "Yeah, bitch, suck it. Suck my dick." On the bed, Dr. Pendergast's hips began to thrust upward as he rhythmically stroked. "Suck me, Tracey. That's right. Suck it." He groaned. On the screen the girl squeezed and massaged the stranger's balls while his glistening cock pumped furiously in her mouth. "Open your mouth," the man said, growling, "I want you to taste my cum."

Dutifully, the girl opened her mouth as his cock spattered her face and mouth and bathed her perfect tits in his sperm.

"Oh… damn… Traceeeeeyy," Dr. Pendergast cried. With a final lurch and bellow, thick ropes of cum shot from his cock and bathed his chest in white silvery cords of gism. Tracey's knees shook, and her body bucked on top of her expert finger fuck. Her cream soaked her panties and bare thighs as she watched the perfect cock erupt, wishing that she, like the girl on film, could catch her lover's white-hot lava in her mouth. Dr. Pendergast lay watching the screen, slowly moving his hand over his still-hungry cock as the actress rose to the bed on her knees, her skirt raised to her hips, displaying the bare, smooth, golden-brown globes of her ass.

The camera panned up between the girl's open thighs to display a hairless brown-and-pink swollen pussy. The man climbed onto the bed, the glistening head of his cock poised to enter her from behind. He surged forward, plunging inside her. The man shouted, "Damn!" as the girl purred and mewled. She rocked her body back against him, working her hips from side to side as she moaned, "Give me more, baby. Give me more."

Dr. Pendergast groaned as he watched the beautiful temptress taking pleasure from the stranger's pistoning cock. He groaned as he gripped his hardened member, "Can you take all this, Tracey? Huh? I'll fuck your little pussy 'til you can't move, 'til you scream," he said, moaning as he pumped his cock in time with the fucking on the screen. The scene onscreen coupled with Dr. Pendergast's words, which were not meant for her ears, sent another shockwave through Tracey's cunt so strong that her knees buckled. Her legs shook, and she moaned ecstatically.

Suddenly Dr. Pendergast bolted straight up in the bed. Tracey covered her mouth a moment too late. She didn't see him grab for the towel or rummage through a dresser drawer and pull out a handgun. Tracey had already stepped back into the hallway and rushed quickly toward the staircase.

"Stop," she heard his voice boom as she ran toward the stairs. "I have a gun and I *will* use it."

Tracey tried to stop her momentum but her heel stuck on a loose nail then cracked. She tripped on the carpet at the head of the stairs then fell, tripping down the next four.

"Stand up…slowly," she heard Dr. Pendergast's voice direct as he kept the gun trained on her.

She rose slowly, speaking rapidly, "Dr. Pendergast… Maurice…it's me…Dr. Kelly. I-I called you. I left a message…about my purse…" she stammered.

Dr. Pendergast lowered the weapon and heaved a deep, ragged sigh. "What are you doing in my house?"

"The lights were on. The door was open. No one answered when I called out, so I came upstairs and followed the light," Tracey said nervously.

"You were in my bedroom?" he asked warily.

"Outside the bedroom," she said. "I was going to wait until you got dressed then call out again, but then…"

He looked down the stairway at the voluptuous spy. His eyes were drawn first to her pitiful expression, then her melon-sized breasts, which had sprung free of the confines of her blouse during the fall. His eyes rested there for a moment before they were attracted to the blood on her knees.

"You're bleeding," he said dryly.

"I'm fine," she replied, hobbling toward him on her broken heel. "I just need my purse."

"Come sit," he said as he headed toward the bedroom. Tracey nodded and followed after him.

When they re-entered the bedroom, the girl on the screen was riding the man hard and furiously as they both moaned in pleasure. Dr. Pendergast hurriedly switched off the DVD as Tracey sat on the edge of the bed. He rushed off then returned from the bathroom wearing a robe and carrying cotton balls and a bottle of witch hazel. He knelt at her knees and applied a moistened cotton ball to the first bleeding knee. She bit her lip to keep from sighing as his large strong hands took hold of her calf. Her shirt was torn open, but she didn't bother to cover herself, especially when she saw that Dr. Pendergast's eyes were drawn to the chocolate pleasures he found there.

She leisurely leaned back a little and parted her thighs. The pungent smell of her sex wafted into his nostrils, and he unconsciously licked his lips. The university community was small, and Tracey had it on very good information that more than three years had passed since he last smelled the fragrance of a woman's pussy. His hands slid from her calves to her thighs. Tracey spread her knees farther. Dr. Pendergast breathed in. From his position on the floor, he could easily view her scantily clad pubis. It would have taken no effort at all right then to press her back onto the bed and push his tongue inside her. Tracey could see in his eyes that he wanted to suck on the puffy lips and lick the length of her opening, that he wanted to fuck her hard and solidly. She could plainly see that he wanted her there with him all night to scorch the sheets with their passion and to quench the flames in their sweat. She knew that he wanted to hold her afterward and wake up in the morning, not alone. At that moment, looking in his eyes, she knew that he wanted exactly the same things she wanted. But what she knew Dr. Pendergast wanted and what he ultimately did were two entirely different things. He took one last look at the wonderland where she wanted him to spend all his waking moments then quickly wiped her second knee and stood, abruptly. "I have not seen your purse, but I will help you look for it," he said dispassionately.

Tracey leaned back on the bed, propping her knees to provide him a better view of her treasures. She smiled coquettishly, then asked matter-of-factly, motioning her head toward the TV screen, "Do you always call my name when you watch?"

"I know many women named Tracey," he replied and shifted uneasily. Tracey could see his cock beginning to swell. She then cooed slowly, still with her legs propped and ample breasts exposed, "Ohhhh? Is that so?" She flashed him a mischievous smile, "Well, at any rate, I wouldn't be opposed to us spending some time together."

Dr. Pendergast's breaths came heavier as he watched Tracey's exposed body on his bed.

"Well, thank you, Dr. Kelly," he answered as he tightened his robe around him, avoiding looking at her, "but I am not interested in you in that way," nevertheless, his breath came a little harder and the bulge under his robe became more pronounced.

Tracey nodded knowingly, exhaled softly then rose from the bed, embarrassed. She had given him every opportunity, basically thrown herself at him while he was obviously aroused; still, he was not interested. She tucked her tail between her legs and pulled her clothes together.

Dr. Pendergast watched as Tracey quickly arranged her clothing. Due to the tear in her blouse, her bountiful breasts tipped with dark raspberry-shaped nipples were covered awkwardly. His cock continued to swell watching her heavy thighs and ass move under the tiny skirt on her way to the door.

"I hope this won't hurt our professional relationship too much," she said as she moved in front of him. "I'm so sorry about barging in tonight. I'm sorry about all of this." Tracey apologized profusely as she hurried toward the door.

"It seems to me," Dr. Pendergast intoned sternly in that deep mellow voice, "that your apology rings less than sincere."

"Excuse me?" Tracey spun to address him, a little off-kilter and extremely taken aback.

"As I recall," he continued, "for the past three years that I have been here, you have done everything in your power to induce me to have sex with you, Dr. Kelly."

Tracey was stunned. Of course she had hoped that he knew, but she certainly didn't expect him to be so direct about it.

"Do you have any idea how much misery you've caused me? Do you have any idea how many extra classes I have taught and papers I have written to spend extra time in my office and in research to avoid all your little suggestive statements, erotic poses, and romantic gestures?"

"Well, you never seemed to respond either way," Tracey defended. "I didn't know whether you were just ignoring me or if you were truly unaware."

"I have been aware since the first day we met," Dr. Pendergast thundered, no longer masking his irritation, "I have many family members who rely upon me and others who look up to me and are proud of my accomplishments. To have lost this position because of a fleeting tryst...I refuse to take that chance.

"I understand your position. What I did was unfair and inappropriate, and I apologize," Tracey said, knowing how precarious things could be for a professor who had yet to achieve tenure. She had lived through those years and shuddered at some of the things she had done to placate the "powers that be" before her tenure was granted.

"Your apology is accepted." He nodded.

She heaved a heavy sigh and continued, "In addition, I apologize if I gave you false impressions about American women. There are many very demure women, even here at the university, I just don't happen to be one of them.

"So I noticed." He smirked.

"Don't get me wrong, Dr. Pendergast. I'm not some dimwitted floozy. I do my job well—"

"—I have never questioned your intellect, Dr. Kelly, or your capacity as a professor. I have had the opportunity to read some of your journal articles. I found them quite engaging and informative, but your professionalism in the classroom is not what we are discussing."

She tripped over her words, flustered, trying to make him understand, "I didn't think I was harassing you…It's just that… that I thought I recognized something… a spark, an attraction."

Tracey knew she was babbling, but she wanted to explain herself. She wanted to find some way to justify all the actions that must have appeared juvenile and overbearing, knowing that she would never be able to, so she stopped trying.

The two stood inches away from each other as a long, uncomfortable silence descended. Before the silence became unbearable, Tracey turned and resumed her trek to the door.

"Are you really sorry?" Dr. Pendergast finally broke the silence and asked.

Yes. Tracey was sorry. She was sorry that she was caught, sorry that he rejected her, but she had no regrets about seeing what she saw of him that night. She wanted to be able to explain it in a way that didn't make her sound insane. But as she turned to answer him, she was met with a vision of Dr. Pendergast that rivaled her wildest fantasies. His robe was open; his beautiful body was covered in a sheen of sweat; his long, thick, throbbing cock bobbed up toward his flat belly. "I mean…really sorry?" he asked as he moved toward her.

"Yes," Tracey whispered, barely able to breathe as he stepped mere inches away and cupped her face in one of his large hands.

"Because if you're really sorry," he continued as he brushed his thumb over her lips, "then maybe we can find a way for you to make amends."

"I thought you weren't interested." She panted anxiously as he methodically stripped off her blouse.

"I lied." He smiled as he bent to one knee and unfastened her skirt, dropping it to the floor. He then rose, running his hands upward over her body. Tracey's hands instinctively reached for his erection. He moaned and pulled her closer to him. It was a moan she recognized…one coming from a man who had not felt a woman's hands on his body for a very long time.

"I want to feel you inside me—now. You owe me," she whispered as she tongued his tiny nipples and slipped the robe off his shoulders and onto the floor, finally baring his flesh in its entirety.

It only took a moment before they were both rolling on the bed, kissing and touching every inch of bared flesh with which they made contact. Dr. Pendergast massaged her breasts and latched on to one of her nipples and pulled on it with his teeth and tongue until she cried out, "Fuck me now, Maurice. Do it—now!"

"I don't know." He smiled mischievously as he moved lower, running his hands down her body, sliding past her thighs, and stopping at her knees. "You've been a very bad girl, Tracey," he said sternly as he pressed her knees open wide, revealing her pussy in full bloom. "I don't think it would be appropriate for me to reward you for bad behavior. Do you?"

Tracey squirmed as Dr. Pendergast breathed in deep while planting a furrow of kisses on her firm inner thighs, which led to the blossom whose fragrance had so deeply captivated him. Tracey wanted him to plunge into her right then, but she could tell that he enjoyed making her wait, enjoyed feeling her move beneath him as she attempted to maneuver her lips to meet with his own.

"Oh Gooooood." She moaned when his tongue began to gently toy with her swollen clit and when his lips sucked seductively on her labia. Her toes curled tightly as he teased her opening, slowly inserting and withdrawing his tongue, tickling just inside the rim and retreating. It was exquisite torture. Each insertion of his tongue was met with a jerking upward stroke from her pelvis, but Dr. Pendergast refused to relinquish control. He wouldn't enter her, not the way she wanted—not yet. Tracey's seduction of him had been persistent…relentless, and her flaunting and teasing had been cruel. Yes, Tracey was being taught a valuable lesson, that turnabout is fair play.

"Please, Maurice. Please just fuck me," she pleaded as her hips tried to break free of his iron grip.

"Patience, my dear Dr. Kelly," he purred as he slid upward, pinning her to the bed, grinding his ready cock into her abdomen, "or I am certain I would split that tiny cunt of yours in two."

Tracey gasped at the thought of the enormous tool pinned tightly against her belly, forcing its way inside her, and almost came on the spot. "I've had bigger," she lied unconvincingly.

"We'll see how much you can take," he murmured in her ear as his hand slid between her thighs. She groaned when he inserted a finger inside, making gentlemanly acquaintance with her quivering walls. "More, baby." She moaned like the girl in the film, and he slipped in another, doing a slow finger fuck, preparing her pussy for his monster cock. The third finger was wedged in, but it was a tight fit.

"You're too small," He panted in frustration as his fingers probed her.

"You're not even trying," she whined as she pressed downward onto his hand to force him inside her.

"I want you to enjoy this," he said, "not send you to the hospital."

"Maybe if we change positions?" she offered and removed his hand. She rolled over onto her stomach, then rose to her hands and knees. She positioned two pillows under each knee and under her chest to give him better access. Dr. Pendergast stood on his knees behind her, much like the man had done to the girl in the film, but there was no plunging and burying himself in her to the hilt. This was slow going.

Dr. Pendergast resumed massaging Tracey's drenched opening, hoping that she would stretch to accommodate his enormous size.

"I'm already ready." She sighed anxiously.

"We'll take it slow," he whispered.

Dr. Pendergast was about to come out of his skin he was so turned on. Tracey was a curvaceous, muscular woman. Looking to be about a size eighteen and five-five, she was what many called fleshy and "big-boned," but against, Dr. Pendergast, she was tiny by comparison.

"You'll let me know if it starts to hurt, right?" he asked nervously as he positioned the large burrowing snake at the doorway of her warm inviting lair.

"Yes, yes," she said moaning, "I'll tell you everything, anything. Just do it!"

Dr. Pendergast grasped Tracey's heavy thighs and pressed forward slowly, working the head of his cock inside her.

"God!" She gasped as he strained forward an inch.

"Does it hurt?" he asked anxiously, kissing the space between her shoulder blades as he throbbed inside her slick, wet snugness. "We don't have to go any farther. This is perfect," he muttered into the soft skin of her back.

"Just a little more," she urged, pushing back against him.

He took a deep breath and plunged forward as her inner walls yielded to him another inch…two inches.

"Jesus," she screamed.

"Do you want me to stop?" he asked as he wrapped his arms around her and pressed even more insistently, easing into her another inch. "Shit, that's good," he cried as she enveloped him, making Tracey giggle. Profanity seemed foreign spewing from his professorial lips.

"It's, it's…really big," she stammered, trying to catch her breath as she balanced her weight on her hands.

I'm going to pull out a little, all right?" he said, panting.

"No! No," she cried, "just a little more. I-I can take a little more."

"You barely have half of it," he warned, licking the sweat that beaded on her back.

"But it's sooo goooood." She moaned, licking her lips. "Just-just a little more."

He didn't have to be persuaded. He pressed forward, and she felt the cave of wonders that was her pussy further reveal itself to him. His body shuddered as three more inches buried themselves inside her.

Tracey moaned, transporting to her own personal heaven as Dr. Pendergast by degrees forced his engorged gland inside her. She knew when she saw the enormous instrument that she had to feel it, had to taste it, had to have it. With more than an inch left to introduce into her hungry cavity, he slid his palms up to her ass and pushed back, pulling all but the head of his cock from the warm confines of her snatch then gripping her thighs again as he pressed slowly…a gradual, even stroke until he was inside her again.

"Omigod," was all Tracey could gasp. Speech failed her.

"You think you can take it all now, Tracey?" he mocked as he again pulled out his entire thick rod, except the head, and in a more forceful stroke imbedded all but the last inch.

"I don't know. I don't know. It's just so, so… much," she cried more in pleasure than in frustration.

"We're almost there," he whispered into her ear as he repositioned himself to make the final thrust of the maiden voyage into her creaming cavity.

"Yes, yes," she whimpered softly as he ran his hand over her breasts then down past her stomach to squeeze her voluptuous pussy lips around her clit.

"I've wanted this for so long," he murmured in her ear as his fingers applied rhythmic pressure.

"Do it, then." She moaned. "Shove your cock all the way inside me."

Tracey squealed as he grabbed her by her shoulders and stroked hard, burying all ten inches of his cock inside her.

"Damn that feels good." He groaned as Tracey began to giggle uncontrollably, gleeful and triumphant.

"It's funny now?" he asked as he administered an open-handed smack to her ass while still buried inside her.

"I was just thinking how we should have done this three years ago."

"Don't worry. We'll make up for lost time," he said as he pulled out and with a deep moan began slowly stroking into her eager pussy.

Tracey's body began to shake. Her arms felt as though they would not hold her weight. Her legs felt weak and useless. This is what she wanted, to feel his power and his hunger, to open herself to him, to make herself his.

"You're so tight." He gasped as he plunged into her with more aggression, increasing the pace of the rhythm he'd set. Her hips gyrated, and her cunt corkscrewed around him, bringing him over the edge. "I-I'm cumming," he groaned as he grabbed at her thighs and slammed upward into her, his back arching and hips thrusting.

"Christ," she shouted, buckling under him. The weight of his body and his hard cock pressing on her clit and her spot sent her reeling into a breathless orgasm. All she could hear was the rumble of his voice vibrating through her saying, "Yes… cum for me, Tracey. Show me how much you want me inside you."

Tracey scarcely recognized her own voice. It resembled something between a mewling whine and a whimper as she moved against him, pressing back to have more of him, pressing down to feel their combined weight on her clit, moving her hips from side to side to feel the scrape of his pubic hair against her ass.

"That's it." He moaned in her ear as he squeezed her nipples, encouraging her to relax, to let go, feeling the intermittent, involuntary contractions of her tight walls around him. Her final shudders left him drained and left her limp, still with his hardness inside her, still with his weight on her. When he tried to lift up, she pleaded, grabbing at his arm, "No… not yet. Don't go."

He rose slightly and pulled her onto her side where he wrapped himself around her. She could feel the pulse of him deep inside her as he softened to semi-hardness, "And where would I go?" he asked. "Everything I desire is right here."

Tracey's analytical mind wanted to determine the probability of success for a relationship that started this way, but her body ignored the griping of her analytical mind and snuggled into the arms of her beautiful ebony god and let sleep wash over her until he was inclined to wake her and take her again.

Thug Bar
by
Winslow Wong

There is a bar on Fulton Street in Brooklyn. It has gone by many names over the years, but to the scores of professional women who flock there after work, it's simply known as "Thug Bar." Lawyers, accountants, teachers, journalists, professionals, and black women of all stripes stop into this little hangout ostensibly for the two-for-one drinks at happy hour, dancing to one of the hottest deejays in town, or the free buffet, but in truth, there's more to Thug Bar than meets the eye.

Most of the women had a different agenda, something a little more sordid. These fine pillars of the community all came for the same purpose: a good fuck. The men who came into Thug Bar were not your typical male who frequented the bar scene through New York. They would be classified simply in the vernacular as thug niggas. They were perceived as hardcore individuals who were very forward in their approach with little need for pretense nor a desire to indulge in any type of bullshit, and according to the women who flocked there in droves, they were, fucking incredible in bed.

Sharmaine Williams made her first foray to Thug Bar because she promised her best friend, Joyce, she would go with her to a spot that really was nothing more than a sleazy dive. Unlike Joyce, Sharmaine was never really attracted to the hoodlums or thug types. She generally liked a more refined man of a certain class and professional status. These street niggas whom she found herself surrounded by didn't meet her standards, but the longer she hung out at Thug Bar, the more she began to see the appeal of these men who had a raw animal magnetism and who lacked the affectations from which so many professional men suffered.

Despite basically becoming a fixture in Thug Bar, Sharmaine held out for a couple of weeks, shunning every man who approached her, often being very crass and abrasive. Many a night, she was a second or two away from getting slapped for the disrespect she doled out to the niggas trying to holla at her, but Reggie, the bartender backed them up with a single look.

Reggie had worked at Thug Bar for many years and was well respected for the work he had put into the street years earlier. People knew better than to fuck with him. Word on the street was that Reggie had taken the bar from the previous owner who owed money on a gambling debt. He just walked in one night and said this is my place and the owner signed over the deed on the spot and then got the hell out of Dodge. Reggie liked Sharmaine and the fact that she wasn't a thug groupie like all of the other chicken heads in DKNY suits and Prada shoes. She was smart and funny and had a mouth that often made him laugh aloud.

"Hey, Reggie, you're a smart guy. Why the hell are you serving drinks in a dump like this?" Sharmaine asked as she sat at the bar one night. Her buddy Joyce was occupied in a booth with her latest boy-toy thug conquest.

"Well, Ms. Big Fancy Attorney, not all of us have the opportunity to leave the hood and go off to work for massa like you," Reggie replied while wiping down the bar.

"Listen, one I don't work for massa. I have my own law firm that I busted my ass building into a successful practice by myself. Two, I was giving your big ass a compliment, but I guess you hear them so rarely, you couldn't tell a compliment if it fucking fell on your ass."

And so it went with Reggie and Sharmaine, jousting and sparring on everything from politics to religion. They both appreciated the conversation and the company.

One night after one drink too many and just tired of going home alone and horny, Sharmaine did something she promised herself she would never do. She slept with a young thug named Scooter who had a large dick and fucked her all night long. What he lacked in technique he made up in intensity and stamina. Scooter hit spots in Sharmaine's pussy that she wasn't even aware existed. He was fucking incredible. The best she ever had, but when it was over, Scooter got up, got dressed, and left. There was no cuddling or small talk. Scooter didn't even ask for Sharmaine's number or say good night. He simply said "later" and walked out.

Initially, Sharmaine felt used. She had had meaningless sexual trysts in the past, but the men were courteous enough to say they were going to call—even if it was a lie. Not once did they ever leave without saying good-bye, much less walk away as if she was just a fuck. That was insulting. Didn't this little hip-hop thug-wannabe know who she was? Finally, Sharmaine realized Scooter didn't know nor did he care. To him she was just some pussy with some serious head skills he fucked.

Sharmaine thought about her evening with Scooter and started getting turned on by the fact that she had just fucked a guy for pure sexual pleasure, with no strings attached. She didn't have to worry about him or his needs. Sharmaine didn't have to worry about anything except cumming over and over.

This was a truly an epiphany for her. She realized that her pleasure was at her control, and if she needed to be fucked well, she knew where to go anytime she wanted.

Sharmaine was now in Thug Bar enough to be known by the regulars. Everyone knew her girl Joyce was a straight-up freak, but Sharmaine tried to remain discreet. Still, she was fucking thugs regularly and was becoming popular among the playas in the club. She no longer had the time to chat with Reggie like before as she became more and more interested in seeking sexual satisfaction.

One night, Sharmaine was wearing a tight red dress that hugged her hips and ass so right that the men were literally drooling on themselves.

They rarely noticed that she was small breasted, barely a B cup. It was always her hips and ass that got her attention, and she knew how to hold it from there. Sharmaine was a bit disappointed with the selection of men that evening—the ones she had fucked before were otherwise engaged, and the new ones didn't hold her interest.

Just as she was about to leave, he walked in. It was like a movie. The light shone on him the moment he entered the vestibule. The patrons in the bar greeted him as he glided past and slipped into a booth in the rear. Sharmaine's curiosity was piqued.

After some discrete inquiries, Sharmaine learned that the suave, handsome stranger was known as Tre and grew up in Marcy projects. The little wannabe thug Hakeem with whom Sharmaine inquired said, "Yo, that nigga Tre's shit is tight. He's a playa on a whole 'nother level."

Hakeem immediately left her side to greet Tre. Sharmaine watched as he leaned over to whisper in Tre's ear. When he was done, they looked in Sharmaine's direction. Noticing this, she turned away and ordered another drink. As Reggie brought her drink, she heard a smooth voice from behind her say, "Put it on my tab." Sharmaine turned to face the stranger and thank him when she realized it was Tre.

His six-foot-two-inch frame towered before her. He wore a white skull cap, leather parka, and a white tee underneath. His jeans were hitched low, and his body was lean and muscular.

"Tre," he said, adding nothing more as no more needed to be said.

Sharmaine savored his voice, which caused a rush of dampness between her legs. She could feel the heat radiate from his flesh, and she momentarily closed her eyes as she inhaled his scent. Sharmaine's pussy throbbed for Tre to do more than stand in front of her. His raw sexuality was overpowering, and if Tre had asked, she would've fucked him right there in front of everyone. Decorum be damned.

After coming to her senses, she was finally able to utter her name.

"Sharmaine," she said with a touch of disdain that hid her true feelings.

"So, Sharmaine, what's an uptown professional like yourself doing slumming in the hood? You're not from around here," he said, giving her a look that made her feel self-conscious about coming to the bar.

"I enjoy coming here," Sharmaine shot back, taking offense at Tre's remark. "What business is it of yours?"

"I don't know. You just seem a bit different from these other trifling tramps that come in here looking to get thugged out. But then again, maybe I'm wrong." Tre got up and returned to his corner seat and held court with his niggas. The way he dismissed her with a single sentence pissed her off. Who in the hell was this fake-ass thug reading her like that?

Fuck him, she thought as she felt the blood rush to her head and her loins simultaneously.

Sharmaine spent the rest of the evening looking into her drink and rebuffing the advances of the numerous men who approached her. She was busy trying to think of a comeback for Tre, anything that would amount to "go fuck yourself," but she was completely disarmed by his admonition.

Sharmaine was angry for allowing Tre to insult her, but at the same time she wanted him inside her warm, wet pussy. She sat aimlessly twirling the stirrer in her drink when she felt a light tap on her shoulder. It was Tre.

"Let's get the fuck out of here," he said as grabbed her hand.

"Okay," she said, quickly dismissing her earlier thoughts of giving him a piece of her mind.

Sharmaine followed Tre as he walked to a Maybach. She whistled in awe because she knew the retail amount for this luxury car was three-hundred-thousand dollars. Sharmaine wondered if Tre was a kingpin or someone big in the drug business and was quickly having second thoughts.

"Where do you live?" he asked once they were inside the car.

"On the Westside. In the seventies," she replied.

"Slumming," he said, shaking his head in dismay, "just like I thought." He turned on Hot 97 and didn't say another word to her for the rest of the ride.

Sharmaine's head swarmed with questions, but she decided it was best to remain quiet.

Tre found a lot still open, parked his car, and gave the attendant a five-hundred-dollar tip to keep an extra eye on his car. Sharmaine was further intrigued by Tre. From the moment he walked into Thug Bar, he commanded respect and was obviously a big timer who didn't take shit from anyone. He was someone to whom people looked up, but there was something about him that was different.

When they got inside her apartment, he tossed his jacket on the chair as if he had been there a million times. He instantly made himself comfortable.

"Would you like a drink?" she asked.

Tre ignored Sharmaine's question. Sharmaine had never seen a man look sexier than Tre did at that moment. Shortly after, he licked his lips, and Sharmaine realized she was wrong, he looked even sexier as he slowly stepped over to her. His walk was illegal. He had just a slight bop to each step, which looked graceful and deliberate. It was as if he knew that when he reached her she would be his.

When he reached her, he placed his hand on the side of her face and gently caressed it then he lifted her head with the lightest of touches so that her lips were poised to meet his. He sensuously licked her lips before allowing his tongue to ease into her mouth. Tre's tongue slow waltzed inside her mouth as he kissed her like no man had ever done before. He held her so tight that she could barely breathe—or maybe it was just the fact that she was swept away by the moment that she was allowing him to completely and totally control her and she couldn't resist. There wasn't anything that she wouldn't do for him. There wasn't anything he asked that she would refuse. She wanted to please this man like she never pleased anyone before.

Sharmaine immediately dropped to her knees and unfastened his pants. She was proud of her head skills. Most times she sucked dick as a way to show off her skills rather than to give pleasure to a man. She always laughed to herself as some poor fool lost it and quickly gave up the ghost after only a couple of minutes of her working her magic. But now Sharmaine wanted to use her skills to please this man whom she had only known for a few hours.

She reached inside and pulled out his dick. His penis wasn't that large, but he was definitely more than a mouthful. Tre remained standing with his hand on top of her head as Sharmaine tried to deep-throat his dick, gagging and choking the entire time. Her discomfort mattered little to her as she inhaled his dick deeper into her mouth. Tre watched in amazement as Sharmaine's mouth worked its magic on his dick. He tried to maintain his cool, but even he had to let out a moan as Sharmaine's tongue made circular motions around the head of his throbbing dick.

Tre knew he wouldn't last much longer if she kept this up, so he gently pulled his dick out of her mouth and lifted her from the floor. He once again kissed her but this time was much more passionate and aggressive. He pulled down the zipper on her dress, and within seconds the dress slunk to the floor along with her undergarments. Sharmaine stood stark naked before Tre. The nipples on her petite breasts were erect, and her shaved pussy glistened with moisture. Her body was picturesque, an ebony version of the famous work of art "Venus on the Half Shell," but she felt self-conscious and vulnerable.

"You're beautiful," he said as he kissed her forehead and looked at her adoringly.

Sharmaine stood still. She wasn't used to conversation, much less compliments from the thugs she had fucked in the past. Even though Tre didn't say much, his eyes spoke volumes, and she realized that he appreciated her in ways the other thugs never had before. His touches and caresses belied his tough exterior. He looked into her eyes as if he was gazing into her soul, into what made her a woman. He was touching her in places that no man had reached, and it both scared and exhilarated her.

"I want you, Sharmaine," Tre said as he held her hands in his, staring into her eyes. "I want every part of you and so much more."

Bring it on, she thought. *Bring it on.*

Tre laid her on the couch, parted her legs, and lowered his head. He was slow and deliberate in his method, gently kissing her thighs as he moved closer and closer to her wet pussy. When his mouth finally reached it, he separated her lips with his tongue and gently slid his tongue into her. He moved his tongue in and out of her wetness. Sharmaine's moans were a guide as he continued to work his tongue in her. He took his tongue out and began to suck on her pussy lips—first the right and then the left and then back and forth over and over.

"Oh, baby, that feels so good," Sharmaine said, moaning gently as she massaged his shaven head between her legs.

Tre moved his tongue to her clit and lightly sucked on it. Sharmaine's back arched upward to meet his mouth, and she held his head tightly to her. Tre let his tongue massage her clit while he fingered her pussy. Sharmaine began caressing her breasts, teasing her chocolate nipples until they stood nice and erect like Hershey Kisses as he continued to use his tongue on her super-sensitive clit and his fingers to hit her hot spot.

Tre had taken her up to the mountain, and Sharmaine let herself go and she came hard as she felt herself screaming out of both pleasure and exhilaration. She held his head to her pussy, never wanting to let him go and hoping this feeling wouldn't end, the rush was so incredible. She couldn't quite believe how he had hit every right note with her from the very beginning.

Tre looked at her and slowly kissed his way up her body until he reached her lips. He pecked her then said with a wry smile, "You ain't the only one with skills."

Sharmaine laughed then she reached over to her nightstand, opened the drawer, and grabbed a condom. She bit open the package with her teeth then quickly slid the condom onto Tre's very hard dick. The condom was lubricated, but that wouldn't really be necessary that night. Sharmaine was so wet her bed was already drenched, and she still had miles to go before she slept.

Tre leaned forward and began to kiss her, his body on top of hers as he just let the tip of his cock enter her wetness. Sharmaine anticipated the requisite thrusting and steadied herself, but Tre surprised her. He just teased her with the tip of his dick in and out of her pussy. This teasing action in tandem with his passionate kissing had Sharmaine in ecstasy overload again. It felt so good, but she wanted Tre to really fuck her, and she begged him to do it.

"Fuck me, baby," she said as she scratched her nails into his back, but Tre didn't stop. He was a man who did things on his own terms and on his own time. He would fuck her when he felt like it.

Tre continued the small, short strokes into her pussy as Sharmaine felt herself cumming again as Tre intended. As Sharmaine was in the midst of the throes of ecstasy, Tre drove his dick deep into her warm, wet throbbing pussy.

Tre and Sharmaine, their bodies totally entwined, made love as if they had been together forever. They seemed to be made for each other as they fucked slow and sensuously. They found a steady rhythm that mirrored each other to perfection.

Sharmaine's next orgasm snuck up on her like a thunderstorm on a hot summer afternoon, gently brewing and building until it could hold off no longer, releasing its deluge upon the earth. As she came, she bit deeply into Tre's chest until she tasted blood such was the intensity of her passion.

Tre said nothing as he continued to stroke into Sharmaine, but this time each stroke was a little more firm and definitive. Sharmaine instinctively pulled her ankles to her head then wrapped them around Tre's neck.

She grabbed Tre's dripping face and gently wiped away the sweat.

"Fuck this pussy hard, baby. She can take it. Fuck her as hard as you want. She's your pussy, baby. Fuck her good," Sharmaine told him as Tre really began to pound into her. Each time Tre stroked down, his groin and thighs would smack Sharmaine's phat ass and would clap as if punctuating the moment over and over. Sharmaine spoke dirty to Tre as he grunted and groaned his way to a nut. Tre's dick grew even harder and thicker as he kept fucking Sharmaine. She knew he was close to cumming. A part of her wished he didn't have on the condom so that she could feel his seed spurt into her, but she still was in enough control to realize that was a foolish idea although the thought did turn her on.

Tre couldn't take anymore. He grabbed her shoulders and screamed at the top of his lungs as he exploded into his condom. Despite the barrier, Sharmaine could feel his dick jerk in her with every spurt into the latex prophylactic.

"Damn, baby," was all Tre said as he lay on top of her for a few minutes trying to regain his composure. He eventually caught his breath and rolled off Sharmaine. He lay next to her, then he stretched his arm out, inviting Sharmaine to lie close to him. Sharmaine's heart leaped as she cuddled next to Tre, and though no words were uttered, actions spoke volumes as Tre leaned toward her and kissed her lovingly on the lips then closed his eyes.

Sharmaine looked over at him, and she thought that Tre looked so peaceful. It was like seeing him for the first time. She knew Tre was an incredible lover, and despite his shortcomings and career choice, Sharmaine realized she had been looking for a man like him—a man who could rock her world—but she also knew there was something more and that she wanted to know who Tre was.

The following morning, when Sharmaine awoke, Tre was gone. Damn, she thought. Why did she think Tre would be any different? Why did a good fuck make her delusional? She should have realized from the beginning that a thug like Tre wasn't going to look at her as anything other than a quick uptown fuck.

Oh well, she thought. It was better that he left. Tre was probably just one step ahead of the police, and she didn't need that in her life. Sharmaine had worked too long and too hard to establish her law practice to throw it all away on some street criminal. Then she thought of the previous night and how perfect it felt, and despite the possible danger, she hoped to run into Tre again.

While taking a shower that morning, Sharmaine couldn't get Tre off her mind, and she came three times, which led to her being late for work. If that wasn't bad enough, she had a big real estate closing to attend.

Fortunately, the meeting wasn't until 3:00 P.M., which afforded her with just enough time to get ready. Her thoughts continued to drift to Tre, and she couldn't wait to hurry back to the bar that evening by happy hour for a possible chance meeting with Tre.

Sharmaine rifled through the papers on her desk and prepared for what she hoped was the quickest closing in history. Her client, Morgan Equities, was selling a building to Stanford Enterprises. "Ho hum," she mumbled to herself as she looked up the buyers' attorney. She wanted to make sure that this deal went through seamlessly and quickly.

Sharmaine called the office of Mulwrich and Mulchahey, one of the largest law firms in the world and asked for Mr. T. Reynolds, the senior partner of real estate transactions. Mr. Reynolds' secretary answered.

"Good morning. I'm calling to confirm the three o'clock appointment. I want to make sure Mr. Reynolds and his team will be there on time."

"Yes, the closing is on the schedule, and Mr. Reynolds will be there on time like he always is," the secretary said, sounding offended.

Sharmaine hung up, giving the woman little thought and immediately began daydreaming about having another episode with Tre.

At 3:00 P.M. everyone was present with the exception of Mr. Reynolds. On the outside Sharmaine remained calm, but inside she cursed Mr. Reynolds and questioned his competence.

Five minutes later, Mr. Reynolds entered the room. He came with an associate in tow carrying the closing documents. Sharmaine was busy studying the paperwork as she said, "Thank you for joining us, Mr. Reynolds," with a pinch of attitude. "Can we get started now? I have a prior engagement this evening."

"Well, whoever he is, Ms. Williams, he is a lucky man," Mr. Reynolds said with a smile. His voice startled Sharmaine and caused her to look up from her papers. She couldn't believe her eyes. It was the man of her dreams. Mr. T. Reynolds was Tre. She wanted to say something, but they exchanged glances, and she knew better. They proceeded through the closing as if their paths had never crossed, and no one would've ever suspected that less than twenty-four hours ago, Tre's dick was smothered with Sharmaine's cum.

Throughout the whirlwind of papers being examined, Tre managed to pass Sharmaine a note.

Sharmaine,

Sorry I ran off last night, but I had a big closing to work on. Wondered if you would be willing to skip the club and just go back to my place and get to know each other a little better.

Tre

Sharmaine's heart was doing somersaults, but she remained professional and calm. She took a blank piece of paper, drew a smiley face on it, and slid it across to him. The other participants at the table paid little attention and were none the wiser. However, Tre and Sharmaine knew they were in for a hell of an evening, as soon as this damn closing was over. And to think, it all started at Thug Bar.

IT Guy
by
Dara Tariq

*N*ancy, this isn't right. I need the graph to the right of the text, not
centered above it, and the spacing is way off. Try using a half-
inch margin. I want this down to one page."

"Yes, Laura. I'm right on it."

Laura Goodwin was about to turn away from her faithful secretary
and head back to her office when she saw the pale, pinched face of her
boss, Hunter Harrison. His whiny voice attacked her senses. "Laura, are
you ready for tomorrow?"

"Have you ever known me not to be, Hunter?"

He looked up to match his five-two gaze to her five-nine one. "Well,
there's a first time for everything. And your last proposal went a tad long.
Try to keep this one down, eh?"

"I'll be ready. Now if you'll excuse us, Nancy and I have work to
do." She turned her back on the short man, and he eventually got the hint
and walked away.

Nancy laughed. "Don't worry, Laura. I'll have everything the way you
like it when you get back from lunch, which by the way, is at Ecco's,
promptly at twelve-thirty."

"Thanks, Nance. I won't be late. You know I love Italian, and Rashelle
is filling me in on her most recent internet catch. I can't wait to hear
about this one."

Laura returned to her spacious office and looked out at the Manhattan skyline. *Nice view,* she thought. *Get back to earning it.* She sat at her computer and tapped out her outline for the next day's meeting. Being the only black executive at her investment firm kept her working hard to prove she wasn't a "quota hire." Being the only woman took finesse to remain attractive and feminine while carrying around the largest *cajones* in the building.

She was so lost in work she jumped when her phone buzzed. "Wassup, Nance?"

"It's noon, and the car service is on the way. Freshen up and hit the streets, boss lady."

Laura made a quick stop in her private bathroom, checked her always-perfect bob, and applied lip balm. At forty-six, she looked thirty-six. She laughed at her reflection and said, "Thank goodness black don't crack." She grabbed her purse and headed for the elevator, calling to Nancy over her shoulder, "Don't let Hunter come around here giving you a hard time while I'm gone either. If that Hobbit comes back, tell him I sold the ring on Ebay."

As she finished her sentence, she ran smack into the IT guy. He was tall and solid and sent her careening off his sturdy frame. He caught her just before she hit the marble floor.

"Whoa. Slow down, ma." He pulled her up then attended to his sagging pants before they, too, hit the floor.

"Oh, Good Lord." Laura collected her purse and pulled her jacket down from its gathered position around her breasts. "Thanks for catching me, but I'm not old enough to be your mother."

He laughed as he straightened his green-and-white Pennington jersey. "Oh no, I didn't mean it like that. It's a term of endearment, like boo."

"And you think you know me well enough for terms of endearment?"

"Well, I did hold you lovingly in my arms. I think we're past the formality of Ms. Goodwin."

"And you are?"

"Jamal." He stuck out his hand. "Jamal Washburn."

Ignoring his outstretched limb, Laura leaned past him to press the elevator call button.

"Mr. Washburn, thanks again for your quick reflexes, but I'm late for lunch. I'm sure you have somewhere you need to be as well."

"Yes'm, Ms. Laura," Jamal said, giving her his best southern drawl while touching the brim of an imaginary hat. "I's just be on my way to fix dees here pikchur boxes. Y'all enjoy dat der lunch of yourn."

Laura tried not to look amused as she watched the baggy jeans confidently walk away.

"Girl, he wasn't on the down low. He was downright flaming." Rashelle tossed her braids over her shoulder and looked around for the waiter. "I need more wine for this story."

"Shelle, you don't know he's gay. Maybe he has a lot of sisters."

"Okay, Laura, let's say he has a lot of sisters. That means he started wearing women's underwear at an early age. The man was gay, and we won't be seeing each other again."

Laura stifled a laugh as she ordered the veal. She sat back in the booth and waited for her friend to order and elaborate.

"I'll have the fish, and pour freely, young man. I had a really bad date last night." She turned to face Laura. "First, he was dressed to perfection: beige, cashmere turtleneck, navy slacks, navy jacket. Shoes were shined and matched his socks and his belt."

Laura looked up from her antipasto. "Wait. His shoes, socks, and belt matched?"

"To perfection. I told you he was flaming."

"Maybe he just reads *GQ*. What else you got?"

"Alright, the restaurant was crowded, and we sat at the bar to wait. Girl, he crossed his legs—not ankle on the knee, legs open, guy style. We're talking full-on crossed, sitting on one ass cheek like Lady Di."

"Oh."

"Oh is right. You haven't heard the kicker. We're walking to our table, and he notices my purse. He says, and I quote 'That Dior bag is fierce.' "

Laura burst out laughing. Dabbing her eyes with a napkin, she said, "Okay, he's definitely homosexual. I'm sorry that didn't work out, but I've told you about that internet mess."

"I know, but what else am I supposed to do? Finding a decent man is like finding a parking spot in Times Square: good ones are usually taken, and the available ones are hard to get into."

"How about you just quit looking? You know things usually find themselves. Men are the same."

"Whatever, Ms. I'm Complete All By Myself. Don't tell me you wouldn't like to cuddle up to some fine hunk of man-meat every now and again."

"I can't lie. I miss the sex of a steady relationship."

"Let the church say amen."

They touched wineglasses. "Laura, you're gorgeous, paid, smart, and funny. I find it hard to believe that you can't find a man."

"I'm already buying lunch, so you can quit with the flattery. Seriously though, I can find a man. The problem is that I want a partner, not a dependent. You remember Jackson?"

"Ooh yeah. He was fine, but you could've put him on your taxes."

"Exactly. I want a man who can challenge me, show me new things, take me places I've never been."

"Do you want a man or a chauffeur?"

"Shut up or I won't share my tiramisu."

Laura returned to work to find Nancy smiling and whispering into the phone. She hung up hastily when she saw Laura approach.

"Ms. Laura, there's a delivery on your desk."

Laura found a single white rose with a card hanging from a silk bow. The card read:

Looking forward to our next trip.

~J

Laura smiled and would've blushed if her chocolate-brown skin was capable. She put the card on her desk, handing Nancy the rose. "If you'd put this in water."

"Yes'm, Ms. Laura." Nancy giggled as she walked away.

"And that's enough of this Ms. Laura stuff. You're not funny." But Laura couldn't stop smiling.

The next day, the presentation went off without a hitch. Even the Hobbit congratulated Laura on a job well done. She knew she grabbed the account and felt like celebrating. She walked to a nearby park, bought an ice cream cone, and sat with her face in the sun.

"Never thought I'd be jealous of a dairy product." Jamal the IT guy stood at her table. "May I sit down?"

"What are you doing here? I didn't know they let geeks out to wile away their afternoons in the park."

"It's information technology specialist, thank you. And I can't stand offices. I need fresh air, sunshine." His gaze traveled Laura's body. "A beautiful view. Now may I join you?"

"Why not?"

"That's encouraging." Jamal's face softened when he smiled. His caramel features were strong and masculine, giving him a hard, don't-mess-with-me look.

"I'm not trying to encourage you. I should thank you for the rose. I was quite surprised."

"Surprised that a man noticed a beautiful woman or that somebody from the basement flirted with somebody with office space?"

"Look, Jamal, I don't fraternize with people in the company. Even if you were on my level, there wouldn't be hope. I'm a few years your senior, and I'm a senior executive. You've been sweet, but what could you possibly offer me?"

"So that's it, huh, Laura?" He pushed his chair back and stood. "Don't underestimate the power of passion. I can tell you've been holding yours in for a while now. It would be nice for us to explore it together. I could show you things. Challenge you. Take you places you've never been."

With that, he walked away.

Laura almost called after him. Instead she called Rashelle.

"He said it. Just like that? I get a confused brother, and you get a handsome young spy."

"Girl, he said it word for word. He was talking about passion like he knew something about it."

"Maybe he does. What would it hurt to try him out?"

"Are you trying to get me fired? He works in the basement."

"You're in no jeopardy of losing that job. You're exceptional at what you do. Period. Worst case scenario, one of the partners finds out and threatens you with it. You leave and start your own firm, which you've been talking about for years. It's time you did your own thing anyway. Girl, fuck that young hottie on the boardroom table."

"I see you've officially gone 'round the bend."

"If he's good, you can have quickies in the office. If he's not, you can just have him fired and forget him. Just promise you'll call me either way."

"Girl, I don't know about this."

"What's to know? He's a fling, not a fiancé. Go have fun. I've got five instant message windows going at once. I'm getting off the phone before I get too confused. Later."

Laura went home, changed into sweats, and jogged until she came to a clear decision about Jamal.

Laura dressed with extra caution the next morning. Higher-ups were getting together to discuss a possible promotion for her, and she wanted to look her best when they called her in to tell her she was a partner. "Believe it and you'll achieve it, sistah." She chose her red power suit and matching fiery Manolos. She felt like a million bucks.

When she stepped off the elevator, Nancy let out a low whistle. "Ooh, Laura, you look absolutely fabulous. If they hand out partnerships for looking fine, you'd own the place."

"Thanks, Nance. Keep hope alive."

Laura was called in shortly after lunch, and judging from the swing in her step on the way back to her desk, things went very well.

"Nancy, pack your desk."

"Huh? We're leaving? But you look so happy."

"We're leaving alright. That corner suite upstairs has my name on the door. This firm is now: Harrison, Baker, and Goodwin."

Nancy jumped up and down, hugging Laura and taking her along for a bouncy ride. "If you quit jumbling my insides, you can check our calendar. I think we deserve the afternoon off."

"No more meetings. You're done for the day."

"Then so are you. Take off, Nance, and thanks for everything. I couldn't have come this far without your hard work."

"Aww, you're gonna make my mascara run. Before I head off, you've got something in your office."

Laura turned and saw a white box on her desk. "What is it, Nance?"

"A box, genius. Are you sure you didn't sleep your way to partner?"

"You better carry your smart behind out of here before I forget all about your raise."

"In that case, enjoy the day, boss lady. You deserve all this and then some." She gave Laura another quick squeeze, grabbed her purse from the bottom drawer, and was gone in a flash. Laura cautiously eyed the box. No markings, no labels. Empty. She opened it and found two beautiful crystal champagne flutes. The enclosed card read:

Congratulations.
Celebrate with me.
~J

Laura flipped the card to find an address on the Lower East Side. She hesitated only briefly before heading to the underground parking garage. The drive was a blur. The neighborhood looked sketchy. Laura collected the flutes from the passenger seat, double-checked the car alarm, and walked up to the entrance of what looked to be a condemned warehouse.

Jamal lifted the large garage door, wearing a sweater and cords, looking casually handsome.

"Welcome." He took her coat and led her into a fashionable loft.

"I love your place. All this open space, and these windows are incredible."

"Thanks. The place was a steal after they busted the sweat shop."

Laura laughed and tried to get beyond feeling overdressed. Her business suit was tailored to her hourglass figure. Jamal offered Laura a glass of wine as she seated herself on a barstool next to the kitchen island.

"Mmm. This is a nice Riesling," she said after taking a sip. "Good choice."

"Thanks. It should go well with the grilled salmon. I'm making a salad, if you don't mind keeping it light."

Laura raised an eyebrow. "Sounds good."

Jamal caught the look on her face. "Forget you, Ms. Bourgie. Like this ghetto boy should only know about McDonald's and malt liquor."

"I'm not saying that. Just surprised, that's all."

Jamal finished dinner and continued surprising Laura throughout the meal. They discussed politics, religion, and racism in America. Laura was enjoying the night and realized they had not mentioned sex at all.

"Well, Ms. Laura, are you ready for dessert?" Jamal led Laura to a spot off the dining area where the floor was covered in large, beautiful pillows covered in silk brocade.

He deposited her with a gallant kiss on her hand. "I'll be right back." He returned with a tray on which he balanced the flutes, strawberries, whipped cream, and a bottle of Veuve Clicquot.

"My favorite champagne no less. You're a spy."

"I'm nothing of the kind. Just wanted to please you, so I asked. Don't blame Nancy for blabbing. She's got your back, and I've sworn her to secrecy."

"About that, Jamal. This can never—and I mean never—leave this room. I'm not trying to jeopardize my partnership."

"Understood. Speaking of partnership, I need to propose a toast.

To the smartest, sexiest, most deserving partner I've ever known."

Jamal's eyes locked on Laura's as she sipped the crisp, fruity taste of the bubbly. "Jamal, I hate to pry—"

"Yeah, right. Your curiosity is vibrating. Ask away, m'lady."

"The flutes. This place. The wine, dinner, champagne. There's no way you could afford these things by hitting control alt delete all day. What gives?"

"I don't sell urban pharmaceuticals, if that's what you're thinking. I'm not eligible for a corner suite like yourself because I didn't attend an ivy league school, but I'm good with computers. I'm self-taught, and there's nothing I can't do. I build websites, networks, make house calls—whatever. Your help desk allowed me to work on the fastest equipment loaded with the latest software. I wouldn't have been able to get my hands on that stuff otherwise. Now that I have the experience, I can name my price."

Laura shook her head, "So you're engaging in corporate espionage. Probably taking equipment, software, and who knows what else."

"No way. I only take knowledge and experience. I'm growing my business."

"Who are you kidding?"

"Maybe I helped them recycle some spare parts they considered trash."

"I applaud your entrepreneurial spirit, but now that my name is on the door, I'd prefer it if you took what you know and got out of the basement."

"No worries. I quit yesterday, right after you told me about your no-fraternizing rule. I walked in with the vision of you and that mint chocolate chip you licked off your bottom lip and told my boss to find my replacement. I'm your IT guy now."

"You think you're my IT guy? What makes you so sure?"

"This." He held her face in his hands and leaned in for a kiss. It was demanding and without pretense. He wasn't kissing her. He was taking possession of her mouth without any hint of tenderness.

He pulled her up roughly and began to undress her. Laura's suit fell to the floor with astonishing speed. Jamal backed her toward an alcove hidden behind a high wall of glass blocks. The most amazing four-poster, king-size bed awaited them. Her underwear went as quickly as the suit. She was positioned against the massive oak pillar as Jamal undressed. He took his time, watching Laura take in his body. Jamal was muscular with an athlete's build: wide shoulders, tapered waist, and strong legs. Laura felt somewhat self-conscious of her more than ample hips and rounded ass. Her breasts were large and full. She tried to cover herself as Jamal's gaze became a stare. He stepped to her in one swift stride.

"What the fuck are you doing?" His voice was raised. Jamal seemed truly angered.

"It's just—"

"It's just what? You have some issues with your body? You want some white model's thin legs or nonexistent ass?" Jamal pulled Laura's hands away from her body. His voice lowered. "I love your breasts. I could spend all day right here." Jamal put his face between the large orbs of flesh and licked the softness he found on either side. "And these hips…" Jamal's hands traveled the arc with reverence. Unknowingly, he caressed the core of Laura's insecurity. She squirmed underneath him as if to escape his embrace.

"Damnit, where are you trying to go?"

"Look, Jamal, we don't have to pretend we're lovers. I'm looking for a good lay, and then we can walk away like nothing happened. Let's just fuck and leave the touchy-feely stuff out of this."

"See, that's your problem. You always want to be in control, but that's about to change."

Jamal had a strange look in his eye as he pushed Laura onto the mattress. He reached under the bed and came back with a handful of silk ribbon. Laura's eyes widened as she realized what was next. Jamal straddled her chest and roughly pulled Laura's arms above her head. He tied one wrist to a spindle in the headboard. He checked the knots and went to work on her other arm. Panic set in as Laura noticed how tightly she was bound. Silk or not, she would not be able to free herself. Jamal tied her feet as well, sitting on her thighs as she thrashed futilely. Laura's anxiety level increased when she remembered that no one knew of her whereabouts. Jamal remained silent as he made Laura captive. She laid naked, spread eagle and restrained on the bed, too stunned to speak.

He stood next to the bed. His voice was lowered and much calmer, but even less reassuring as he said, "Tonight you will learn what it means to lose control. You will beg me for release, and I will ignore you—again and again."

Tears escaped Laura's eyes as she feared the worst.

Jamal's voice softened even further. "Stop that. I'm not going to hurt you—much. You'll ultimately enjoy this." He approached the bed and ran his hand up her thigh. Laura flinched at his touch.

"Damn. You're really scared. I'm sorry, Laura. I assure you you're not in any danger."

Laura pulled against her restraints. She was sure all serial killers used that line at some point. His words were doing nothing to assuage her fear.

She begged, "Please untie me. I won't tell anyone, just let me go. Please."

"Laura, for the last time, this is not about violence. This is purely sexual. Tonight you give up control and try something new. Experience something beyond the tired sex you've had in the past. We'll use a safe word. At any time, you say this word, the evening ends. You can go back to your workaholic life, drab and boring. Your word is *Monday*. You can yell *stop, don't, quit,* or beg me to let you go, and I'll ignore you, but say *Monday* and you walk. You understand that, Laura?"

A quiet "Yes" was whispered in response.

"Then let's begin." Jamal could see her chest heaving with shallow breaths. Her heart must be racing. That should be the end to this adventure, not the start. Jamal moved to Laura's side. He stretched his tall frame next to hers and put his head on her shoulder. She did not recoil from his touch. He said nothing as he deepened his breathing. Soon, Laura was also breathing deep in her abdomen. Laura knew that the evening held many possibilities, but the fact that he noticed her nervousness and helped calm her anxiety spoke volumes. She always had *Monday*, if things got out of hand.

Jamal slowly ran his hand along the side of her naked body, making sure not to touch the traditional erogenous zones. He traced her armpit, the underside of her breasts, her ankle. The skin there, unaccustomed to touch, was sensitive and responsive. Jamal stroked her body gently and slowly. Laura started thinking that this losing control thing was a good idea. He moved to the other side and began again, even slower. She then realized his purpose. She wanted him to touch her dampening pussy, to lick her nipples, to kiss her. And he was avoiding all of this.

"Please, baby. You know what I want."

"This isn't about what you want. Fuck what you want."

He continued his exploration of her body, but this time used his tongue, still focusing on places most people forget: her eyelids and the insides of her wrists. He found his way to her collarbone, sucking the bony protrusion. He traveled to the valley between her breasts. Laura moaned and tried to shift her body so her nipple would meet his warm tongue.

"Bitch, if I wanted it, I'd take it. Now stay still."

Laura, resigned to the feeling of frustration, willed herself to stay in place. Jamal went lower, licking the warm skin below her belly button. He lifted her hips and kneaded the softness of her buttocks. Her skin was so soft. Her legs were parted from the restraints. Jamal moved between her thighs, getting closer and closer to her wet pussy. He licked the inside of her thigh up until he reached the soft down of her pubic hair. He nibbled the delicate skin, backed away from her intoxicating scent, and traveled down the other thigh. Laura pushed her hips forward, silently begging for his tongue to touch her moistened sex. He did not oblige. He continued to move his wet tongue down her leg until he reached the instep of her foot. He paused there, with long, broad, erotic strokes of his tongue. He moved to her toes and sucked them one by one into his mouth. Laura pulled against the wide ribbon, to no avail.

"Oh, God. I want you to fuck me. Pleeeeease?" Laura did not like the sound of need in her voice as she writhed and squirmed. She hoped this teasing would be over soon.

"Begging won't help. I'll fuck you when I'm good and ready." His voice was calm in contrast to her impassioned plea. He straddled her waist and stroked his dick in front of her. It was already semi-hard. Laura watched as he brought himself to his full length.

Laura looked on in stunned silence. He continued to stroke himself unhurriedly in full view of her. He took his dick and rubbed the tip along her stomach, down the line of hair that led to her neatly trimmed bush. She anticipated penetration, but could not have been more wrong.

He persisted in teasing her. Moving all over her, he rubbed his hard dick against her soft skin.

Finally he returned between her open thighs. He rubbed himself around her pussy, spreading the lips, but making sure to avoid her clit. He circled his dick around her wet pussy over and over. Laura bucked against her restraints, begging in earnest.

"Jamal, I need your dick inside me. Stop teasing me. I'm so ready and wet. Fuck this pussy, baby. Please, fuck me."

Jamal moved away from her. Laura thought it was to better position himself for the aggressive fucking that would soon begin. Wrong. His knees straddled Laura's head. She opened her mouth, ready to please him when he slapped her forcefully on the cheek with his hard dick. Her eyes wide with shock, she sputtered with anger, "What the—"

"I've had about all I can take of your damn whining. If I want to hear your voice, I'll ask your bitch ass a question. Other than that, try shutting the fuck up."

She looked at him as if she wanted to set him aflame. Jamal was unfazed. He simply stared at her. Seconds later, he cocked his head to one side and asked, "Are we clear?" Laura nodded silently, aware of the proximity of his dick to her face. She did not take her eyes off his thick penis. She told herself she'd bite it off if he swung his dick at her face again. He stared at her for a long time until she averted her eyes. Satisfied that she understood, Jamal got up and rummaged under the bed again.

Laura saw him approach then felt cool silk on her eyelids. He tied the blindfold securely.

"Can you see me, Laura?" he asked.

"No."

The bed sagged with his weight. He sat very close, barely touching her. "Can you feel me, Laura?"

"Yes." Laura's fear returned. She was thinking that this was a huge mistake. He was taking this too far. She was looking for a kinky adventure, but ended up tied to the bed of a true sadist.

He stroked her breasts, flicking the nipples with his nail. Laura moaned as the desperate need for release returned; her nipples hard as diamonds. He pulled on them, making them even longer. Then she felt something cold and metal being applied to her left nipple. "Oh shit," she shrieked as Jamal applied some type of pincher.

"Did I ask you something?"

"No," she said through clenched teeth.

"That's right. I didn't."

Her nipple was burning, sending jolts of electricity straight to her already excited pussy. She breathed deeply, trying to relax and remove herself from the pain. Visions of *Monday* floated behind the blindfold. Jamal gave her a minute to acclimate to the new sensation. When her breathing was even and the muscles in her face were slack, he went to work on her right nipple. She withstood the application without a sound. He stroked the outside curve of each breast. Laura was getting used to the pressure on her nipples. The flow of blood reduced, the pain decreased to a tingle, which continued to resonate in her core.

"That's my girl. You handled the clamps well. And your nipples are perfect."

The compliment thrilled and angered Laura. On one hand, she was proud that she had not broken down and cried. She was in full control of her emotions. On the other, she was pissed at herself for enjoying the way he spoke to her. She liked the sound of approval in his voice—not to mention the sensations in her pussy. Her mind raced as to what could be next.

A large, cool pillow lifted her hips off the bed and rested in the small of her back. Jamal applied something cold and slippery to the crack of her ass. She was an anal virgin and tensed greatly but said nothing. Laura felt Jamal's fingers probe her rear opening. Slick fingertips fluttered against the puckered skin, setting off fireworks along the responsive bundle of nerves. Jamal pushed a single finger against her sphincter. Again, Laura tensed.

"Breathe in and out slowly, Laura. This won't hurt if you relax."

"Relax? Mind games are one thing, but you want to commit sodomy against my will, and you think I should relax?"

"I haven't done a damn thing against your will. Say your safe word, get dressed, and go. Put on your five-hundred-dollar shoes and clickety clack your fancy ass right on out of here."

"It's just that I'm scared," Laura admitted in a quiet voice.

Jamal's tone softened. "I know, baby. We're trying something new. Challenge yourself. You might like it." He stroked her tight anal entrance lightly, and the fireworks returned with a vengeance.

The tension in her muscles eased, and he slipped his finger inside. Jamal rotated his finger while slowly pushing back and forth. Laura let out an involuntary moan. It was incredibly erotic and felt better than she ever imagined. He inserted his finger as far as it could go and left it buried there, waiting for her muscles to relax further. He slowly pulled his finger out of Laura's ass.

Jamal applied additional lubricant and inserted two fingers. Again, he rotated, thrusted, and rested. Laura moaned, loud and luxuriously, and was instantly embarrassed. She was thankful for the blindfold that partially hid her face. She liked his fingers in her ass way too much. Jamal continued the pattern of twist, thrust, and wait until there was no wait and more thrust than twist.

He removed both fingers and surveyed her ready asshole. She felt something cold and rubbery that increased in size as it entered her. Just when she thought she could take no more, she felt her sphincter close around it. It was buried deep inside her as she felt the base of a butt plug against her cheeks.

Jamal straddled her again, his ass on her chest. He moved his penis above her mouth and outlined her lips with the tip of his dick. Laura attempted to lick him, but he pulled himself out of reach. After a few motions of the cat-and-mouse game, he rested his dick on her lower lip, pulling it down. Her tongue sat waiting, knowing he would fuck her mouth when he was ready. He lifted his hips and lowered his dick into her open mouth.

Laura raised her head and began to suck him. She put forth effort like she never had before. This was different. She felt freed of inhibitions. She could let her freak flag fly because this wasn't real. It was all a game. Besides, she was no longer in control. She was bound and blindfolded, unable to free herself. She was doing these freaky things because she had no other choice. Even more so, she wanted to show Jamal she knew how to give pleasure.

She licked and lapped at his hard dick, making delicious, wet noises. She craned and strained her neck to stroke him fully with her willing mouth. He regretfully pulled out, lifted his dick, and placed his balls on her tongue. She licked eagerly, applying suction and pressure with her mouth. Jamal returned his dick to her lips and thrust himself deeply into Laura's mouth. She could feel him deep in her throat.

He grabbed a fistful of her hair and pushed himself farther inside. Her head trapped by the mattress and his hand in her hair, she could not move back from the onslaught of his dick. His rhythm varied, and she did not have time to prepare her throat as her gag reflex set in. He had both hands in her hair now, fucking her mouth violently.

"Take it all, bitch. Yeah, just like that..." Laura did her best to relax and let him have his way with her. She could feel his balls tighten against her chin and knew he would cum soon.

"Swallow it." Laura had never let a man cum in her mouth and was nervous about the taste. She need not have worried. He was so far down her throat, his hot cum never touched her tongue.

"Aw, fuck." With another grunt, he pulled out of her mouth. She could still feel the weight of his legs and knew he was watching her. She made a show of opening her mouth and licking her lips to prove she had done as instructed. She tasted his salty cum for the first time. She felt him leave the bed and heard footsteps moving away from her. Laura heard water running then a glass filling. She heard Jamal's return as he drank greedily. God, she was thirsty. He was teasing her again. Drinking loudly and not offering her a drop.

He put the glass down noisily on the nightstand. She could hear water sloshing. She couldn't wait. "Can I please have some water? I'll do anything."

"I already know you'll do anything. You don't really have a choice, do you, Laura? But I'll let you earn your water."

He moved between her legs, his face mere inches from her sex. She could feel his breath on her wet pussy lips, the air cooling them.

"I'm going to lick this pretty pussy of yours, and you cannot cum. Cum and you'll be punished. You can speak, but you will not orgasm. Understood?"

"Yes, Jamal."

He lowered his face to her soaked, hot pussy. He lapped at it with his tongue spread and flat, taking long strokes, starting at the bottom and working his way up. He placed his thumbs on either side of her clit, releasing it from its hiding place. Jamal moved his tongue around the throbbing button until Laura's head moved wildly from side to side. Her moans and sighs told him his pace was right.

He bent his head lower and licked her puffy brown outer lips, sucking and pulling. He spread them to reveal her inner lips, a darker brown, wet and slick with her juices. He did the same, licking and pulling. He spread her inner lips to reveal her pink, smooth center. He inserted his tongue and felt the soft, smooth texture.

"Oh God, that feels so good. Lick my sweet pussy."

Jamal, urged on by Laura's comments, decided to up the ante. He reached for the butt plug and pulled it out slowly. Laura gasped when she felt the explosion on the nerves of her sensitive anus. Jamal tongued her spread pussy and rotated the butt plug, inserting it deeply and pulling it out slowly. It was too much for Laura.

"I'm gonna cum. I can't stop it."

Jamal bit down on her clit. The pain brought Laura back from the edge of climax. She pulled her hips into the mattress, afraid of further retribution.

"You'll cum when I say you cum. Not before."

He reseated the butt plug firmly inside Laura's ass and shifted his weight. He brought the glass to Laura's face and placed it next to her cheek. The coolness was wonderful.

"Open your mouth."

Laura did as instructed as Jamal poured a mouthful. She swallowed and opened for more. The water was incredible. She licked her lips, collecting any drops that might have missed their mark. Jamal leaned over and kissed her. He let his tongue slip between her moist lips as he buried his hands in her hair. She felt passion, not just dominance. She moaned into his mouth and knew, at this point, she could cum from his kiss alone.

He placed the glass back on the nightstand before placing himself between her gaping thighs and rubbing the swollen head of his dick on her wet pussy. Laura smiled and moaned softly as Jamal rocked gently. She could feel his hard dick against the butt plug planted deeply inside her backside.

Jamal leaned back to untie her ankles. He rubbed the chafed skin briefly and placed her feet on his shoulders. He flicked his fingertip against her clit while he plunged forcefully into her dripping pussy. He leaned forward to untie her wrists, which brought a brief scream from Laura as her thighs rested on her nipple clamps.

Jamal removed the blindfold and looked deeply into her eyes. Laura saw an intense passion in his stare that she never knew possible. Jamal fucked Laura with reckless abandon. Her moans were taking him to another level.

He reached forward and with both hands, undid the nipple clamps. Laura screamed loudly as the blood returned to her assaulted nipples.

"Cum now, Laura." Pure electricity traveled from the tips of her breasts straight to her clit. Her eyes widened as the most forceful orgasm she had ever experienced racked her body. Unintelligible sounds escaped her lips.

Laura wrapped her legs around his back and clawed at the sheets, her head rolling from side to side. She whimpered in ecstasy, an overwhelming feeling of fulfillment rumbling within her.

"Let me hear you. Don't hold it." Laura let go and moaned in earnest. She'd always been embarrassed by how loud she got during sex, but it seemed to drive Jamal on, so she stopped caring. If only she knew the effect it had on him. The sound of her sexy encouragement caused a vibration to begin in his pelvis. It resonated through his hips and into his dick, which got harder as he fucked her.

He rolled over on his back, taking Laura with him. She folded her legs on either side of him and began a luscious dance on his dick. She didn't hop up and down, but ground into him deliciously. The butt plug also rotating inside her tight ass. Her clit rubbed against him when she leaned forward, and she increased the circumference of the circles she created with her hips. Her breasts were above his mouth, and he began licking and biting her chest, avoiding her sensitive nipples.

He gripped her ass and pulled her away from him, almost releasing his dick from her warm sheath. She found the movement very pleasurable and repeated the stroke herself. Laura leaned back with her hands on the bed behind her and brought her hips back and forth, experimenting with a stroke that just barely kept his long dick inside of her. She was exceptionally wet, and their fucking was noisy. Jamal watched as his dick, shiny and slick with her juices, disappeared in her searing pussy over and over. Leaning back this way, Laura's clit was without stimulation. She reached down and fingered it herself, moving her hand in fast circles while continuing to rock on his throbbing dick. She finally came again, throwing back her head and moaning loudly. Her breasts were shaking from the spasms she experienced, her nipples like hard bullets. She continued to rub herself slowly as Jamal could feel as well as see and hear her orgasm. She collapsed on top of him, licking and kissing his neck and shoulder, still breathing noisily through her mouth.

He took her waist in both of his strong hands and flipped her over. He pulled her up onto her knees and pushed down on the back of her neck, keeping her shoulders on the bed before positioning himself behind her and easily sliding inside. He fucked her with long, smooth strokes until her moans fused and became a lust-filled melodious song.

Laura reached for sheets, pillows, the headboard—anything to hold on to for fear she'd be lost and never find her way back. Jamal watched the muscles in her back move and stretch and traced his fingers along her spine. He grasped her hips for dear life and increased the pace that was still agonizingly slow to Laura. She began to push her ass against him, another orgasm brewing just under the surface. She knew a good, hard, punishing fuck would take her over the edge again.

Jamal reached around and put two fingers flat on her clit and pressed down, making the same circles he made with his dick inside of her dripping sex. She arched her back, and her moans increased.

She would cum that way: under his hand and on his dick. She pressed back against him as her orgasm poured over her. Her shoulders dipped back onto the bed as her breath came in heavy gasps. Satisfied she was spent, Jamal stopped holding back. He fucked her hard, slamming into her ass. The noisy sounds of her wetness and skin slapping skin took the last of his control. His dick jerked and shot thick streams of cum into her waiting, clutching pussy.

He threw back his head and yelled loudly, giving in to the raw power of his orgasm. They both collapsed, and Jamal spooned against Laura's backside, "That's my girl." He kissed her neck while he ran his fingertips lightly across Laura's sweaty skin. She continued to experience the tremors of aftershock that accompanies really good sex. Exhausted, it did not take long for Laura to fall asleep, snoring softly.

Jamal whispered Laura's name, and she did not answer. "Get some rest, baby. Tonight was only the beginning. I'm going to do everything I can to make you mine."

Pulse
by
Anna J

The night belongs to me. After dusk, once the sun dips down behind the city and the concrete cools, it's my time to shine. When you can hear the pulse of the city coming alive under the drone of the worker bees, you can feel it in every step you take. Clothes start to come off as both men and women make the transition from "business casual" to "club sexy." I can feel the beat of the drums in my veins…The night belongs to me.

After putting in eight long hours at a nine-to-five I'm just holding on to because I have a car note, my flesh comes to life as the evening breeze caresses my skin, leading my feet to a happy-hour spot before I head on home. A big beautiful woman I am indeed, I turn all kinds of heads as I make my way down South Street. The sway of my hips is being watched closely by every man on the strip. The women around me are seething with envy because they can only dream of being as voluptuous as this Virgo. No effort, only sex appeal dripping off me like chocolate ice cream running down the side of a cone. So sweet…

My stiletto heels keep a steady rhythm on the pavement as I step to a beat that's only in my head. Oblivious to the world around me, I keep walking until my body pulls me into the place where I will be relaxing for the time being. A few glance my way as I step into the dimly lit building, some turning back to their dates in a dismissive fashion, unaware of what they're missing out on: Black cherry, slightly pink on the inside, juices that run like a faucet all night…you can only wish of sampling this black berry pie. Too cute to assume that it's possible you don't want me, I make my way to the bar where I rest my ancestry on a high stool, the bartender giving me his immediate attention.

Staring at my chocolate-lined lips and the dip in my shirt, my servant asks what I will be tasting as he steals a peek at my tattoo. Full breasts filling out the barely there fabric shielding my flesh, I lean forward flirtatiously so that he can get a better view as I softly ask for a Slow Screw. Not wanting to pull his eyes away from my outer beauty, he turns to mix my drink, dropping in an extra cherry just for me. Teasingly, I tie the stem into a bow using only my tongue, further adding to the mystery.

Swaying in my seat to the slow reggae beat that has just filled the walls of the building, I slide off my stool smoothly, making my way to the dance floor. The only one out there, and eating up the attention, I dance seductively for my chocolate servant like we are the only two in the room. Floating on the lyrics that are exiting the speakers, I continue to dance nonstop, shaking and popping it, showing the room that us big girls know how to drop it like it's hot.

Moving seductively as the deejay switches to a calypso beat, I speed it up with him, extra light on my feet. The occupants of the small bar sit back in awe, trying to figure out how I can move so fly in the sky-high sandals I'm dancing in. I simply show them the confidence of this Virgo. I show them that there's nothing to be scared of, and that they don't know exactly what they're missing.

While in the beginning all of the men were sitting back swearing to the high heavens that they would never be with a "big" girl, all of them are now sitting with their mouths wide open, quickly rethinking what their type may be. As the drums slow down, I find my way back to my seat, not a bead of sweat on my pretty head as I wrap full lips around my drinking straw, giving the occupants of this space one last look at my gorgeous ass.

Taking a look around the room, deciding to make my exit none too soon, I flash my smile for all to see as I retreat with all eyes in the place on me. I hear the drums instantly when my foot touches the pavement, my hips swaying to their own rhythm all the way back to the car. My engine beating to the tune in my head, I slip down the street discreetly on my way to my house so I can fall back and just be me.

I pull up to a chocolate rainbow in front of my building. A sea of mixed chocolate muscles from sweet vanilla to baker's dark. The caramel in between is just what I need, but deciding against it, I slide through on my quest to just be me. Checking the mail, and then running a bath, I slide thick thighs into the water. Its warmth caresses me like an old lover patiently waiting for me to get home and glad to see me when I get there. Toni Braxton is singing about speaking in tongues in the background. My head finds the massage pillow as my body sinks into my lilac-scented bath water, my eyes closing, releasing the stress of my day.

Don't need no Caller ID 'cause I won't have anybody interrupting our call.

Talk dirty to me, baby, without talking at all…

Humming along to the music, I trace with my finger what's familiar to me. My fingertips roam over my curves, caressing firm fudge-colored nipples before finding their way between soft chocolate thighs. I continue my journey of self-fulfillment without opening my eyes. The music is my man tonight, and my hands become his as he parts the Savannah and dips into the valley of my forever thirst quencher. My eyes stay shut tight as I imagine his lips taking hold of my clit, me holding the side of the tub tight with one hand so my feet won't slip as my other hand holds the door to ecstasy everlasting open for him.

His tongue sliding across my panic button, I just about have a fit as I explode, depositing vanilla ice cream on his tongue. The music fading into another song, my heart returning to a normal rhythm, my wet bathroom floor… I can't even be mad as I cleanse my body four times like my momma taught me, then tiptoe to my bedroom to finish the job.

Spread out on three hundred thread-count sheets, I reach into my end table drawer where he rests patiently, always ready for me when I need him. Ten inches of flexible, vibrating magic that lasts as long as my D batteries. The vibration on my lips is too much as I dip my snake into my cave, making it wet all over. Pulling my legs up to my chest, I relax my muscles and slow my breathing, letting the vibration take me to levels seemingly impossible to reach.

He makes me want to do things I'd never do for anyone else. I'm in trust with him because he does whatever he has to do to please me. He does things to my body that cause instant explosions back to back. In my mind, his tongue feels hot on my skin, and his hands explore every inch of me. He talks to me in a deep baritone voice that drives me crazy while he's stroking me.

His request of "give me that pussy" never goes unanswered. My lips open instantly in anticipation of him filling me with his deliciousness. His vibe is electric, and I can feel him wrapped around me, even when he's not present. His thick chocolate lips are smooth to the touch as he wraps them around my clit, and his tongue makes me sing soprano. His long fingers play me like a piano, causing me to hit high notes as our bodies become one.

Only for him, I allow him to watch me please myself. I repeat for him exactly what I do when I'm thinking about him at the times when he's not around. I slow it down for him so he can see how he makes me feel. I show him how bad I want him inside of me, contracting inside of my walls until I cream all over him. My eyes are closed and my head is thrown back as I softly moan, whispering to him how I want him to take me. I open my lips so that he can see my cream ooze out, my clit pressed between my thumb and forefinger. I dip my finger into my cave and hold it to his lips so he can sample my nectar because I want him to want to taste me.

For him, my knees are pressed to my chest, my panic button fully exposed. I want him to want his tongue inside of my walls. I want him to want my fingers gripping his dreads as he drowns my clit. I want him to want to be inside of me because, baby, we are good together. I want him to want to make me moan from pleasure and squeal with delight, and quiver under him as he plunges in and out of me with long, steady strokes. I want him to know that I've never been made love to, and I thank him with all my heart for the experience.

He makes me feel sexy from the inside out. He makes me feel like I can conquer any fear that I believe exists. He understands my confidence and doesn't shy away from my pride. He believes in my dreams and never disappoints me. He's my Adonis, and I'm his queen. He makes me want to taste him from head to toe and linger around the middle longer than necessary. He makes me want to deep-throat him so that the head of his gorgeous dick is acquainted with my tonsils.

He makes me want to tease him just beneath his testicles with the tip of my tongue before diving in for a rim shot. Only for him will I continue to orally please him until his seed is coating my taste buds. For him I make good use of any lubricant. With him, there are no limitations. He glides into my back door patiently with the skill of an excellent lover.

He makes me feel like I'm floating on clouds, even though he resides in my mind. He makes me feel alive and satisfied and energetic all at the same time. Only for him will I slide down on him in the riding position, teasing the head first before I take the plunge. For him, I feed him both nipples at the same time as I tighten my walls around him. He makes me feel like it's never too soon to cum because he'll make sure I'll cum over and over. He moans in pleasure so that I know I'm pleasing him, too. He says, "Give me that pussy," and I do.

Only for him, I let my wild side out, and it's cool because he has a wild side also. I'm twisted into all kinds of compromising positions because I want him happy. For him I finger-fuck myself as he watches from the end of the bed because I know it turns him on. I lick my juice off my fingers then tongue kiss him because he likes the taste of me. My vibrator is just an enhancement because he knows he can never be replaced. He knows that sucking on my toes heats up my entire body, and for him, I gladly masturbate because he likes watching my expressions when I explode.

For him I lay on my side with my legs wrapped around his back. I hold the lips of my vagina open so that all of him can fit in me. He knows I want his finger in my asshole, and he gently slides it in, causing all kinds of havoc in my erogenous zone. Only for him, I whisper for him to take me because a whisper is all that's needed. I don't need to be loud for him to hear me because he can read my thoughts. And once I close my eyes and morning comes, I tuck him safely in my drawer until next time, because I'm almost certain we will meet again.

I can hear the drums almost instantly when my feet hit the soft carpet in my room, and I make my way to clean up the mess I left in the bathroom the night before. Only eight more hours until the workday is over, and just like all the days before, the night belongs to me. I fly into work, feeling like a caged bird, and none too soon, it is time to go, and the cage is opened…this bird is set free. My feet lead me to where I need to be, and I don't hesitate to step into the humidity of the spot for the night, the drums beating…pulsating inside of me.

It starts innocently enough. He watches me watching him from across the room. I am so caught up in the color of his eyes, it seems as if no one else exists. We make our way to the dance floor, our bodies liquid. A dance made for more intimate surroundings is performed right there in the smoke-filled lounge. I should stop him when I feel his right hand graze my nipple, but I am mesmerized. We make love on the dance floor, and it feels oh so good.

His tongue tracing my earlobe sends a delicious sensation down my spine, causing instant wetness. Wrapping my right leg around his waist allows his smooth fingertips to tease my wet triangle as we rock steadily to "Like Glue" by Sean Paul. We are the only two people in the room…in the universe. The beat of the drums heavy like our pulse beating wildly echoes in my head upon orgasm, making it feel like we are levitating. If anyone is watching, we look like one well-carved sculpture instead of two individually beating hearts, intertwined, fitting perfectly together.

The song ends much too soon, and the magic of our embrace is temporarily interrupted. My body still tingles from the sensation of him being so close to me. I am suddenly embarrassed and quickly flee the scene. I look back one time, and we make eye contact before the crowd rushes me through the door. I yell back to tell him my name, but my voice is lost among the beat of the drums. Every day after that is sheer torture and wonderful bliss. I want so badly to put a name to the face I made love to every night. I go back to the lounge every day, hoping to see him. Hoping we can meet again on the dance floor and make magic one more time.

I find myself there one Saturday night. Three months have passed since we last made eye contact, and just as I am about to give up, he walks in. My heart rate quickens as he approaches me. I can't breathe, and all those nights I've spent masturbating with his face in mind appear briefly before my eyes. I know in that instant I won't let him get away again. He plays it cool as he stands next to me and asks what I am drinking. "Slow Screw," I whispered in a husky voice only he can hear. I notice for the first time that when he smiles, he has dimples. I resist the urge to put my tongue in one of them.

We tease each other into a heated frenzy the entire night, once again realizing the songs end much too soon. Just as we are about to part, I whisper in his ear that I know a place where the music lasts an eternity. Curiosity brightens his eyes, making gold streaks stand out among their gray depths. We were on our way to Seduction 101.

I feel him watching my ass as we leave the lounge, the scent of our bodies lingering around us. Deciding to take my car, I play devil's advocate and let him drive. As soon as we exit the parking garage I have his zipper down, and him in my mouth. Deep-throating him only heightens my orgasm as I am simultaneously stimulating my clitoris in the process. Im not stopping until I swallow his cream and he delivers just as we approached the on ramp.

Half-hour later, we pull up to my door. No introductions or ice-breakers are necessary. We are ready, and it is time. I feel him undressing me with his eyes all the way to my bedroom. Once inside, we waste no time stripping down to our birthday suits. His body looks like it is hand sculpted. His skin glistens like warm caramel, enticing my taste buds.

I listen to the cars pass as I try to steady my breathing.

His eyes tell me what to do. I lay down on the bed to let him handle his business. I can feel his essence wrap around my toes, and work its way up my chocolate body as he takes control of my clit. Mmm…mmm…mmm…and damn, because I know this is heaven. He strokes me into an uncontrollable orgasm that has me screaming out for help.

The feel of his tongue against my triangle has me just about going crazy. He makes me cum over and over until my heart feels like it will burst in my chest. Sliding one finger in me, then two, someone on the outside would have thought I was being murdered. If only they knew, if only they could feel the pleasure I am receiving. I lay there spent while he caresses my nipples. As he takes both of them into his mouth at the same time, I am suddenly happy I opted to use the chocolate-flavored body cream.

I want some doggy style like you wouldn't believe, but not before I get the chance to turn him out. I'm a firm believer in "you do me, I do you." He circles my belly button with the tip of his tongue before diving in, and I stop him before he can go back down. Now it's my turn.

I can't wait to taste him, and go right to his dick. I remember thinking his precum tastes like Hershey syrup. It takes a little effort to get all ten inches in, but I am cool once I get a rhythm. I want him inside of me so bad I can taste it, literally. Cupping him with warm hands, I massage his sack, never losing rhythm. Taking his balls inside of my mouth one at a time, I let my tongue explore underneath. He feels my tongue venture around the rim of his asshole, and before he can say anything, I dip in one time before making my way back up. I smile after deciding he isn't ready for that just yet. I want to control how soon he puts it in, but he flips the script and flips me over.

I have an instant orgasm when I feel the head of his dick graze against my clit. With just the head, he presses in and out of my contracting walls while smacking me on my ass. I try to back up so that he will be all the way in me, but he won't oblige. This is his show, and he runs it how he sees fit. It isn't until I start contracting faster, indicating an orgasm, that he gives it all to me. He strokes me for what feels like forever. Damn, I'm getting hot just telling the story.

Now on my back, he spreads my lips and teases me with the head by putting it in slowly. When it is all in, it is on. We make love so intense it feels like we are levitating. He sexes me with long, slow strokes, and it is driving me crazy. Watching us through my ceiling mirror turns me on even more. My body shakes, wanting release as I watch him work magic on top of me. The voyeur in me wants to watch us in the side mirror while I ride him. I ease down on him so slow it is killing me. It is like there is a red heat surrounding us. I place my hands on his stomach for leverage, because my back is to him. Sitting up with my feet planted firmly on the bed, I switch between taking it all in, and only the head.

Rotating between a fast and slow pace, we work ourselves into another screaming orgasm. Still on his back, I swing myself around so that I sit on him sideways and continue my act as a rodeo queen. "You better fuck me good" is all the warning I give him. He will never forget me once he leaves here, and that's a promise. I turn around so that I am facing him and wrap my legs around his back—a total 360. Giving it up like I'm not going to see tomorrow has him calling my name and stuttering. As calm as I can, I get up and position myself at the end of the bed and bend over to receive him from the back.

I play with my clit and suck on my nipples simultaneously while he pleasures me by inserting his finger into my asshole. This dance has to be forbidden. We maneuver into the doggy-style position on the bed, and he plays with my clit from behind moistened by our juices running down my legs.

He starts tracing my butterfly tattoo with his tongue, and that makes me explode even faster. He holds on to my hips as we make our way to orgasm number nineteen. All of a sudden, I hear a phone ringing, and he starts fading. The ringing gets louder, and I jump up out of my sleep mad as hell because I was about to cum again.

"Hello?" My phone ringing does not amuse me. The numbers on my clock read 11:25 P.M., and everyone knows not to call after ten during the week.

"I'm sorry…did I wake you?"

"Hell yeah. Who's this?"

"Savion." Chocolate. That's the only word that comes to mind when I think about him. We've been kicking it for a few months now. I have a key and everything. He's hooked a sistah up on the oral sex tip, but we have yet to get it in.

"Hey, wassup?"

"I know you said not to call after ten, but I needed to see you."

"Now?"

"I know. Can I come over? I just want to hold you."

At first I think this dude is plain crazy, but I realize I was just hugging my pillow after the most erotic dream I'd had in a long time. Maybe he can quiet my body down.

"Sure. Come over."

"I'll be there in five minutes."

Savion lives all the way across town, so he must have already been on his way. I jump in the shower real quick to make sure the nana is tight, then I lotion my body with his favorite scent, Sweet Pea from Bath and Body Works. Just as I slip my rose-colored chemise over my head, I hear his car pull into my garage. I have the door open before he gets the chance to knock. He walks in all sexy, like only he can.

"Mmm…mmm…mmm…girl, look at you. You make it hard to be a gentleman."

"You don't look too bad yourself."

Savion is dressed in a pastel yellow Polo T-shirt and khaki shorts. His canvas Polo sneakers match perfectly with his shirt, and both sport the same light blue horse on the side.

I turn my back to him and let my gown fall to the floor, remaining only in my silk thong underwear. I bend over, giving Savion a full view of my wet pussy as I step out of my thong and crawl across the bed. I've never been shy, and I am not starting now. I lay back on my pillows, which makes my hair surround me like a halo.

As not to constrict his view, I pull my knees up to my chest and spread my legs wide. I stick my middle finger inside of my contracting walls and use my moistened finger to stimulate my clitoris. I close my eyes and moan as I take my nipples into my mouth one at a time.

I open my eyes to watch Savion undress. In one fluid motion his shirt is over his head and his shorts are on the floor. He puts his head between my legs and buries his face into my perfectly trimmed pubic hair. His tongue plays circles around my little man in the boat. I spread my legs wider to give him more access. He puts his finger inside of me, and I grab his hand so I can taste it. Going back down, I hold my lips open for him. He lets go a steady stream of cool air, then covers my clit with warm lips. My senses are like a live wire as I squirm under his tongue. Sucking on me softly, I gyrate my hips against his face, as he moves his lips in a side-to-side motion.

Savion gets up on his knees to get a better view, and I finger myself for his viewing pleasure as I dip my middle and ring fingers into my walls while my thumb strokes my clitoris, turning him on. With my free hand, I hold my left nipple to my lips, using the tip of my tongue to moisten it before taking it into my mouth. Still fingering myself, Savion takes hold of my clit once again, causing an eruption of all sorts. My body is aching to have him inside of me.

I take his ten inches into my hands and put my lips to it. After gently rolling his testicles around on my tongue, I lick him from the base of his soldier to just under the head. I like an audience, and every time he closes his eyes, I stop. What's the use in being down there if he won't watch? I deep-throat him until I feel him release in my mouth, and I make sure to swallow every bit.

His soldier jerks around in my hand, ready for more. I want it from the back, so I get up on my knees and put my ass high up in the air for easy entry. In one swift motion, he is inside of me, and we are rocking the boat. I love rough sex, and he gives it to me just the way I like it. He is smacking me on my ass and fingering my asshole, making me explode all over the place. We go at it for hours, and our final orgasm makes us collapse into sweet bliss.

Just as I am readying myself for more, Savion starts to fade. I wake up because it sounds like my phone is ringing again. This is getting old, and I swear it is going to be a problem. All this cumming is wearing me down, and the real thing is just what I need.

I call Savion's house to see if he will answer the phone. I hang up when I hear his sleep-muffled voice and get ready to head over there. Deciding to do the damn thing right, I shower and shave, ridding my body of any unnecessary hair. After I get out of the shower, I lotion my body with Moon Dust. It gives my skin a nice smooth finish with just a hint of sparkle. Thigh-high stockings and a garter belt are all I wear under my trench coat. No bra, no panties. Six-inch heels complete my outfit, and I make my way across town.

Having vowed to never use it, I pull out my spare key to his condo and walk straight to his bedroom. Hoping in the back of my mind that he doesn't have company, I open his room door to find him sleeping. Closing the door gently behind me, I turn the lamp that is by the door on low, and that wakes him up.

"What are you doing here?" he asks as he looks at me while trying to adjust his eyes in the darkness.

Instead of responding, I walk over to his CD collection and pop in Janet's *The Velvet Rope* CD. Skipping down to track number nineteen, "Rope Burn," I position myself at the end of his bed with my back facing him as the song begins to play.

Gyrating my hips in a slow circle, I remove my trench coat first, revealing my lack of clothing underneath. I small smile plays across my lips as he watches me perform. When Janet sings for her lover to "tie her up," I cross my arms at the wrists above my head as if I am tied up to something, while continuing to move my hips to the music. Keeping one hand tied up, I take my other hand and use it to massage my dark nipples before inserting both of them into my mouth.

I dance my way over to where he is now sitting up in the bed, his erection evident. Pulling back the covers, I can now see he is bulging against his satin boxer shorts. I flick my tongue across his nipples one at a time, then straddle him. Still moving in beat with the music, the sensation of my clit rubbing against his boxers is causing major friction. I push both of my nipples together and feed them to him. His tongue feels so nice on my warm skin.

Savion reaches into the drawer of his nightstand and pulls out a black silk scarf. The song is near the end, and he picks me up and lays me on the bed. A wet spot is where my clit was just resting. He takes the scarf and uses it to tie my wrists to his headboard. I just close my eyes and go with the flow. Trailing butterfly kisses down my stomach, he gets right down to business. My clit is highly sensitive, and him humming against it is taking me to the edge quickly.

"Eat up, boo. It's all yours," I say, and he doesn't stop. My hands are tied to his headboard, so I can't grab the back of his head like I want to. Before I can protest, he gets up and lights a candle.

He covers my eyes with a second silk scarf, enhancing my other senses. I want to watch, but this proves to be even better.

I hear a faint buzzing in the background and smile, full of excitement. I know it is my favorite toy, and I spread my legs in anticipation. He lightly touches my clit with the silver bullet, sending shock waves through my body. I'm moaning like crazy as he simultaneously teases me with our new toy and the tip of his tongue. I can feel myself about to explode, and he can, too, as my clit stiffens under his tongue. My legs are now up to my chest.

"Is this how you want it?" He takes hold of my clit, his tongue like fire against me.

I tell him I'm almost there, then I feel something cool slide into me. If I could have gotten up I would have. The sensation of cold and hot is too much, damn near bringing me to tears. He moves the ice-cold object in and out of me slowly, until it feels warm like my insides.

"You better fuck me good," I manage to get out between short breaths.

I feel the weight of him climbing on to the bed. Positioning himself between my legs, he holds my ankles up to the headboard, gaining total access to my cave. With long strokes, he gives me what I asked for—for hours. The entire time my hands are tied to the headboard, he puts me in all kinds of compromising positions.

Lying beside me, he takes me from the back, playing with my clit until I come. Removing one hand from the binds, he lets me turn over so that I lay flat on my stomach because he's chose, the anal entry. Pulling me up off the bed, he takes me with my toes pointing to the ceiling and has me creaming all over the place.

He knows how I like it and unties me. I wrap my legs around his back and contract my walls because I know he can't handle it. A switch in his rhythm tells me he is about to cum. He pulls out of me and leans back on his knees. Placing him inside of my mouth as far as I can take it, I stroke him with both my mouth and my hand until he satisfies my thirst.

Without saying a word, I get up out of the bed and put my trench coat back on. I kiss his lips as he lies in bed, trying to catch his breath, and I make my exit the same way I came in.

Know Your Role
by
Jamez Williams

The analog clock read 12:00 P.M. as Shannon glanced at her dash. Its light green hue mimicked her mood as she smiled with anticipation. Her meetings at the firm had gone well, and she had secured two more lucrative deals. She was on the fast track to a major promotion, and she knew it.

The higher-ups should be pleased, she thought as she turned the corner and turned up the volume on the radio.

Her car rested at a red light as she started to think of what the rest of the afternoon was about to bring She was only moments away from a meeting to which she had been looking forward all week, and she grew warm with anticipation. Stephan was someone she had met at an exclusive Black Card event. He was there offering a keynote speech and showing some of his award-winning photos to some of the city's most important urban dignitaries. She remembered how dignified he looked as he stood prominently and spoke about the Black Card community and its plans for the future. She took it that he must have been involved on the board somehow, but she had not seen him at any of the previous events.

Sometime during the night, their eyes met, and he coolly excused himself from his company, walked over, and introduced himself. He was six-one and modestly built. She knew by his looks that he kept himself fit and healthy. His hair was fine, jet-black, and he sported a close-cropped, well-groomed Van Dyke. It perfectly complemented his smooth brown face and outlined his semi-full lips. His voice was strong, and he spoke with controlled eloquence—bold, succinct, and sure. Each time he spoke to her, she became more enthralled with him.

She had looked at those lips and instantly imagined his mouth caressing her vagina. She almost felt his tongue separating her lips and inserting to her moist folds. She was wet, and her nipples had started to swell, and he knew it. His smile was penetrating with even white teeth. She could tell that he had some work done, but it sure looked good on him.

Stephan had dark brown eyes, which looked both mysterious and sure. He used them to outline her body strategically as he spoke. They showed appreciation, moved over her face, to her neck, down to her breasts, then back to her lips. She loved the way he noticed her as he spoke. She was mesmerized and kept thinking about how the night should end. As someone once said, a woman knows within five minutes if she is going to fuck a man. She definitely had an answer when it came to him: yes.

As the night went on, and after many conversations, he had taken her by the hand, licked his lips, and motioned with his head toward the door as if to say, "Shall we leave?" The warmth of his hand on hers had made her feel comfortable. A smile had crept up her face as she bowed her head slightly as one would do with a schoolgirl crush. He had noticed her unspoken acceptance and verbalized his request one more time.

"I have a room at the Marriott just up the road. I know that line sounds a bit cliché and somewhat crass, and for that I should apologize, however, we could get something to eat, maybe a drink or two, and take this conversation further. I don't bite," he had stated with surety.

"Sure, as long as all we do is converse," she had said slyly, hoping that biting would be on the menu.

"Definitely," he had answered in a tone that said, "Yeah, right. It will."

She had let out a slight laugh to let him know that she knew how the game was played. Hell, she had even written a few chapters herself.

"Let me just tell my company that I'll be calling it a night, and I'll meet you at the coat room," she had said.

"Agreed. I'll be waiting with bated breath," he had retorted as he had released her hand and walked across the floor toward the entrance.

The rest of that night was almost like nothing Shannon had ever experienced. Stephan was methodical and intense in his lovemaking. He had her pulling down curtains, speaking long-forgotten foreign languages, and smacking her own ass. He had licked, sucked, and fucked her until she forgot her name. Even after moments when she thought she got the best of him, he had sprung tricks that were more intense on her ass. His tongue was majestic to say the least, his penis divine, his focus...extraordinary. Moreover, after that night, she was hooked, and that episode had started the beginning of their six-month relationship.

"Here We Go" by Minnie Ripperton and Peabo Bryson started playing as the light changed, and she pressed on the gas as she returned from memory lane. She could not think of a more appropriate song and turned up the volume again. "It's a lazy afternoon," Minnie crooned in her sensual voice, and the irony of the moment could not be more poignant. Shannon's pussy started to throb, and her nipples started to perk as Peabo added his vocals, and she knew that the day was about to bear more fruit. Once again, she smiled as she pulled into the driveway of Stephan's home.

After pulling around to the back of the house, she killed the engine and stepped out of the car. She wore a black business suit with a modest split on the skirt, a silk solid lavender blouse that contrasted slightly where her nipples resisted the fabric. Her feet rested in a pair of Manolo Whipstitch Halter pumps that subtlety flexed the muscles in her calves and gave them a sensual look. Her strong legs gave hint to the La Perla undergarments she was wearing—a sexy two-piece chemise set that looked great across her dark nipples and prominently showed her thatch of hair just above her vagina. She was happy with the set and knew that once Stephan saw it, he would be happy too. She was bad, and she knew it.

She popped the truck with her remote, walked toward the back of the car, and pulled out a wooden picnic basket and a small overnight bag. She stared at the sky and let the warmth of the season shower her for a moment, letting it caress her from the top of her head, down her face, neck, and shoulders, across her breasts and arms, down her back, behind her calves before resting on her feet. She imagined that the sun's rays were Stephan as she got her bearings and walked toward the back entrance.

Memories of their last intense session crossed Shannon's mind as she placed the key into the door, turned the lock, and entered the kitchen. She put the basket on the counter, and moved back toward the door to punch in the alarm key code: 1-0-6-9 #. Shannon laughed out as she realized what the code meant: ten inches for his penis size and sixty-nine for his favorite position. It was evident as daylight, and she loved them both. She knew that it was more than a coincidence. That's just how Stephan was with his offbeat, subtle humor.

Shannon knew from Stephan's earlier phone call that he would be a little late as he had a few details from a fashion spread photo shoot on which to work. He said that he would not be long and should arrive only moments after her.

"Make yourself at home," he had offered during their phone call. Shannon took time to settle in and tour the rest of the house before he arrived. As she walked out the kitchen and into the dining and living rooms, she noted that his décor was well thought out with a minimalist approach. She was impressed more with the depth of this man who not only commanded her waking moments but her libido as well.

In the immaculate living room, somewhere in the background, she heard Pat Methany's "Chris" playing from his stereo. Leather couches and an ottoman, a plasma television, and a fine glass cabinet adorned the room. With long steps, she walked over to the bar and poured herself a glass of cognac. Shannon glanced at many of the photos that adorned his walls. He had been all over the globe and had done quite a bit of photojournalism, but these photographs were stunning and sensual. His walls were covered with prominent black-and-white photos. One in particular was a striking picture of a woman's left breast. The solid-frame image was enough to catch Shannon's breath and command her eyes' focus. Its intent was luring. The breast was dark with a prominent, thick nipple. It was perfectly round and beautiful at which to look. Perfectly poised and captured for all eternity. The breast and areola shone against the moisture that covered the beautiful, unblemished dark skin. Beneath, it read "Heart of Tunisia." Shannon's arousal grew.

Another photograph displayed a woman's full lips, while another captured an image of woman's vagina, partially shorn and elegant. A small thatch of hair just above the fold reminded Shannon of her own vagina, and when she acknowledged the beauty of this woman's pussy, she appreciated the beautiful complexity of her own even more. She massaged her nipples through her bra, then licked her middle finger gently and placed it in her panties as she spied a picture of a penis arched downward with a significant sized bulb on the end of its length. The phallus hung low and heavy while being displayed from the right side. It was full of minute veins that created avenues along the length, offering shades and subtle contrasts. Shannon imagined her lips parting and filling her mouth with penis, attempting to engulf the whole thing. She found herself giddy as she eased her hand farther into her panties, found moistness, and fondled her clitoris. A warm tingling feeling engulfed her as she came.

Shannon darted back toward the kitchen on unsure legs. Once there, she grabbed the picnic basket from the counter and placed it on the kitchen's island. With a quick smile, she opened it and started to remove the contents: cheese and crackers, a bottle of wine, two pieces of cheesecake covered with strawberries, two wineglasses, cutlery, and her secret weapon: full in-season strawberries smothered with chocolate liqueur sauce. She proceeded to carry her edible weapons upstairs to the bedroom. Once done, she ran back to the kitchen to get her overnight bag and complete the rest of her kinky plan.

Shannon removed her jacket, which she dropped onto a chair by the door, and unbuttoned her blouse. Her blouse fell a few feet from her jacket. The same went for her scarf, skirt, shoes, then her silk stockings. She was leaving a trail of breadcrumbs for Stephan to follow that led from the kitchen to the living room, where she would be waiting—libido willing and legs wide open. She sat, sipping her Cognac, and closed her eyes. The time was 12:22 P.M.

Something cold brushed up against Shannon's cheek, startling her. She realized she must have fallen asleep. Groggy, with Cognac swimming through her, Shannon attempted to adjust her eyes. Sunlight beamed through the window and washed across her face, obscuring her vision. Cold once again brushed her face, and she attempted to brush it away. Her hand met something hard, just underneath her left eye. She shifted her head to the right and squinted against the sunlight, finally realizing the source of the cold object. It was a gun.

Shannon jumped back onto the couch and attempted to scream. Her mouth gaped open, but nothing came out. Her heart rate escalated as she cringed and threw up her hands in a defensive motion. She brought her knees toward her chest in an awkward fetal position.

Again, she attempted to scream as she kicked wildly. The Cognac glass shattered as her heel connected with it and hurled it across the floor. Breaths shot out, and she began to hyperventilate. She focused with frightened eyes on her assailant as she said a silent prayer.

"Bitch, please. Can the dramatics and stand up," a woman's voice said slightly above a whisper. It was deep, sultry, and deliberate. Shannon lowered her hands slightly and focused on from where the voice was coming. The woman stood about five-nine, three inches taller than Shannon. A dark blue leather wraparound raincoat contained her frame. She wore her hair in shoulder-length locks tinged with brownish-red hues. She had dark, almond-shaped eyes, modest cheekbones, and small, full lips that complemented her cinnamon-colored skin.

She stood there unblinking, looking directly at Shannon with an intent and possessed stare. Shannon looked at the intruder, at her shoulders

and down her arms. Her left hand held what appeared to be four mul-
ticolored silk scarves; her right, a chrome 380 handgun.

"What…what …do you want?" Shannon managed to ease out.

The intruder sucked her teeth, let out a sly, crooked smile, and tapped
the gun on her hip several times. Her left foot followed suit. Shannon
noticed she wore black leather mules and had strong calves, like a dancer.

"If you're looking for Stephan, he should be here…shortly. I was
getting ready to leave. I just came to drop something off. Are you a
friend of his?" she asked nervously, her eyes steadily on the gun. Her
heart continued to race. Tears began to well in her eyes.

The intruder spoke. "I see judging from your attire—or the lack of—
that you came prepared to have fun. He told me that you were a looker.
Shit. You're sexy as hell." Her voice grew deeper and sultrier; she was
enjoying this. Shannon felt uneasy as the intruder's gaze began to scan her
body. She began to nod as she twirled the scarves in a circular motion.

"You know, when he first asked to me attend this little session of
yours, I almost declined. However, he convinced me that it would be a
world of fun, something to expand the horizons, so to speak. Freaky
bastard he is. I happen to like that, and here I am." The intruder took a
few steps forward; Shannon backed away.

She continued, "Shannon, right?" She extended her hand. Shannon
reluctantly returned the gesture, and the two shook hands.

"You know who I am?" Shannon asked.

"Of course I do. I know everything I need to know about you.
Girlfriend, there's no need to be afraid. I won't hurt you; besides, this
will be a night for both of us to remember." A deep smile crept across
her face, exposing her beautiful teeth.

Shannon found a little bit of comfort in her response. Her initial
reaction began to fade quickly. More questions arose in her mind, but she
thought better than to ask them. She knew Stephan was a freak and felt
deeply that he had something to do with this. She'd fooled around with
role-play before, but never with a third person. *This will be interesting,* she
thought. "Why the gun?" she inquired.

"You're supposed to be my hostage. Let's just say that I have a flair for the dramatic. It provides, shall we say…a bit of ambience, don't you think?" She waved the gun in the air playfully. "Besides, there's nothing like a damsel in distress. You've been a very bad girl, and I'm here to punish you."

The way she said "damsel" melted away the last bit of Shannon's defenses. She pronounced it as though the word itself was liquid. For the first time, Shannon noticed a slight accent, but she couldn't place it.

"Where is he?" Shannon asked as she stood.

"He'll be along shortly. Now, I'm afraid that I'll have to tie you up and prepare for his arrival. Please turn around and put your hands in front of you."

Shannon complied. The intruder put the gun in her pocket, took the scarves and began to wrap them carefully around Shannon's wrists and hands. The intruder looked into Shannon's eyes deeply and said, "Trust."

One simple word was all it took.

Shannon understood and accepted the word as the final knot was tied. She instinctively turned around and gave her back to the intruder. Shannon became excited. Her breaths quickened to nervous, shallow bursts, causing her breasts to rise erratically as her eyesight faded behind the silk. Her hearing began to cloud as she felt a knot tighten with a gentle pull. Submission was never a consideration before, but this form was rather comfortable, she thought.

An arm gripped silken-bound hands and brought them up from her waist. The silk flowed over her shoulders, cascading across her breasts and reawakening her budding nipples. Shannon was titillated and couldn't wait for Stephan's arrival.

"Follow me," Shannon heard the intruder's voice say through the silk, near her ear; she complied.

Shannon could barely hear the awkward footsteps that she took as the stranger led her across the room. She could make out the tapping of each step the two of them took as each heel hit the bare wooden floor. Although her hearing was masked slightly, she knew they were only two people walking. That realization brought her more comfort, and the butterflies in her stomach started to settle. She grew hornier with each step and began getting moist with anticipation. She wanted to be tongued, sucked, and penetrated, and she wondered what Stephan had in store for her.

A door opened and kind hands led her down several steps. She heard slight music somewhere in the background. Beautiful smells filled the air, and it was warm. They stopped walking.

Shannon's senses increased as she was blind and her hearing limited. She did not know where she was but imagined her surroundings. She knew it was a room downstairs in the basement. Shannon heard her captor walk around her several times.

Fingers grazed across her neck, and instinctively her shoulders rose. Her senses betrayed her as her body became taut. She forced herself to relax and take deep breaths.

Her bra fell away as something sharp tore through it. Shannon gasped loudly just as a strong arm reached around her and grabbed her breast. The arm belonged to a man.

"Stephan." She moaned as she craned her neck back to receive him.

Shannon's nostrils flared as she inhaled his cologne. The warmth of his chest pressed into her bare back. Fingers began to massage her left breast. Sensory depravation increased her sensitivity to touch. She was becoming intoxicated at his feel. His breath grazed the back of her neck as he reached in front of her and put his fingers into her panties where they found moisture as they slightly penetrated her outer lips. Her knees weakened.

Shannon was beginning to open up more to accept the fingers deeper into her hot pussy. Blood flowed, swelling her clitoris, and she imagined Stephan's tongue flicking wildly across her vagina. She was ready, but not quite.

Two soft hands placed themselves on Shannon's hips. She realized that this was the part where the intruder got involved. Fingertips slowly peeled off her panties while gentle bites paraded across her back. Soft whiskers tickled the crest of her ass, and a warm tongue traveled down her back. Shannon stood naked and elated in just stockings and two-inch pumps. Prickly bouts of electricity shot from her hair follicles down to her toes. Her nipples swelled more as they filled with blood.

Soft lips gently kissed her breasts, and teeth caught nipple. Mini bites commenced. A tongue circled, causing heated breaths to escape pursed lips. Lips moved to shoulder, from shoulder to neck, from neck to ear.

"Trust," she said in an accented whisper.

Shannon nodded.

Strong hands once again surrounded Shannon as they picked her up and walked her across the room. Hands still bound, she felt his musculature against her sensitive flesh. His heat traded with hers, and their skin danced for a short time. Long strides stopped suddenly and her lithe body was lowered onto a set of cushions. Shannon's body molded into each cushion that surrounded her as her arms were hoisted above her head. The cushions were soft and fragrant. She felt a tug as one of the scarves became taut. Her legs were gripped and separated by strong hands. Silk was wrapped around her ankles, and her legs were pulled farther apart and tied taut. Shannon couldn't move; her heart raced.

Music started to play in the background, and Shannon couldn't recognize it through the scarf. It sounded like slow drums and violins. The music was inviting and warm, she thought. She began to relax as something warm drizzled across her breasts. She jumped, and it took a moment before she noticed a scent. It smelled like cinnamon and vanilla, and she realized it was massage oil.

Two sets of hands began to slowly massage her breasts. The feeling was smooth and intoxicating. Palms went above her breasts, massaging her shoulders, then back down to her areolas, circling the dark circumferences. A mouth engulfed her nipple as a hand fondled the other. Hands continued to lightly brush against her as her skin heated up.

Shannon began to writhe and moan audibly. As a firm tongue danced across her breasts; another created a line up above her knee. That tongue traveled up her thigh until it met her inner bliss. Quick kisses peppered her vaginal lips as fingers separated her folds. Mouth met clitoris and sucked lightly. Light sucks grew faster and harder as she playfully resisted. Each lap captured her wetness and savored it. Shannon moaned loudly as if in pain, but her face told a different story. She was enjoying having two people pleasure her at the same time.

"Trust," she said, moaning as she began to cum violently. Her body shivered as the mouth began humming on her clitoris. Moisture eased gently down her lips. Fingers inserted into her wanting pussy caused her to fight against her restraints. She pulled her arms and attempted to kick her legs to no avail. The pair continued to assault Shannon's senses with their sexual prowess.

Shannon's vagina pulsed when she felt thighs positioned over her face. Some slack was given to her hand restraints, offering a little movement. She breathed deeply as her head was pushed in between the thighs. Another deep breath intoxicated Shannon with the sweet aroma of sex. Her mouth found soft, sweet-smelling lips. Her tongue cautiously darted out as she tasted another woman for the first time. The taste was succulent, and Shannon continued to lick the inner folds of her captor—first with slight awkwardness then with more intensity as she found her bearings. Moments later, Shannon's rhythm took shape as her tongue probed farther into her captor's warm pussy.

Juices slid down her chin as Shannon found the clitoris. She licked and captured it in her mouth and began to hum on it; mimicking what was happening to her down below. Hands gripped her head and offered direction. Shannon's long tongue found the center again and ventured inward to hot, moist lips. Thighs became taut as her captor began to grind her mound gently into Shannon's face. Tongue continued to fold in and out of succulent sweetness, sending waves of ecstasy up through her captor's body. Fingers gripped Shannon's head firmly as the grinding increased. Moans started escaping with each gyration. Screams escalated above Shannon's head. She imagined strong thighs tensing. Shudders came in waves and orgasms exploded as both women came in fiery bursts.

Breathy pants emerged in the room as one woman collapsed next to the other. Her captor leaned over and whispered in Shannon's ear, "Trust."

Once again, Shannon nodded in agreement; "Trust," she whispered back.

Restraints slackened as Shannon was twisted and her body turned over. A soft wedge was positioned underneath her stomach, offering her ass to the heavens. Still breathing heavily, she heard a package rip open. Her female captor massaged the nape of her neck and blew softly on her back. The mild, cool breath was welcomed down her shimmering spine.

Her breath caught momentarily as she felt her ass grabbed my hungry hands. Her cheeks were separated as hot tongue met ass. Her stomach tightened as gasps broke free. Its serpentine movements danced strategically around her ass, occasionally circling her anus. Fingers gripped tightly as the tongue moved deeper into her ass. Shannon's voice froze deep within her throat. Sweat poured from the side of her head, and she shuddered as she came.

Her thighs were once again pulled apart, and her ankles were fastened. Blind, Shannon imagined taking Stephan's dick into her mouth. Her daydream quickly evaporated as she felt the lips of her vagina pushed apart by a swollen penis. Mild pain shot through her midsection as the long, thick member penetrated its way deeper into her. Swollen vaginal lips braced themselves against the friction caused by the condom. Lubricant drizzled down her ass as his frequent pumping continued. Friction gave way to smooth sliding as the lubricant took hold.

Shannon bucked as his strong thighs met the sides of her ass with each thrust. His intensity increased as he grabbed her shoulders and penetrated deeper. Fingers gripped as his plunging continued. He was large, and Shannon became more aroused. Her ass moved in gyrations as she attempted to match his passion.

Shoulders were released as fingers ran down her back. She arched in slight discomfort as the pain gave way to pleasure. Thoughts ran wildly through her head as she tried to understand his intensity. Something about it was familiar. They had been together sexually numerous times, and although great, it never came close to this. Whatever the case, she was turned on and loved how Stephan was fucking her. She reemerged in the here and now as he fucked her harder and harder. She started to cum wildly. Fingers massaged and entered her ass. She attempted to run away but failed to get far.

"Damn scarves," she said to herself as she tensed and let out a loud yell. She wanted to participate freely and was becoming frustrated at her inability to move. She tugged at her hand restraints; they did not budge.

The pounding continued.

"Shannon," the woman's voice said, "say his name."

Shannon bucked wildly, throwing her ass at Stephan. His penis went deeper into her, and she felt his balls hitting underneath her ass, almost touching her clit.

The syncopation of her movements matching his made her breaths quiver. Her hands shook as she screamed, "Stephan."

"Again...say his name again."

"Stephan," she said again. Tears started to seep through her blindfold. She smiled and began to cry at the same time. She loved the feelings that were flowing through her body. She continued yelling his name repeatedly as she came one after another. Her fingers dug deeply into fabric as he forcefully slapped her ass. Another hand reached down and tugged at her stockings, causing them to rip. He continued fucking her; she felt his dick began to swell. She moved her ass more and threw each gyration into him at each plunge. She wanted him to explode inside of her.

His grip tightened around her waist as he began to increase his thrusts. They continued until she came hard, and he quickly pulled out. The wedge was removed, and Shannon crumpled among the pillows. She could hear his breaths from across the room. They were long and loud. She wondered what he was thinking after he took her close to the edge. Shannon closed her eyes and smiled.

Shannon, exhausted, weakened, and covered with sweat became

hoisted by her waist by arms that felt as thick as cables. Her limp body was carried and placed into a chair. The leather fabric was cool against her skin; her breathing coming under control. Arms and legs were once again restrained. Calming fatigue ran through her body, and she could not remember the last time lovemaking had been this intense. Her body was ravaged, and it showed. She felt heated lines down her sides where nails left their marks against braised skin. Her breasts were tender from the forceful sucking, and her ass was sore from the constant smacking and grabbing. Sensitive legs felt the remnants of fabric from where her stockings were torn. The room was pungent with sensual smells as her head swam in a maelstrom of ecstasy.

As Shannon sat, glistening from sweat and massage oil, she wondered why Stephan had pulled out when he did. She wanted to feel him swell deep inside of her before his release. Stephan had never made love to her that forcefully, she recollected as a post-orgasm shiver ran through her body. That was unlike him, she thought, but was not too concerned. She was amazed at how well he knew her body. He orchestrated a sexual symphony that rivaled no other. All she knew was that she did not want this day to end.

Her head was pulled back into the chair, and full, hot lips met her throat. The elongated tongue caressed the length before it found a succulent spot on which to rest. Hands went to breasts as lips moved to meet her own. Shannon tasted herself on the lips and tongue. The tongue probed deep into her mouth, and she sucked it gently. She loved the sensations it brought. Marvin Gaye's "I Want You" piped through the speakers replaced the previous Moroccan drums. The song was almost through before Shannon started to mouth the words.

The music faded as Shannon sang the chorus. She wanted Stephan. Her every thought encompassed portions of him, and she knew she was hooked and didn't even care to fight it. Once again, hands caressed her blindfolded face. Her disheveled hair was stroked as the person started to undo the knotted eye restraint. Soft, gentle tugs led way to silk falling down her face and into her lap. Her forehead accepted the coolness it encountered. The silk was warm and moist with perspiration across her thighs. Hands moved to her shoulders.

Her eyes attempted to adjust. The lighting in the room was dim but significant for her to see clearly. She blinked several times to get control of her vision. Her ears were alerted to moans coming from in front of her, and Shannon took a few seconds before she realized they were coming from a television. She turned her head to scan the room, and there were no sign of her female captor. The volume on the television increased. She looked deeply across the room and noticed two figures fucking across fifty inches of screen. She smiled at this new dimension of pleasure because she was a big fan of porn, and Stephan knew it. She shared many secrets with him, and he used many of them to his advantage that night. She smiled and continued watching.

Pulsing, once again, started to commence between her legs as she watched the man on the screen insert his penis deep within the woman's ass. She got hot as he gently inserted himself in and out of her, and increased with more controlled ferocity. The woman let out incredible moans with each deep, deliberate penetration. Her cries cracked several times as he drove himself deeper and deeper into her ass.

Shannon was a freak for this type of action, and it took a moment before she realized that the figures on the in the movie were her and Stephan. She let out a slight laugh at this realization, and her arousal intensified. She knew that this was from when they went away together for the weekend a few months back. She wanted so bad to touch herself, but her arms were still tied to the chair. She tried to twist them free.

The images changed and offered her a view of her taking Stephan's penis into her mouth. She sucked the head gently and licked the length of it. Then the video cut to her taking him deeply into her mouth. Wetness glistened along his thick length, causing Shannon to get deeper into her mode. She ground her pussy into the leather chair, bringing little pleasure to the passion that erupted below. Hands on her shoulder released themselves, and her lover moved from behind her. She was anxious to see him and wanted to be free. Hers was a want that needed total participation. She wanted more. Her lover left the shadows and emerged before her, face to face. Her breath caught.

Shannon took two deep gulps and gasped for air as she looked into the very familiar face. A loving one she had known and made love to constantly. This face that caused her so much ecstasy and brought tears to her eyes. She began to sob. A smile crept across a visage that she loved, who in return loved her back unconditionally. The face belonged to her husband, Darius.

Darius was supposed to be away at a business meeting, yet he was there. She did not know how or why, but he was definitely there in the flesh. His six-one figure stood inches from her face. His dark skin glistened against the light, exposing all of his fine musculature. His dark eyes met hers with strict dedication, and they spoke without speaking. His stare spoke volumes, and she understood fully what his eyes were saying. She now recognized the feeling of familiarity that she experienced. She was both scared and ashamed. The thought of her being in Stephan's house temporarily escaped her. She wondered what had happened to him. The bigger issue surrounded the look on her husband's face and her tied securely to a chair.

Shannon broke her gaze sharply as she heard footsteps coming down the stairs. She had not heard her leave, but her captor returned. She was dressed in a matching sheer boy-short combination and drinking something from a chilled glass. As she crossed the far side of the room, Shannon brought her attention back to her husband who had yet to break his penetrating gaze. His gentle eyes were afire, and his wonderful smile was nearly nonexistent. She lowered her head.

Darius looked down at Shannon's naked hand, particularly at a specific finger. His eyes found bare skin. He continued to stare at the naked finger, his eyes narrowed, and an audible breath escaped his lips. He returned his gaze, twisted the visible wedding ring on his finger, turned away sharply, and began to walk across the room toward the woman. Shannon watched his naked ass flex with each stride. Fear crept up her throat, and she cursed herself for removing her ring. His stride ended in front of the woman, who only moments ago had her pussy in Shannon's mouth. She offered him the glass; he took it and began to drink. His lips left the glass and met hers. Their tongues intertwined as they kissed passionately. Shannon's attention left Darius again and focused on the woman.

Their lips parted, and Darius leaned against the closest wall; his stark nakedness partially hidden by the lack of lighting. The woman walked toward Shannon slowly with a wry smile painted across her face. Her body was magnificent to say the least. Shannon saw how her dark nipples strained against the sheer fabric. They were big, and her breasts were full. There was a slight bounce when she walked, and Shannon's eyes absently followed.

Her midsection was flat and firm, and she possessed a fair amount of muscle. Lines of separation were prominent all the way down to her waistline. Her boy shorts held a powerfully built ass. It was round and solid and connected to a commanding set of thighs. Her skin looked like brushed cinnamon. Her body was curvaceous, athletic, and sexy. She was so fine it was disgusting. Shannon's brow furrowed as she allowed herself to get angry at this woman's physical beauty.

The mystery woman was still looking pitifully at Shannon as she undid her bra. Large, dark breasts fell from their sheer housing. Panties separated from supple ass and eased sensually down toward her ankles. They met the top of her mules, and she kicked them toward Shannon. Underwear landed on her exposed lap on top of the silk scarf. The mystery woman turned and walked away. Darius sauntered out of the shadows and met her halfway.

With a quick drop, she balanced herself on her mules, took Darius' penis into her hands, and placed it hungrily into her mouth. She slowly swallowed it completely in its semi-flaccid state. Her lips met testicles as she relaxed her throat to accommodate him. With each pulse into her mouth, Darius' size increased. Her hand reached up and fingers surrounded his girth. Veins pumped more blood into his manhood as she increased her oral stimulation.

Shannon grew warm as she watched this woman pleasure her

husband. She watched as arm muscles flex elegantly with each pump. She noticed full lips embrace width and cheeks collapse to contain firm penis within moist walls. Moans escaped mouths and locks were held firmly in masculine hands. Tender fingers held his chest and massaged his nipples. Ass muscles grew tighter and stance became more rigid. Darius grabbed her locks tighter as he released himself full into her mouth. Her eyes became enlarged as she held his load. She was determined not to spill a drop and massaged his balls as if to drain him dry. He pulsed and shook until she released him, stood, and licked her lips. Shannon was livid and began to feel fire heat up her crotch.

Darius composed himself as he shot Shannon a look. Shannon stiffened. She couldn't identify what the look meant and wasn't about to ask him. No words were spoken yet between the two; concern met her heart. Their eyes met once again, and she began to wonder when exactly he found out about her and Stephan. Feelings, barely contained, were on the surface with a mix of confusion, fear, and arousal. A day meant to steal away had turned into an offbeat nightmare.

Darius reached for the woman, and she extended her hand. Once met, he led her over to a bed that was across from the mound of cushions. Passionate kisses were once again exchanged and naked, heated flesh began to intertwine. Cabled forearms pressed flesh closer and tighter toward bare chest. Penis lengthened and moisture dripped from her hidden pockets. Shannon's line of sight was directly in view.

Naked back was placed onto the bed; slow and deliberate movements took court. Calculated caresses and deep-throated kisses propelled Shannon's discomfort. Darius completed the kiss and lay back onto the comfortable-looking bed. Teeth under painted lips took hold of a wrapper, and a slight pull released a condom. Delicate hands firmly grabbed base as latex slowly unfurled over swollen head. Slight effort eased the rest of the condom down the shaft. Gentle tugs tested its hold; a lubricant bottle emerged from underneath the fluff pillows. Focused feminine eyes continued to lock on her husband.

Shannon's eyes narrowed as she witnessed her husband's penis stroked up and down by another woman. She attempted to speak but found no voice. Tears streamed down her cheeks, dripping off her chin. Darius smiled.

Fingers spread delicately across his oily shaft in a steady rhythm. Thick thighs replaced hands as they lowered slowly down his manhood. Pleasurable moans exited his mouth. His hands met hips and pulled them down his length to complete the union. The end of the slide brought glances from both participants toward Shannon. Hips began to move.

Darius reached up and took a dark nipple to his mouth. His tongue playfully tickled it, creating ovals around cinnamon circles. Feminine sighs embraced the action, and hips moved up and down. The gyrations increased, causing heads to fall back and breasts to bounce wildly. In one move, Darius flipped his partner onto her back and pushed her legs up with his. Calves met arms, and he plunged himself deeper. More blood flowed down his shaft, and she smiled. He smiled back. He stared over at Shannon, pushing himself deeper and deeper into his partner. She began to moan louder, and her hands reached for his mouth. Teeth gently bit fingers; moans became whimpers. Darius released his gentle clench and offered his tongue to her open mouth. She accepted; her legs rose above his shoulders. His strong pumps increased.

With a strong push, she playfully pushed Darius up and out of her. His breathing came long and full. His eyes met her breasts as he reached for her throat. Fingers brought her neck toward him; his mouth opened to accept. Salty perspiration met his tongue as he attempted to swallow her throat. Her head went back to offer him a canvas for his tongue to paint. Lips pursed as his introduced them to her neck's length. Her arms encircled his head and back, pulling him closer. He moaned into where her neck and shoulder met. She released him with feline grace, elegantly throwing her leg over his head and rolling quickly, landing on all fours.

He looked over beautiful dark skin. He admired how full her ass was and lusted after the dark crevice separating her cheeks. Her magnificent ass invited him to her moist pussy. Her ass wiggled as manicured hands pulled it apart, exposing her anus and vagina. Darius bent down and offered her ass one long, sensual kiss. It writhed as warm tongue cascaded over its fullness. Fingers separated begging lips. Darius nodded.

Darius looked at his wife one last time before he entered the captor's wet, hot, waiting vagina. He slid in with no resistance and worked his hips to meet succulent ass. He wanted all of him inside his sensuous partner and wanted his wife to know. His eyes held lust as he began to thrust himself inside cinnamon-coated essence. Movements began to take control as sweat appeared on his face. Her ass moved in unison and welcomed his swollen member. Twin moans escaped both mouths as eyes closed. He thrust deeper, and she accepted him.

His force became undeniable with each continued thrust. His partner's eyes began to tear, and she smiled. Her lips formed a quivering circle as she pleasantly cried out. Her ass rose higher into the air as Darius forced her shoulders down with the palms of his hands. Her arms splayed across the bed and her fingers grasped handfuls of linen.

"Damn, baby…fuck me," she strained through tight lips. "Make me yours, baby. You own this pussy, baby," she continued as her English accent escaped. Shannon noticed it, too, as she continued to look through blurry eyes.

His performance continued; he moved faster and with more zest. Her plea was accepted, and his ass became tight as he held her down. His stomach hardened, separating deep muscle, and striations shot across his chest and arms. His body glistened with sweat while his face became distorted with shameless pleasure. Her cries became more audible and frequent with each penetration; her ass bounced wildly, causing ripples along her body.

His fucking went nonstop for several more minutes. Sensual cries, tears, and verbal commandments were continuous.

"Punish me," the woman screamed out in a cracked voice as his dick went deeper and touched all her walls.

Shannon looked into her adversary's eyes and knew what she was feeling. Jealousy and hatred rested on her shoulders as she realized it was not the other woman being punished sexually, but herself.

Cinnamon-coated arms pushed forcefully against the bed. She held herself firm as she rotated her ass around Darius' penis. She balanced on one arm, grabbed her right breast, and pinched her nipple forcefully, squeezing it harder. She screamed with abandon as she was nearing the point of no return.

Darius grabbed a fistful of her locks, tugging her head back. He placed his other hand underneath her arm, holding her shoulder. He placed himself flatfooted on the bed without losing his stride. Using her body for balance, as locks contrasted against his dark hand, he thrust faster and faster. Her cries became uncontrollable as she reached back and intertwined her arm around his for stability. He felt himself get warm as his dick started to swell. An intense feeling took over from his head, worked down his chest, across his nipples down to his back, and through his engorged penis. His asshole tightened as he released himself deep within swollen pussy. Intense screams erupted through the air. Man and woman both reached their sexual heights and alerted the world. Their battered bodies collapsed as fast breaths and post-orgasmic twitches commenced.

Darius pulled himself out and forced himself to his feet. Weakened as he was, he still looked strong as he worked himself upward. His breathing raised his big strong chest. He walked steadily over toward Shannon; his dick still partially swollen and shiny with love juices. He stood upright and looked at her face. He glanced over his wife's beautiful skin and body and remembered all the things he loved about her. She was stunning and smart. He pulled off the condom, tossed it onto the floor, pulled off his wedding ring, and thrust it in her face. Her eyes widened.

She looked at the ring and the word etched into its platinum surface; "Trust." She knew the moment she looked into her husband's eyes what this involved. Trust had been violated, and she was sorry for it. They had a certain code that they lived by that went beyond marriage; most swingers had a strong understanding that was not to be broken. She broke a primary rule that stated "No outside relationships." She had met Stephan at a swinger's party and did not adhere to the mandates. Her own selfishness and libido had put her in a position where she now had to pay the price—the price of infidelity. Tears flowed freely down her eyes as her husband turned and walked away. He placed the ring on the far counter, and he reached for the woman with the cinnamon skin. She handed him his clothes, and they walked up the stairs hand in hand. Darius glanced at his watch as he disappeared. He did not look back.

Shannon had had the fuck of her life, and her pussy still throbbed. She had witnessed some of the most intense lovemaking she had ever seen, coming from the husband she swore to love, who, from this point on, would now give it to someone else—just like she had. Turnabout was fair play they say, she thought. She cried hysterically as she heard a car pull away in the distance as another one entered the driveway. It was Stephan.

The time was 4:15.

Sweet Surrender

by

Scottie Lowe

Have you ever had a secret? Have you ever been haunted with thoughts that aroused you and scared you at the same time? Thoughts of pleasure that made you feel uncomfortable? Have you ever been tortured with thoughts that turned you on that you wouldn't want to admit to anyone else?

Greg had such a desire. Actually, it was more like a painful secret, one that he could barely acknowledge himself. It was virtually impossible; it was unthinkable for him to contemplate. Real men would never have thoughts like that, not real hardcore brothas like himself. He did everything he could to suppress his thoughts, deny his feelings, and ignore his longings. In real life, Greg projected the opposite of his real desires. He wasn't even aware of when the fantasies first started. Afraid of the implications and ramifications, he did everything possible to create another reality. It was essential for him to manufacture a truth in which his fantasies would not haunt him, a reality in which "she" was not there.

Greg was a better-than-average-looking, extremely intelligent, mad cool brotha. He was a ladies' man for sure, but that wasn't his fault. He was six-two, 220 pounds of sculpted ebony, baldheaded, and penetrating green eyes. His eyes were obviously some sort of genetic mix-up from a recessive slave master gene, but it separated him from the rest.

He worked out every day to keep his body together—six-pack, chiseled chest, his shit was tight. He stood out in a crowd—in a word, he was fine. A graduate of Yale Law, Greg was a successful attorney. He was a fraternity member, played ball with the boys on the weekend, upstanding, a really genuinely nice guy. In his lifetime, he had had more pussy than he knew what to do with. Name a fantasy; Greg had done it— twice. Threesomes, group sex, sex any and every place you can imagine, in fact, he had done every wild, nasty, kinky, sweaty, hot sex act humanly possible. Now, his own secret perversions were driving him to distraction. The more he tried to suppress them, the more the images and sensations crept into his head.

She stalked him: his dreams, his thoughts, and his fantasies. This vision, his goddess, his perfect woman crept into his thoughts when he least expected her to. She was always there, possessing his perversions, lurking in the recesses of his mind. In fact, it seemed that the more stress he was under at work, the more his thoughts drifted to his secret. Sometimes at night, Greg would stay awake as long as possible watching late-night ESPN, avoiding the bed at all costs; afraid to go to sleep because he knew she would be there, behind his eyes as he drifted off into a peaceful slumber, only to torture him with pleasure untold. Even though she was completely a creation of his imagination, he knew everything about her— what she looked like, the way she moved, what she smelled like, her every desire—and he also knew how to satisfy them all. He could feel the intensity of her stare and the caress of her touch. It was too bad she was just a fantasy—or maybe that was a good thing.

Greg needed to get out. He had a case he was litigating, and it was a career maker or breaker. If he won, it would be what he needed to set the stage for the rest of his career. There were complications with the opposing counsel and it was starting to look like it was going to end up being a knock-down, drag-out fight. There were rumors that the litigants on the other side were bringing in some hot-shot, heavy-hitter attorney who had a reputation for taking no prisoners. It was some mystery lawyer who supposedly had never lost a case and dotted every *i* and crossed every *t* and left no stone unturned in order to get a favorable judgment.

Greg needed to get out to release some of the tension because he was working twenty hours a day trying to prepare for the case that could make or break his career.

The list of invited guests at the record release party that Friday night read like a who's who in the social registry of hip-hop. Everybody who was anybody was there. The label had rented the club for the entire night, and Dom P flowed freely. Greg was dressed head to toe in Emporio Armani, and he showed up slightly after eleven o'clock. He mixed and mingled with the best of them, one of the perks of dabbling in some entertainment law every now and again. Of course, events like this one drew the most beautiful women, wearing next to nothing, looking to get a record deal, be in a video, or end up hot and sweaty in the back of a Bentley with the rapper du jour.

This night was no exception. Fly honeys were everywhere. He would never admit it openly, modesty prevailing, but Greg was always the best-looking brotha wherever he went. The ladies were in competition for his attention, and to Greg, they were toys with which to be played.

There was one young lady who stood out. She was wearing a short skirt and didn't really care who saw that she was without panties or thong. Somehow, she had made her way to the VIP section of the club and was flashing shaved pussy and fat ass for anyone who wanted to look. Her titties were so big for a woman her size, they looked fake. The way they jiggled and bounced in her skimpy little top left no doubt in anyone's mind they were real fo' sho'. The fact that she was so breathtakingly beautiful was what set her apart. Perfectly packaged, she could easily be considered in the ranks of Aaliyah, Jennifer, and Janet, minus the refinement. Fellas and ladies alike were intimidated by her looks. All the other females in the club were either openly hating on or lusting after her. Guys were buying her drinks and flashing cash like there was no tomorrow, trying to impress her. All the men in the club were dying to step to her, but they were afraid that if they approached her and she laughed at their advances they would never live it down. Greg had no such fear.

Greg positioned himself directly in front of her. They made eye contact, and the stage was set for an evening of intense sexuality. She was sitting on a couch and he was directly in front of her in a chair separated by about ten feet or more. She opened her legs to reveal her surprise. Even with the dim lights of the club, he could see the reflection of the silver bar that had pierced her clit. People started to gather around and take notice, at first inconspicuously, then more voyeuristically. The chemistry between the two of them was electrifying. Greg kept his distance—he knew how the game was played. The young lady was desperate for his attention; she needed him to want her. She pulled her skirt up to her waist and nonverbally dared anybody else to come near her. Her gaze was focused completely on Greg.

He mouthed the words, *Fuck yourself,* and she proceeded to do so. She spread the lips of her pussy with her left hand and rubbed her clit with the index finger of her right. She seductively rubbed her pussy up and down, dipping her finger inside. Her finger was coated with juices, and she made a point of sucking them off like she was sucking a dick. She loved all the attention and the admirers. All the while, not twenty yards away, people were dancing to the latest joint from DMX, totally unaware. The nameless beauty was forming quite a crowd around her with her performance. People had now formed a circle, waiting for more instruction from Greg. Everyone watched in silence as she got more and more into fucking herself, but the effects were taking their toll. Hard dicks were protruding from the latest Sean John, Enyce, and FUBU gear. The ladies were discretely stimulating themselves, afraid that if they were too conspicuous, people would think that they were desperate for attention. If there hadn't been metal detectors searching everyone at the door, you could have cut the tension with a knife.

Greg was amused. He yielded his natural power over the woman from across the room. With a snap of his fingers, he signaled for someone to move the table that separated him and his new friend. Immediately, brothas lifted the decorative but substantial coffee table out of the way and where it disappeared was anyone's guess. By this time, the woman was fingering herself like crazy. She had spread her legs wide and was fucking herself with reckless abandon. She had three fingers thrusting in and out of her pussy and was rubbing on her clit. She reached down and shoved a finger in her ass, and the entire crowd gasped for air with her, like they felt the same sensation. Greg stood and took out his dick. He moved closer to her—within a few feet—and started stroking it, and everyone could see the girl's look of desperation. She shut her eyes and started ramming her finger in and out of her ass. She was breathing hard and lost in her own pleasure.

Greg could tell she was about to explode, and he said, "Don't you dare cum. Stop right now. NOW!"

She couldn't stop. She was too far gone. She needed the release. Her ecstasy and pleasure were not of this world. Greg signaled the two women who were closest to her to grab her hands and make her stop.

"Restrain her. Don't let her move. Hold her arms." The two women appeared to be in their own trance and followed the orders without hesitation. They grabbed her by her wrists and pulled her arms to either side of her. It was too late. That was enough to send her over the edge, and the waves of pleasure came crashing down on her. She moaned like a wounded animal. Her body convulsed with rapture. Cum was dripping out of her pussy. It took all the strength of the two young ladies to restrain her. She was babbling and screaming, "Fuck me. Fuck me damnit. Ride this pussy. Use it. Stick it in me—now."

Greg had seen this look of desperation so many times before. They were women with the look of need on their faces. She had a need to be pushed farther than she had ever been pushed before.

Sensing the direction things were going, Greg signaled the makeshift bodyguards to release their captive. Unsure of what to do next, she simply waited for Greg's next command.

"Crawl to me," he said. Like a panther, sleek, Black, and sexy, she crawled on her hands and knees to him. He grabbed his dick and held it in her face. The crowd drew in closer, fully aware that any live sex act in the club would not only get somebody arrested, but close the club down and result in mad fines and negative publicity, no matter how much the party promoter had paid to rent the club.

Kneeling before him, the woman waited for her next instruction. She felt honored to be at the feet of this mysterious stranger, even though she was quite sure she would never see him after that night. Greg held his dick to her lips. He took the tip between his fingers and squeezed it causing precum to ooze out.

"Tongue-fuck the slit."

With that, the woman stuck out her tongue and began to seductively lick Greg's rock-hard dick, trying to get the tip of her tongue in his piss hole. The sensation was enough to make Greg's dick throb and jump. He was stroking his dick, milking it, forcing out more precum.

Up to the challenge, she was licking it up like it was the sweetest honey. She stuck out her tongue and licked Greg all the way from his balls to the head of his dick, including his hand as he continued to jerk off for the crowd.

Overcome with lust, he grabbed her head, pulled her by her hair, and slid his dick deep in her mouth with one thrust. Her mouth felt like a hot, wet, tight pussy. She was sucking his dick like a pro. Her tongue was swirling around the shaft as her lips kept up a steady, rhythmic sucking. Her spit was all over him, and if you listened closely, you could hear her slurping noises even over the music. She kept her eyes glued on Greg and eagerly awaited his next command.

Greg was on the verge. The inside of her mouth felt like hot silk. The cum was boiling up in his nuts, the sack drawing up close to his body. Lights were flashing, the music pumping, and he was thrusting in and out of her mouth. She had taken him deep. He was fucking her face. "Yeah, suck my dick. That's right, swallow my joint whole." Greg closed his eyes and concentrated on the beautiful woman sucking, licking, and swallowing his dick. The sensations were incredible. The suction felt like he would never get head this good again in his life. He grabbed the back of her head and started to pump his dick in and out.

He opened his eyes to see the reaction of the crowd. He glanced around him, just to see who was watching and a striking woman caught his eye. She didn't fit in with the rest of the crowd; she emanated an air of sophistication and distance. It was her aura that made Greg feel like he was looking at the woman of his dreams. She was staring through him, watching the entire scene. Greg gasped for air and wanted to scream out to his fantasy woman. As quickly as she was there, she was gone. She disappeared into the club.

Distracted and positive it was the woman of his dreams, Greg lost all his concentration. The woman before him meant absolutely nothing. He wanted to run after his mystery woman, call out to her, find out who she was. All of his secret fantasies and desires started flooding his mind. The woman sucking his dick no longer aroused him. He grabbed her head and groaned out loud.

Everyone watching knew exactly what was happening. Greg and his dick-sucking friend knew differently. Greg faked it. He pretended to cum. Actress that she was, the young lady didn't let on any differently. She couldn't see what had happened, but she had sucked enough dicks to know something was weird, so she just played along.

Greg grabbed his still-hard dick and put it back in his pants. He didn't even wait for her response or to see what was going to happen to the horny crowd. He was off in search of the mystery woman. He looked in every corner of the club. He even went into the employee-only areas and the ladies' room. He was crazed. He wasn't even sure what he would say to her when he found her. No luck. She was nowhere to be found. Once more around the club, just to make sure, he emerged out into the night, desperate and confused. Had it all been a dream? Did he make it all up? Did she really exist? Greg was dazed. He began to wonder if he had really seen her at all. Maybe it was just his imagination playing tricks on him. When he really thought about it, he was convinced it was really all blown out of proportion. The woman in his fantasies was his creation; she didn't really exist. He stood in the night air trying to convince himself he was making it all up. He was kicking himself for running out on ol' girl in the club. She would have been an interesting depository for some of his frustration. For a minute, he thought about going back inside, but he knew that she could never satisfy his real appetites. He was distracted. For an instant, he recalled the sensation he felt when the ominous stranger made eye contact with him. It was as if she could see right through him. She was not affected like the rest of the crowd. It was as if she was taking notes, objectively observing. It was more than apparent that she saw through Greg's façade. She saw what no one else could see. Greg shook his head, trying to dissuade himself from such thoughts. He was really losing his mind. There was no way anybody could affect him with only thirty seconds of eye contact. He felt pretty sure he was losing his mind.

He realized that he had been standing outside in the warm night air for about thirty minutes, just lost in thoughts and fantasies. The only thing that snapped him back into reality was the insistent need in his pants for release. His dick was pulsating, demanding his attention. He summoned for the valet to get his truck and did his best to keep his erection from showing. Once inside his vehicle, the tinted windows shielded him from the rest of the world, but not his fantasies. She was calling out to him now; he could feel her fingernails down his back, her breath as she whispered nasty things in his ear, her hand wrapped around his dick. He was driving around aimlessly in a daze, not knowing where to go. All he wanted was for his thoughts to go away. The high beams in his rearview made him snap back into reality. He realized that he was in the red light district of town. It couldn't hurt to stop off, pick up a magazine or a video before he went home to take off some of the pressure.

As secure as Greg was with his sexuality, when he sought out release for his secret desires, he was intimidated and scared. He was sure no other brothas on the face of the planet shared his thoughts. He entered the store and looked around. No one was there except him and the tattooed white guy behind the counter. He made his way over to his favorite section of the store. He wanted to just take it all in, stand there and look at all the images. Too bad they were all white people on the boxes, but at that particular point and time, he really didn't give a damn. Greg's dick was still hard, with no signs of going down any time soon. He heard the chimes on the door signal that someone else had entered, but he didn't turn around. He was going to pick out a magazine and a flick and be out. *Ahhh, decisions, which one to choose,* he thought.

He was just about to pick up his selections when an arm reached across him and grabbed the exact same video.

"I always find that true female domination comes from the softest whisper, not physical force. Don't you agree?"

It was "her." He was frozen. No, it couldn't be. How? What the . . .? The blood rushed to his head, and his ears were ringing. His heart was racing. His heart was beating so fast, he felt like he was going to faint. His mouth was dry. There was no way he could form words to speak.

"I asked you a question. Aren't you going to answer me?" she said.

All he could do was just stare. She was exactly the woman of whom he had dreamed. At five-eight, around 135 pounds, she was a size four— no, maybe a six. Her skin was the most perfect color of mocha, flawless, and it looked so smooth, like a baby's. Her naturally curly hair was pulled up and secured in a severe, dramatic style, but he could tell that the second she let it down, it would go back to Africa, in its most beautiful state. She was dressed in a sexy black suit, probably Calvin Klein; it was severe and sophisticated. Her hosiery shimmered off her perfectly sculpted calves, making him think they were silk and that she'd them picked up in Paris on her last trip abroad.

Her shoes were definitely Italian. The black leather of her pumps framed her perfect size seven foot like it was a work of art. Her most striking feature was her eyes—jet-black and mysterious. They were so deep, so mesmerizing, Greg was jealous and captivated at the same time. He looked into those eyes and found his true home.

"Greg, are you going to answer me?"

He was snapped back into reality. "Wait, how do you know my name?"

"I know quite a bit about you, Greg. It wasn't too hard to find out.

You have quite the reputation. I would suggest in the future that if you want to remain anonymous, you shouldn't have women suck your dick in the middle of a very public club. I guess you aren't going to answer my question. Oh well, have a nice night."

"No, wait," the words came tumbling out. There was a panic in his voice. "Ummm, yes."

She looked at him with disgust. She didn't have to say anything. Greg lowered his eyes and addressed her again. "Yes, I think that the true female dominant can control with just her will—manipulation if you must, not force." Greg was rather pleased with himself, considering all the blood was not flowing to his brain, but rather his other head.

She put her delicate hand on his arm and leaned close. He could feel her breasts gently pressed against him. Her lips were near his ear. "How do you suppose you should address me when you speak to me, Gregory?"

There was no fucking way this was happening. No way in hell. Greg managed to squeak out something about not being sure, about not knowing too much about this sort of thing, not knowing her name.

"Too bad, Greg. I thought you had promise." With that, she turned and started to walk away.

He couldn't let her walk out of his life again.

He was sure it was "her." He yelled out to her again, "No, please wait. Tell me what I should call you. I don't know."

The guy behind the counter was hanging on every word. He had put down his magazine and had moved closer to hear every word that was exchanged between the two late-night customers. None of that mattered to Greg right at that moment. She didn't turn back. She put her hand on the door and pushed it open, the chimes ringing in his ears. He ran after her into the night, into the dark and desolate parking lot. She was putting her key into her car door when he called out to her again, "Wait . . . Please don't leave . . .mistress."

He stopped dead in his tracks, waiting for some form of acknowledgement from her. She turned and stood in silence. He walked

over to her, his eyes on the ground. "Good boy. I'm proud of you."
She reached out and put her hand in his pants pocket. His erection was
more than obvious as she got his keys and said, "Come on. Let's go."

She walked over to his truck and got in on the driver's side. Nobody
had ever driven Greg's truck before, except an occasional valet. Greg
quickly got in on the passenger side and sat in awe as the woman adjusted
the seat and mirrors to suit her. Just then, her cell phone rang.

" . . . This is Chantal . . . no . . . I'll be in in the morning." She turned
her head and examined Greg's demeanor and expression. "I need to get
a lot of work done so I'll probably be there the entire day. Have all the
files that I requested and be prepared to pull an all-nighter. I don't really
care that it's a Saturday. Be there tomorrow at 8:00 A.M., and be ready
with the things I asked for."

How incredible could this woman be? Greg wondered. She was a
woman in control, and that made Greg's dick leak precum like a faucet.
They were off. It only took a few minutes to figure out that she was
driving to Greg's home.

"Wait, how do you know where I live?"

She didn't bother to respond. Greg had never even been on the
passenger side of his own truck. The view was intoxicating. Here was
this magnificent woman controlling him, and he wasn't even sure how it
had happened so fast. He was unsure of what to do with his hands. He
was nervous and fidgety.

"Caress my thighs, Gregory."

"Yes, mistress." He wanted—no, needed—to say it now. He placed
his hand on her knee, and electricity shot through his body. The muscles
in her thighs were tense. He gently caressed her leg, scared to move up
too high and risk offending her. He was drunk with lust. This was the
most exquisite sensation he had ever had in his life. For a brief second, he
got lost in thoughts of why he so desperately needed to be controlled by
a strong Black woman. This was not the time for such reflections. At the
moment, all he could think about was the unbelievably stunning woman
who was capable of controlling his every move. He was caressing her

leg softly, getting more and more comfortable with that fact when his hand encountered skin. He realized that she was wearing stockings. "Mmmm." He whimpered like a baby. Chantal laughed out loud. Surely, Greg had seen dozens of women in stockings before, but this had affected him in the most intense way.

They were in his carport before he knew it. All the details of how they got inside his condo were a blur. All Greg knew was that he was in his bedroom with this magnificent woman, and she was undressing in front of him like this was her home.

She unbuttoned her suit jacket and revealed the most magnificent set of 36 Cs known to man. They weren't too big, not too small—they were just right. They were beautifully encased in the most expensive black La Perla bra ever made. Her nipples were works of art poking through the lace. They were perfect peaks of sensuality to cap off those smooth, brown tits. Her stomach muscles showed evidence of many a personally trained workout. She turned around, unzipped the back of her skirt, and slipped it down her legs.

The matching panties were French cut, so much more sophisticated than the all too popular thong. Of course, a garter belt held up her stockings. Her ass defied words, although if one were to try to describe it, they would probably use the words *soft, round, high, big,* simply a beautiful representation of Black femininity.

She moved about the room comfortably. Emerging from the walk-in closet, she held several belts and ties. Her taste was exquisite; they were the most expensive imports from his collection. She arranged them at the foot of the bed.

"It's showtime, little boy."

It sounded comical coming from a woman of her stature compared to Greg's size. He had a look of confusion in his eyes. He was watching all of this transpire as if it was a movie happening in his own bedroom.

"Undress." Her command was simple and to the point.

Completely aware that there was a strange woman giving him orders filled Greg with pleasure. Greg had only dreamed of giving up control before. All of his sexual life, he was the predator. A few months earlier, he had begun to fantasize about what it would be like to give up control—to be used if you will. He didn't even want to think about why these thoughts thrilled him so. He did know they were extreme. He wondered if this woman would truly have the power to take him there.

Chantal taunted him. "Would you like it if I humiliated you like you did that young lady at the club?"

Perhaps out of habit, more out of fear, quietly, he whispered, "No."

"Excuse me? I don't think I heard you correctly. Do you think I'm here to play games with you? If you don't want me here, I can leave. I don't need you, need I remind you? You created me. I'm your fantasy, not the other way around." Greg panicked. There was no turning back. If he let this opportunity slip through his fingers, he would never forgive himself.

"Yes, mistress, I need you to use me. I crave your domination and control." He was reminded of his command to undress. His hands were trembling. The buttons on his shirt seemed outrageously small. He took off his shirt and stood motionless and speechless.

Chantal walked around him, admiring his smooth brown chest, strong arms, and broad shoulders. She picked up one of the belts, folded it in half, and gently touched it to his lips. She leaned close; her body heat seemed to scorch his skin. She whispered in his ear, "I said undress."

He felt awkward but he knelt to take off his shoes, then undid his belt and kicked them to the side. He had never been more proud of his body at that moment. All of his hard work had paid off because his mistress looked pleased. He reached into his boxer briefs and grabbed his shaft. It had never felt thicker. He couldn't resist stroking it just a little before he hauled it out. He finished getting undressed and stood there before his mistress, erect in more ways than one.

She walked around him, examining him from every angle. She caressed his chest and arms, ran her hand over his stomach, pressed her body against his back. She walked over to him, dragging the belt behind her. As she circled him, Greg stared at her ass in awe and disbelief.

She sat on the dresser and spread her legs wide.

"Crawl to me."

It took a minute for Greg's brain to register what she had said. He wasn't even thinking as he put his right foot out. "I SAID CRAWL. You do understand what that means, don't you?"

This was it, the deciding moment. Greg had to decide if he wanted all of his fantasies to come true at that very instant. Could he really give over his power to a woman, be controlled, dominated by her? Chantal took the belt and flicked it against the dresser with force. "Crawl—now." It seemed like a million miles between him and this powerful Nubian queen—no, goddess. Again, Greg didn't know what to do.

Chantal spread her legs even wider and slid her finger inside her panties. She was rubbing her clit, and Greg wanted to see, up close and personal.

This time, it was only a whisper. He wasn't even sure he heard her correctly. "Come here, little boy. Come to Mommy." In the perfect act of submission, he got down on his hands and knees and crawled toward her.

Kneeling before her was an indescribable sensation. Chantal took her pump and placed it squarely on his shoulder. Never taking her finger off her clit or her other hand off the belt, she got into pleasuring herself. Her heel was digging into Greg's flesh but the sensation was pleasurable. He could smell pussy in the air—sweet, sexy pussy. His mouth was watering.

She was keenly aware of his position and her control over him, so she just leaned her head back against the mirror and rubbed the sensitive spot between her legs with passion. He was whimpering, and his neck was strained upward because she was positioned higher than eye level. She took her fingers and slid her panties to the side.

Beautiful was not the word to describe her pussy. Rather than being shaved, it seemed her baby-soft hair naturally tapered to her mound. Her outer lips were delicate and fat, but they closed perfectly to hide her deepest recesses. Her inner flesh was the most glorious pink, and he could tell how wet she was from the way it shined. Her clit was the size of the very tip of his pinky, the perfect bundle of nerves just waiting to be sucked. It peeked out from under its hood and called to him. Greg swallowed hard. His knees were hurting, his shoulder was in pain, his neck was cramped and his dick. . .there weren't even words to describe it.

"Greg, you want to lick my pussy, don't you? You need my pussy, don't you?" He had waited his entire life to be subjected to such treatment. In his mind, he was going over how many times he had been the controller. Now he was being controlled.

"Please, mistress, I need nothing more than to taste your sweet treasure." He wasn't even sure those words were coming out of his mouth.

With the flick of her fingers, Chantal unhooked the straps of her garter belt. She looked down on him with pride.

"Remove my stockings with your mouth. And be very careful not to run them."

The rush of adrenaline was out of this world. Chantal took the belt, placed it along the spine of his back, and slowly pulled it toward her. Her touch was so excruciatingly light it was painful. Greg swallowed hard. He was careful to use only his lips, not his teeth, lest he ruin the delicate nylons. She dug her heel in deeper to his shoulder. He couldn't resist using his tongue to caress the smooth flesh of her legs. Laughing at him, she kicked off her heels and helped him take her stocking the rest of the way off. She placed her perfectly pedicured soft toes on his lips and teased him. Instinctively, he began to lick them. He was using his tongue and lips all over her sweet toes.

Chantal was caught up in her own rapture. "Mmm, Greg, did I tell you that you had permission to pleasure my feet that way?"

Greg panicked. He knew the unspoken code, even if he had only experienced it in his mind before. "I'm sorry. Please forgive me. All I wanted to do was to give you pleasure."

"You understand that I'm going to have to punish you, don't you, Greg?" she whispered.

His dick got harder than before, which he didn't think was possible. Chantal went into a little speech about pleasure and pain, but it was strictly for her amusement. Greg couldn't hear a word. He was off in his own world. She signaled for him to follow her. She made him kneel on the bed.

"You've been a bad boy, Greg. I'm going to have to spank you, and you understand that I don't want to, but I have to."

All he could do was nod, but she accepted that as sufficient.

Whap! The first blow came without warning. The sting spread throughout his entire body. There was no doubt that he experienced the feeling as pleasure, but he cried out in pain. "More, please mistress, more." He didn't want to think about what any of it meant. All he knew right then was that he had never felt safer—or sexier. He didn't have to be in control, and that felt good. It felt damn good. To know that this woman could take him where he'd only dreamed was beyond his wildest fantasies.

Whap! Whap! Whap! The heat spread across his ass. She was steadily raining down blows on him, and he was overflowing with emotion. *Whap,* more pain. *Whap, pleasure, Whap,* ecstasy. Before he knew what hit him, Greg screamed out, "I'm cumming." His gism came spurting out. Never in his life had he ever cum without direct stimulation to his dick.

Chantal moved to take advantage of the situation quickly. She turned him over and secured his arms to his four-poster bed with his ties. Facing the head of the bed, she climbed on top of him and placed her pussy just inches from his mouth. He could see it, smell it, he could virtually taste it. What he couldn't do was touch it. His arms were tied so securely, he started to panic. What if she was crazy, out to hurt him seriously, rob him? What if . . .

He was distracted by her lowering her pussy down onto his mouth. As much as his mind was racing, he could only concentrate on one task at that particular moment. Slick, that was the sensation he felt. Her lips parted, and he gained access to her sweet treasure. It was so slippery, and sweet, and earthy. Heaven. She obviously knew what she wanted him to do because she worked his mouth like a fine-tuned instrument. She moved back and forth, up and down, riding his tongue, lips, and mouth like a champion rodeo rider.

Greg did everything he could to work his mouth and make his lady cum. He nibbled on her fat lips, licked her slit, tongued her hole, and sucked her clit. He was not going to stop until she filled his mouth with nectar from the heavens.

She was pulling on her nipples and getting all worked up. Her moaning became louder and louder, her hips were grinding away. "Greg, do you like being used?"

All he could do was moan and lick and suck that much more. His arms were aching, his jaw was tired. He had no choice. He pointed his tongue and tried to fuck her mercilessly with it. Rhythmically, she bounced up and down. Greg's face was wet with her desire. She coated his lips and face with her sweet sauce. She was teasing him. She rubbed her clit and moved her pussy to within inches of his mouth. Fuck, if he could only move his arms, grab her hips, and pull her to his hungry mouth. Unconsciously, Greg was thrusting his hips, begging for her to please put her pussy back on his mouth. "Please, may I have more?"

"No, baby," she cooed. "It's time for the ride of your life." Chantal climbed off Greg, walked to the foot of the bed and grabbed another belt. Greg's dick jumped, remembering the indescribable pleasure he had experienced just a short while before with that accessory of pain. Chantal surveyed her prize. Here was this fine specimen of Black man, fine beyond description, lying helplessly tied to his own bed. He had eight inches of fat meat sticking up proudly from his body, betraying his true feelings. She grabbed another tie and secured it around his eyes. He begged her to let him see. All he wanted to do was see.

Silently she just walked around the bed, examining her "victim." She ran her fingers over his nipples and pulled on them. His body twisted and contorted to the pain. She took the belt and lightly rubbed the leather over the fronts of his thighs and across his hips.

"Are you scared, Greg?" Chantal gently rubbed the belt over his dick and balls. Words were stuck in his throat. She climbed on the bed and started using her tongue to tease her little boy. He didn't know from where the sensations were coming, or where the next one was going to land. She licked his lips, reminding him of the intense pleasure he had experienced just minutes before. She ran her tongue down his neck, across his shoulder blades. She sucked and bit his nipples. Greg couldn't take any more.

"Please, mistress. Please, fuck me. Just fuck me. Use me to make yourself cum. Please." This was it, the defining moment of truth for Greg. He was helpless, and he loved it. He had no control over his body or his reactions. At that moment, the words came pouring out of his mouth. "This wasn't supposed to happen to me, yet you've done it. My fear at this moment is what happens if I submerge myself completely and never return. I've gone to a place where I feel this restriction has become my freedom and where I gain so much pleasure from satisfying the very person who has claimed me. It is no longer about the satisfaction of my pleasure, but I have begun to enjoy the sensations that cause your pleasure. The torments I feel are now delicious. I truly loved what I used to do, but will I love this more? That is what scares me. I know how arousing desperation feels. I know how utterly tempting complete and total submission is from both sides of the coin. This . . .there truly is nothing like it. I don't want to lose this anytime soon. Please, mistress, you have my control. I pray you use it wisely."

Greg's arms were fatigued and tired from pulling against the restraints. He was paralyzed; he couldn't move. The sensation of being restrained was almost too arousing. Chantal straddled his body, placing her hot pussy inches above his dick. She put her delicate hand around the base of his dick. He wanted to see but he had no say in the matter. All he could do was wait. Enjoying her power immensely, Chantal rubbed the head of his dick back and forth on her slit. The heat was intense, and Greg cried out in anguish. She used it to masturbate herself; really, the vision of him squirming around was more arousing than anything else. She reached back and played with his balls, rolling them around between her soft fingers. Without warning, she slammed her pussy down on Greg's dick, and they both moaned in sweet agony.

Greg felt like his dick was wrapped in the hottest, wettest, tightest piece of heaven he had ever felt. Chantal knew that she had met her match. His dick penetrated her like none she had ever had before. They fit. They fit perfectly as a matter of fact. It was a dance of lovers where they worked out a perfect rhythm. She started bouncing up and down; he began thrusting into her, trying to throw her off. She held on, and his dick hit every hot spot she had. She leaned close to him and started pinching his nipples and grinding her pussy all over his dick, just using her muscles to squeeze and work it. She was masterful in her control. Just when she thought Greg could handle more stimulation, she started fucking him again. His breathing was out of control. He felt lightheaded. His nuts were aching from his dick being hard so long, but he had never felt so much pleasure. Harder, faster, stronger, there was no holding back. Up and down she rode him. Her face was hot, and her body was covered with sweat. She was going to time it just right. "Okay, motherfucker, tell me now, whose. . .dick. . . is . . . this. . . ?"

At that moment, he knew how the woman in the club felt. "Oh fuck." Neither one of them could take it anymore. Pleasure—pure, sweet, unadulterated pleasure—washed over them at the same time. The boiling cum shot so hard up out of Greg's dick, he felt every single drop coat her insides. She squirted. Her cum flowed out of her body, coating Greg all over his thighs. He shook, out of control. Before he drifted out of consciousness, she untied his arms, and he cradled her to him, wrapped in the essence of each other, completely.

The morning sun shone through the window and warmed Greg's skin as he began to wake up. His arms were sore, his dick was still hard, and his ass was tender. He knew she wouldn't be there when he opened his eyes, so he just lay there, trying to put it all in perspective. He had really been dominated, and it was all he had hoped to experience. He knew at that very moment that he wanted to go further. He got up and looked around for the note that he knew would be there. Sure enough, taped to the bathroom mirror was a business card. Chantal Moore, Esq., Attorney at Law. He flipped the card over and it simply said:

Counselor,

In the courtroom, we shall be equals. In the bedroom, you will be my possession. Either way, prepare to battle.

Raw

by

Kenji Jasper

I'm laying here in an all-white room with steel-rod drapes and starchy sheets and breathing through the clear mask over my face. I imagine that first bullet spinning toward me, racing from the barrel to that point of entry between my ribs. I can still feel it tearing through me to come out the other end. I still feel the burn. I still see my blood all over me. I still wish I could've done things different.

Every few hours, the nurse comes in. Her name is Tamara, and she's this tall Jamaican broad with skin like midnight. Her titties look perfect in that bra beneath her uniform. Her lips are thick and pouty. And that damn accent. Dear God, that Kingston accent.

When the lights are out, I think of her pussy lips spread open by my tongue, of me burying my tongue in her wetness, working my index finger back and forth in her ass while she does her best to swallow me whole on the other end. I think of her cumming, her spilling across my face as her thighs tremble, of her begging me to fuck her deep, to push up into the places her man can't reach 'cause he ain't got the length or width. I think of those long, elegant fingers stroking me until I leave a white trail down her throat. But I shouldn't be thinking about any of that because it's those kinds of thoughts that got me in this room in the first place.

I ain't gonna tell you my name, just in case I decide to be stupid and

go out and do it again. But I will say that I was born in DC, up off Blair
Road, near the funeral home and the Fort Totten train station. I'll tell you
that I'm thirty-four years old and that I got a little girl somewhere named
Candra. She got lost in the shuffle when her triflin'-ass momma got my
visits revoked after she found out I was fucking someone close to her,
the girl that came out of her momma two years after she did. But see,
that's another story. All this is just to let you know who I am. What I'm
'bout to tell you is how I got here.

Brooklyn

I got this job at a TV station, a good job at one of the Big 3 that paid
about seventy grand a year before taxes. That was more than enough to
keep me out in the nightlife whenever I needed.

I hadn't been in New York too long. I was twenty-four, and six
months fresh off a discount flight from Houston, where I had gotten my
first job right after college. There was a girl back there, a girl with the
tightest abs I'd ever seen. She used to love it when I came on them. She
used to love it when I watched her rub it into her skin then licked her
fingers clean.

I had never cheated and never lied. I had loved and gotten the best
lovin' possible on the face of the earth. I'd taken all the money from my
tax return and bought her a little ring, a little $2,763 piece of my love that
I was sure she'd keep forever.

But what she told me was that she wasn't ready, that twenty-one was
too young for her to make a decision like that, especially when she hadn't
finished school yet. That was what she said, but what a little bird told me
was that there was another nigga with more cake in his pockets who had
made some bigger promises when I wasn't looking.

He had taken out a loan against his house to buy her an Acura Legend
with all the trimmings. How he did it without his wife knowing was
beyond me. He'd done it, and then he was doin' her while I was working
third shift at my little job at that local cable channel. The truth came out

when she turned up with the clap and I didn't. Apparently he'd been making a lot of promises to other sweet young things as well.

I couldn't look at her after she told me. I couldn't even see her as the same person, like this hooker was living in the house me and my baby had built, and I couldn't get her to leave. So I did the leaving. Shot my résumé out across the world and took my seventy-G-a-year payday in the Rotten Apple.

There were times I used to wake up crying. Other times I was punching walls with bare knuckles just so my joints could pay for it in the morning. Night after night, I parked myself on a barstool and threw them back until I went broke or the bartender kicked me out. I rarely even looked at anyone because I was still living in the past, still remembering when I'd dream all day about the smile on my baby's face when I came home from work in time to make love with her before she had to go off to her job.

But drinking away the pain only brought me an extra twenty pounds and a stomach ulcer. Needless to say, I hung up for something better. I got into this book club—you know one of the ones where you read a different book every month and then talk about it. Join one as a black dude, and there's never more than one other brother there. Even if you look halfway decent, you've got five to ten sets of female eyes on you. They study your face, maybe imagine whether they want to fuck, though they wouldn't tell you one way or the other if you paid them.

The funny thing is I wasn't even in the club for the women. I liked reading. It was some real calming shit to do after a long day of working with stupid-ass people who believed their own hype. I liked disappearing in the words and becoming whoever was telling me the story. On this particular Thursday, the group was going through one of those relationship books, you know the ones where the girl writes three hundred pages on all the ways the dude fucked up, the kinda shit broads with problems write hoping that other women with the same problems will read it and agree and make them all feel better about themselves.

I knew better than to come out swinging when talking about a book like that, so I waited for them to come to me. I waited for them to ask me how I felt about it, then I told them that most men don't understand how women need passion, how a soft touch and a few words can mean more than the greatest fuck alive. I told them that so many of us grow up without fathers that we have this false idea of what being a man is, and what a man does, and how he's suppose to treat his woman.

Some of them agreed and others didn't. We went back and forth about the issues until it was way past the usual meeting time. We even said we'd have a part two the next time around to finish the discussion.

As I was leaving, this girl named Katrina tapped me on the shoulder. We were having the meeting at her crib that night, this little two-bedroom not far from the Triboro Bridge. She had a car, and she wanted to know if I needed a ride since I was going from Harlem all the way down to Brooklyn. She said she was going that way, so I gladly accepted the offer.

The rest of the members left, and Katrina and I stayed along with one other girl, Tanay, who said her boyfriend was picking her up. Tanay is around five-one, black and Dominican and maybe a size fourteen, a thick girl who has two kids at home and a boyfriend who works a lot. Katrina is light-skinned and slender, five-nine with long legs, a cute little ass, and no breasts to speak of. I only noticed the way you have to notice as a man, because it's there and you can't help but to look.

So I was sitting in a bean bag chair and the two of them were on the sofa. Katrina offered me a drink, and I took a shot of Hennessy. Tanay said she didn't drink, but had a glass of white wine anyway. We talked about the book club, about whom we liked and whom we didn't, about the books we read and the ones we just skimmed through. Then we got on the subject of relationships. Katrina hadn't had a boyfriend in three years. Tanay wasn't happy, and I kept thinking of the love of my life back in Houston, the one I still couldn't get over, the one who wouldn't marry me because my pockets were too shallow.

We had more drinks and more after that. We talked about love. I missed it. Katrina missed it. Tanay said she couldn't miss it because she'd never had it. Her kids came out of lust and bad rubbers. Her commitments were the best way to keep the bills paid.

After drink number three, Tanay burst into tears. She knew her man wasn't coming to get her. She only said that so she could have a little time away from it all, to talk to some nice people. I reached into my pocket and found the sack of herb I bought earlier in the day. I asked if they wanted in, and everyone agreed.

Just as my high kicked in, Katrina kissed Tanay. It was a soft kiss at first, nothing drastic. But Tanay came back at her like she hadn't been touched in years. My high had me wondering if any of it was real and if I'd ever get back to Brooklyn—until their clothes started coming off.

Katrina peeled away Tanay's bra and rubbed the naked nipples against her face. The mother of two reached under her skirt and started to touch herself. Katrina removed her own top and bra as she traced the length of Tanay's rib cage with her tongue. I started to harden. The girls kissed again, sucking on each other's tongues as if I wasn't there. Katrina grinned and announced that she hadn't had a man because she was into girls.

The next thing I knew, most of Katrina's face was between Tanay's thick thighs. They were both moaning, their eyes closed, dissolving into a moment that I got to watch like something on The Hot Net. Katrina pulled away from her meal just long enough to tell me to fuck her. I barely had my pants down before Tanay was coming as if it was the first time in her life.

I was harder than I'd ever known as I entered Katrina. Her muscles were so toned that I struggled to keep from coming in the first thrust. But I found my rhythm. I pulled and pushed myself in and out as my partner started to suck Tanay's toes as she murmured something about wanting some too. After the perfect amount of time, Katrina pushed me out of her and told me to take care of Tanay, if I knew what was good for me.

I was so high, I barely knew where I was, but I got to Tanay in time to see Katrina roll over on her back as she began to put fingers inside herself. Tanay grabbed me headfirst but guided me toward her ass. She said she liked it that way. I knew it kept the risk of a baby by another daddy out of the equation. And from what I heard, that's the way Spanish girls liked to get down.

It was my first time doing it that way and that hole felt better than I could have ever imagined. Katrina was breathing heavily on her back. I could see the orgasm building as every part of her began to flush.

It arrived almost exactly as mine did as I spilled all over Tanay's thighs. The head rush sent me backward, and I stumbled to the floor, next to Katrina, who kissed me on the mouth and smiled. "It's always good to have a boy in the group," she says.

Los Angeles

Two years later, I got promoted and became an executive producer on a TV show everyone watches. I was twenty-eight, and I lived in a crib that cost a quarter of a million in the Valley. I did yoga every morning on a deck with wood brought over from Japan. I lived with a Southern Belle from Mississippi. She had an accent like Whitley Gilbert from *A Different World* and titties like the black chick from *Ali McBeal.* She made jewelry and gave good head while I was pulling in a half a million a year.

I ain't one of those dudes who tripped about money. I met Maya at this poetry thing down in Leimert Park. She was there at the mic with this skirt that went down to her ankles and a baggy-ass top that didn't show anything. Still, there was something about her that was even sexier than watching Katrina and Janay all of those years before. She had this confidence, this determination, the kind of shit you want in the gene pool so you can pass it down to your kids.

She'd been living with me for six months, and we'd damn near renovated everything but the grass on the front lawn. When I wasn't working, we'd puff a J right after dinner and watch movies from other places that you had to use subtitles with.

Only thing about her was that she wasn't into much between the sheets. One of those straight missionary kinds of girls who grew up thinking that sex was a dirty matter best done as quickly as possible. Needless to say, doing it was always the same thing, the same kind of way. Passion was what she put into her poems, never into me. To top it off, she went to bed at ten. I was a night person who didn't have to be in until ten in the morning.

Maybe it was the gleaming bright future of a dream that kept me around. All I could see was our little babies and her being there no matter what went down. If I lost it all, I knew she'd be there regardless. That was some rare shit you didn't just throw away because the pussy wasn't mind-blowing.

I spent a lot of time driving around late at night, up and down Hollywood Way and then over the hill onto Sunset. Sometimes I'd get out and hit the bars, the Red Rock, The Whiskey, The Pearl on La Brea. It never really mattered what the crowd was like. I just liked the people. I liked to watch them move and smile, to see what they wore and the way they cut their hair. Their conversations never meant anything, but it was L.A. Nobody's words meant anything.

"What you doin' in here?" the bartender asked me. She was the color of caramel with round hips and a derriere the size of two basketballs stuffed into a pair of tight black pants, and flats to match. Her eyes were narrow and sleepy.

"People watching," I said.

"That explains the lime and seltzer," she replied, "but can you do me a favor?"

"What?" I asked.

"Tip me like it's a rum and Coke."

I smiled. She smiled. We smiled. Then I put a hundred on the bar and told her to keep them coming until I said so. There was something about the way her thighs shifted that told me she liked it, that I was not what she'd come to expect in this place, that she wanted to know more. But she had a bar full of people to appease, so it took some time.

It turned out she was managing the place until the owner and the regular manager got back from Oakland, which meant that she had to close every night and then get up for auditions in the morning. Of course she was an actress. She'd come close to getting the part Kandi Alexander has on *CSI*. She was in the final three for the part of the dyke on *The Wire* and just did a commercial for Sprint PCS that was gonna give her enough money to take an extended leave of absence from this place she'd come to hate.

I told her that I was a writer for a network TV show, but that I didn't like to talk about it. She told me she didn't like to know what the men she liked do for a living. It was closing time when I told her I had a girlfriend. I was next to her when she was locking up the place and telling me she didn't care.

She undressed me slowly in the bedroom. She had speakers from her stereo in all three rooms of the house, so Abbey Lincoln was just about everywhere. Close up she smelled like Halston, or maybe it was Chloe. The walls were bare except for these little abstract sculptures she said her father made. I peeled her out of her pants to see that her toes were painted green. I sucked each one, then licked each instep as if it was made of sugar.

She tasted just as sweet as her lips covered mine, as her thighs clamp around my ears. A nipple hardened in each of my palms as I squeezed. She stroked it like it was the most precious thing in the world. I sucked her clit as if there was something priceless inside.

Her ass was too big for hands that could palm a basketball. But it was so firm that my sweat bounced off it. We'd fucked through an entire CD when she told me she was on the pill, that I didn't have to worry. I told her that she was a gift from God.

The next thing I knew she was on top of me, riding my length like her favorite toy. I could see her smiling in the darkness. I could see that it hadn't been this good for either of us in a long time. I blacked out when I came into her the last time and opened my eyes in her arms. She said she envied Maya for having me. I told her I envied Maya for believing that she did.

She wrote down a number that I tore into pieces at the closest stoplight. No need to torture myself. No need to torture her. I needed to tell Maya I couldn't do it anymore.

DC

In my hometown, snow only comes once or twice in a season. Businesses close early. Schools shut down. People stay inside except for shoveling out their cars. I was thirty-four years old and just back in the country from two years in Costa Rica. I bought some real estate, opened a little shop for all of the surfers and a cozy restaurant for all the lovers on their getaways.

I got sick of the TV business. I got sick of so much money for something so meaningless, so I sold my house in the valley, stacked a cool three million and disappeared. This was the first Christmas I'd been home since I was twenty-seven.

My mother was happy to see me. My father was still in the grave where I saw him on my last visit. I have a brother doing life in prison for shooting a cop. I have sister who runs a nonprofit for social change. She doesn't speak to me because I got rich in Hollywood. She doesn't speak to me because in her eyes I'm part of the problem. Christmas dinner was mostly conversation between my mother and my sister and my mother and me, and the food.

I had no regrets about leaving home after college. I had a degree under my arm and about a thousand dollars in graduation money. Houston was cheap and warm, and I heard it was where all the girls with the phattest asses lived, so I gave it a shot. When I fell in love with that would-be fiancé I called to say I was never coming back. Now I was back and looking like a fool. My sister was struggling not to laugh at me.

The turkey and stuffing and sweet potatoes are good, but the green beans had been cooked flabby. My mother asked me if I was going back to Cali. I told her I didn't think so. I was going to buy some property close to home, rent it out, and just live life. Maybe I'd write a book about it all. Maybe it was time for me to settle down.

My mother said I needed to go church. My sister said I should invest my money in the community. After dinner, I gave them their Christmas gifts. My sister's was a check for twenty grand. My mother got diamonds for her ears. I told them I was going out to see friends and would be back later. They both knew I was lying.

White Christmases are rare in DC, so it was hard to believe that I walked out into falling snow that was actually sticking. I was brushing powder off my windshield when someone called my name. I spun around to see the first girl I ever loved, Maxayne Washington, who used to live across the street.

Every dude has a girl like Maxayne. You know the one you play doctor with and kiss just to see what it feels like. She was the first girl I ever put my fingers in. But we never did it, even though we wanted to, because we were both almost always with people for my whole time in the city.

"What you doing back home after all this time?" she asked.

"Waitin' for you," I said. The funny thing was that part of me meant it. "Merry Christmas then. You still livin' around here?"

She explained that her parents, who were older than mine, passed away just after my father. One in '02 and the other in '03. In true love, one can't live without the other. Or at least that's what some people say. She invited me inside, and I accepted.

Her place was cluttered with old memories. She still had every little picture her parents took of her. Maxayne was an only child so they treated it all so preciously, because they never ended up doing the parent thing again. She has a ten-year-old boy named Alonzo whose father's been inside for the whole length of his life. She worked at the Department of Transportation and went to school at night for her master's.

Maxayne's skin was the color of honey, and her eyes were a sweet caramel. Her breasts were about a handful. Her ass was a polished thing of beauty. But it was her smile I loved the most because it reminded me of home, of my father, and a whole life I tried to forget after high school. Looking at her, I remembered when we kissed on the boat where our prom was held. Even though we brought different dates, I remembered that night at the Branch Avenue Lodge when we tried to lose our virginity only to get the call that our time was up before we got the courage to go past kissing.

She told me she was married for about two years to a dude who was kind of a stalker. People she worked with would see him hiding across from her car in the building parking lot. Some days he knew more about where she'd been than she did. But what took the cake was when he showed up at the strip bar on girls' night out. That was too much. That shit was way too much.

When I heard about him, I got a weird feeling, but I sat next to her on the couch anyway. She smelled like sandalwood and jasmine, but her navel tasted like peaches. She pulled the shirt over my head before I could get to it. I pulled off her panties even while I was blinded.

She took me into her mouth as if that's all I wanted. But knowing DC niggas, I was sure that's all she was used to. She moved her jaws around me like a seasoned veteran. Just the right rhythm. Just the right speed. The hair that was hers within the cornrows felt like silk. My head fell backward as she pulled away for me to let loose and caught me all in her hand. I don't know what she did, but when I next looked, her palms were clean, and she was on top of me.

I lifted her up and down as our weight forced me back against the couch. She called my name unlike any woman I'd ever known. I held one nipple to suck with one hand while the other played with her pearl down below. After what seemed like forever, she finally came, her spasms so severe that I had to catch her before she fell to the floor.

We smiled and embraced. It all felt just right. I'd gone a thousand miles to come back home and found what I was looking for right across the street.

I didn't know what it is when the door came open, but I did notice that the shades in the living room weren't drawn. Anyone who wanted to see us from the street had it all in view, including the ex-husband who couldn't get over old endings and new beginnings.

I never saw the gun, only the look on her face as she took three slugs.

Only one went into me. The rest took her heart instantly. I never saw his face, which makes me the worst witness alive.

I never get to tell her how much I loved her when she couldn't be mine. A black millionaire would have to come back home to get shot. I laughed at the thought as it all faded to black.

I came to nearly two days later. I had a punctured lung and massive blood loss. My sister was asleep in the chair next to my bed, a copy of some self-help book about how to say you're sorry fanned open in her lap. The room was all white and the sheets were starchy. If I'd stayed at Mama's on Christmas, none of it would've ever happened.

I was not well enough to see Maxayne buried. I didn't remember enough to fully answer any of the cops' questions. I told my mama and sister it felt like I was dying inside. I spent an hour a day crying my eyes out when no one else was looking.

I could accept that Maxayne was dead. I could accept that the bullet was less than an inch away from taking me out. What I couldn't accept was what came back in my blood work, those three little letters that say more than anything else.

For the rest of my week I ran back through all my partners. There weren't that many, so it wasn't that hard. It was only in New York, L.A. and at home that I ever went raw. It was within these three episodes that my fate got sealed.

Luckily I had the money for the treatment. Luckily I had family and friends who cared. But there's not as much to be said for brief moments of pleasure when you look at a life as a whole, a life free of a designated death sentence.

I stayed home for six months and wrote a book about it all. It got bought for a huge amount of money that I didn't need. I toured the country and revisited all three cities where the scene of the crime might've happened, searching for a face to match all the words I had inside myself, words that only made sense to the person who did it. But no one showed—until Houston.

The bookstore was still empty after a half an hour. It wasn't uncommon in cities that weren't big on books, especially when you're nobody famous. I thought about signing some copies then leaving, going back to my hotel or someplace close for lunch. But she came through the door just as I was leaving. She came through the door hoping to catch me in time.

She eventually married the man who gave her that Acura. He also gave her two kids and a house outside the city. But all those trappings didn't make his last gift any easier, three little letters three months before he gave out completely. The kids weren't infected, and her insurance was good. She was like me, always reliving the old moments because new ones wouldn't come, or at least not without bringing death along with them.

We had dinner at a steak house after my signing. She still had the ring I had given her with my itty-bitty tax return. She still had the letters she had written me after I was gone that she never mailed. She still kept a picture of me.

I can't say that it's going to be perfect. I can't say that this second time we can't lose. But I can stay that it's nice to find a family when you come home, ready-made and waiting just for you.

Bus Route 69

by

Goldie Banks

*B*yanca's pussy glistened with wetness. If she could put her finger or better yet, his dick inside of her to ease the monthlong yearning, she would. Byanca was quickly becoming accustomed to the sticky substance that formed between her legs every morning after getting on the bus. She parted her thighs slightly, allowing the cool breeze from the air conditioner to seep between them, giving her momentary relief, but it didn't ease the throbbing from her clit.

Byanca had faithfully boarded the 69 bus to work every day at 7:30 A.M. for two years without fail. However, one month earlier, her trusty alarm clock didn't go off at its appointed time. Apparently the wiring in the building where Byanca resided needed an electrical upgrade because sometime during the middle of the night they suffered a power outage. Byanca ended up catching the eight o'clock bus, causing her to be late, but it was worth it. From that morning forward she made it her business to be late and catch the eight o'clock bus. Being the head woman in charge definitely had its privileges.

Byanca hadn't been in a relationship since she took the senior vice president position two years earlier. Her hectic schedule didn't allow much time for anything other than work. Her personal life had become predictable and redundant. Work was no longer fulfilling since she had no one in her life with whom to share her successes. The moment she laid eyes on the driver for Bus 69, she knew what was missing from her life and just who she wanted to fill the void.

The bus driver made her wet just thinking about him. She didn't know if it was his sexy voice and the way he greeted her daily or his smile, his dimples, his muscular body, copper complexion, and the sexy tattoo on his bicep, or the way he smelled like Nautica Cool Water. It could've been any number of things triggering her pussy to become moist, morning after morning. Whatever the case, Byanca had to see him, and her pussy wanted to feel him. Byanca wanted to taste, feel, and have a full orgasmic experience with this stranger.

Two weeks after seeing the driver, Byanca decided it was time for a makeover. She went on a shopping spree with a personal shopper, followed by a facial and a new hairstyle. It was time to do something with her hair, which she always wore piled atop her head in a bun. If she was going to get the man she desired, she needed to improve her wardrobe and do something with her long, thick mane.

The next week, Byanca's highlighted tresses flowed past her shoulders, and her off-the-shoulder blouse revealed her tan lines. Her skirt hugged her hips, and when she lifted her leg to climb the stairs, the material hiked up a few inches, revealing her toned thighs. To Byanca's dismay when she stepped on the bus, the driver greeted her the same way he always had. He didn't do a double-take, stare longer than usual, or give her any extra attention. It was as if she hadn't done anything special. Byanca paid her fare and found a seat beside a man who couldn't take his eyes off her, but she wasn't interested in him. She wanted the driver.

The following day, Byanca went back to putting her hair in a bun, but she kept the new wardrobe. It was prime time that she updated her gear.

By the fourth week, Byanca had lost hope and returned to her 7:30 A.M. ritual. The eight o'clock ride proved to be a tease, and Byanca didn't think she could take seeing the eight o'clock driver without lusting after him. It was more than her pussy could bear.

Nevertheless, Byanca couldn't get the driver off her mind, and she didn't know why. She could get just about any man she desired, yet she sought this blue-collar driver who wouldn't give her the time of day. Perhaps, it was the chase. Whatever, the case, Byanca dreamt of putting his fat—she was sure it was fat—dick into her mouth and licking the tip of it with her pointy tongue. She wanted to graze his dick from the tip down along the shaft to his balls.

Friday night found Byanca hanging with her friends, Kama and Jacinda. It was girls' night out, and Kama was able to score them V.I.P. passes to an exclusive album release party, which was held at the prestigious Cipriani's on Twenty-third Street in Manhattan.

The deejay played all of the latest jams, and though many people chose to be flowers on the wall, Byanca and Jacinda decided to be the first to step out on the floor. Byanca was never one to wait to be asked. If she felt like dancing, she did just that. Within five minutes, a few more brave souls joined them. Moments later, the floor became filled with gyrating bodies.

Byanca closed her eyes as she allowed the music to sway her movements on the floor. Her black fitted knit dress hugged her body like a glove, accentuating the fullness of her hips and succulent breasts. Men all around the room watched as this gorgeous specimen danced to Mary J. Blige's remake of "I'm Going Down." Most of them were too afraid to approach her because Byanca looked as if she coined the phrase "too beautiful for words." The other men were too turned on and awestruck to request a moment of her time.

One man finally worked up the courage to ask Byanca for a dance. She was so entranced by the song she barely felt the tap on her shoulder. After several more taps and realizing this intruder was not going to let up, Byanca finally turned around. She decided not to flip out just in case the person who desired her attention had potential.

Before Byanca could utter a word, the man asked, "May I have this dance?"

After recognizing the familiar face, Byanca's voice got caught in her in her throat. She began to cough and lightly hit her chest in order to resume breathing properly. Too embarrassed to answer, she merely nodded and accepted his extended hand. As soon as their bodies met, Byanca became aware of her pulsating pussy. It began throbbing intensely, and her nipples hardened beneath her dress.

"You smell good," the stranger whispered in her ear.

"Thank you. You do too," Byanca managed to say seductively.

"I miss seeing you," he said.

"Really?" Byanca asked, surprised.

"Who wouldn't miss seeing your beautiful face?" He planted a soft kiss on her temple and pulled her into his wide chest and her ripe nipples brushed against his body.

They continued to waltz to the song, enjoying the moment. Byanca closed the space between them and placed her head in the crook of his neck, savoring him. Within seconds she felt him become erect. He palmed her ass and rubbed it in a circular motion. The desire to have him inside her magnified, and she thrust her pelvic region against his. His dick became even harder and began throbbing. Byanca spread her legs and did a slow grind against his dick. The tempo of the music changed, but they were in their own world and continued to slow grind in the middle of the dance floor.

Byanca moaned quietly. She had been rubbing her clit against her dance partner's dick, and the friction caused her to have a mini-orgasm in the middle of the dance floor.

"Are you okay?" he asked, sounding concerned.

"Oh, I'm fine. Just a little hot."

"You wanna get outta here?" he asked.

"Sure. What do you have in mind?" Byanca asked curiously, recovering from her orgasm.

"I don't know. Whatever you wanna do," he said with a mischievous smile.

"Okay, give me a sec. Let me run to the ladies' room then I gotta tell my friends good-bye."

"Cool. I'll meet you at the entrance."

Once they were outside, he turned to Byanca. "Did you drive?"

"No, my girlfriend drove," she answered.

"No problem. We'll take my car. Did you decide where you want to go yet?"

"The bus depot," Byanca replied shyly.

"The bus depot. Why?"

"I've been dreaming of fucking you on the bus for weeks now. Is it still open?"

"Wow." Her response caught him off guard. "It's open 24/7. It's a little risky bringing you there, but if you're down, I'm game."

They hopped in his black-on-black Range Rover and headed toward the depot. He turned on the radio and hit the CD button. The SUV was quickly filled with the smooth tunes of the late Luther Vandross. The volume was reasonable enough for them to delight in conversation, but they rode in silence.

When they arrived at the bus depot, he pulled into the lot and parked his vehicle in the employee section. He released his seat belt, got out of the car, and walked to Byanca's side to open the door. He extended his hand to assist her while she climbed out. They walked through corridors of buses and walked in the shadows, avoiding the possibility of being seen by anyone. They finally got to a row of B69 coaches, and when they got to what must've been his regular bus, he opened the doors.

"Come in," he said, escorting Byanca up the steps.

Once inside, he tipped Byanca's head to meet his and sensuously licked her lips before allowing his tongue to ease into her mouth. His tongue slow waltzed with hers as he kissed her sensually. They kissed, tasting each others sweetness, probing the tantalizing recesses of their mouths.

Byanca's nipples stood erect, and her pubic region glistened with moisture. He reached inside Byanca's dress and found her crotch. He massaged her clit, and it hardened against his fingers. He pulled the fabric off one shoulder and kissed her bare skin. He did the same with the other side and eventually eased the dress down until it slinked onto the ground. Byanca's body was picturesque, but she felt self-conscious and vulnerable. He stared at her bounteous display of feminine shapeliness.

He continued tracing her body with kisses to show his approval.

He returned to Byanca's breasts and placed a large nipple into his mouth.

"Oh," Byanca said, moaning, "it's been so long since they've been sucked properly. I want to suck you." She unzipped his pants, and his erection swung freely, only inches from her mouth. She smiled as she appraised his well-hung penis. She took in a deep breath and savored the smell of his maleness, and the aroma made her pussy become even wetter. Byanca took his manhood into her warm mouth and delicately ran her tongue around his velvety head and licked the drop of precum that had oozed out of the slit. His dick slid easily into her eager wet mouth. Byanca began jerking the erection with her hand as her head moved up and down the shaft. She could feel him beginning to tense, and before she could go any further, he removed his dick from her hot mouth.

Byanca watched as he grabbed his dick and began stroking it with smooth pistonlike movements. She began furiously fingering her slick pussy while watching him get off. A low moan escaped his lips while he masturbated himself to a dramatic climax, and sperm shot from the tip of his cock onto the floor. Byanca didn't want any cum to go to waste and hungrily licked off the last vestiges of it from the head of his dick.

"It's my turn to taste you," he said and placed her in the driver's seat. He parted Byanca's legs and began eating her pussy. His tongue slid between her lips and sucked on her clit. Byanca began caressing her breasts, teasing her mocha nipples until they jutted like Hershey Kisses as he continued to pleasure her sweet spot. He had her ass in the palm of his hands and massaged her cheeks while his tongue played with the folds of her pussy. He tongue-fucked her, burying himself deep in her wetness. Byanca tried to pull his face even farther into her pussy. She panted as his tongue flicked over her very erect clitoris. She couldn't take it and came hard as he licked her to ecstasy. Byanca couldn't quite believe how he had hit every note with her from the very beginning.

Before entering her slick, hot center, he rubbed the tip of his cock against the swell of her pussy. She whimpered with pleasure. He gently eased himself inside in a slow, steady tempo. Their bodies intertwined as she joined his rhythm.

"Damn, your pussy is so wet and tight."

"It's all for you, baby. I've been dreaming of this moment."

"Is it what you dreamed?" he asked as he continued to pound her sweet pussy.

"More," she whispered.

As his dick pumped in and out, his finger played with her clit, causing her to swear and claw at his chest. He became even more turned on and flipped Byanca onto her stomach and rammed her pussy from behind. He watched as her fat ass jiggled, and his nuts grazed her ass with each stroke.

She closed her eyes as he slow-fucked her. They changed positions, and she knelt over him and raised herself up and down on his rock-solid dick. Her hips were pressed against his while he busied himself and inserted one breast in his mouth and fondled the other. Byanca continued to bounce up and down on his member.

Byanca's pussy convulsed, and she came with a rush of passion and pleasure that she had never experienced before, and when he came, he held her in a tight embrace. They remained cuddled, slowly regaining their senses and strength.

"What's your name?" he asked, glancing at her quickly.

"Byanca."

"Pretty name. I'm Bryonn. I know it's a little late for introductions, but—" They both laughed.

Bus route 69 would never be the same.

More & More

by

William Fredrick Cooper

The thought of his chocolate wand sliding inside of me, moving like a carousel—up, down, all around—brings a wicked, antici-patory grin to my face, not to mention the throbbing and flow it invokes below. I can still envision the warmth of his tongue as it did its erotic dance, causing me to scream out in passionate agony. In fact, I'm starting a minor flood just thinking about the feeling. A warm sensation flows through you when a man licks you from clit to anus. Your body moves involuntary while your toes curl and your hips arch. You want to hump the hell out of his face as well as swallow his long, hard magic stick simultaneously.

Last night, he stroked me in every way imaginable. Fast and slow, hard and soft, in circles, up and down, from the missionary, doggy-style, in my soaked tunnel, and other places. He hit my cunny so well I experi-enced memory lapses, forgetting places, time, dates, and years.

I rode this man mercilessly, making my ass bounce as he stroked me from below. I had electrical currents—no let me rephrase that, shocks—shooting through my body, causing violent shakes and pleasurable quakes. Contracting my wall muscles around his steel, his heated satisfaction insu-lated me, and I felt complete. And just when I thought it was over, he grabbed my ass and drove his dick in me ferociously. Sure enough, an-other set of currents had me screaming, squealing, and damn close to death. Now I can relate to what those nymphs on *Desperate Housewives* are thinking when they encounter a true master of his craft. Can you feel what I'm saying? I couldn't get enough.

I wanted more and more of him.

Ladies, what do you do or say when someone who has entered your life is fulfilling all of your fantasies? You don't say shit. You just enjoy every minute of his presence and savor each encounter. Whether his appearance is momentary or lasting, your body is under a spell, and the breathless orgasms that leave you are followed by an incredibly sublime peace.

This is what happened to me, and it all started with a dance. A dance after a rejection, that is. I'll never forget the pain left from that Thursday phone call from Granville. My cup of patience was already at its brim as he worked two of my last three nerves. He had proposed a couple of months back, and he began the disappearing act that men do when they experience cold feet at the thought of marrying an independent Black woman. It was bad enough the poor soul was taking those blue tablets to keep up with my insatiable sex drive; and then had the nerve to lie about it when I found the Viagra in his medicine chest.

When I asked him about the pills, he peered deep into my eyes and said, "They're not mine."

He could have told me the truth, that he was experiencing inadequacies. Let's be real, the chemistry wasn't there. Not only did I have to get acclimated with something pale and pink inside of me—he was a white man, girls—but I had to get used to a whole different rhythm. I could have been patient and understanding. After all, I did love him. Shit, maybe I could have done something like the trick I learned from my cousin where I could deep-throat a nice-sized piece of steel and testicles at the same time. I respect a man's candor, but when he flunked my honesty exam, the voice in my head screamed "Strike one."

Strike two came from his poor imitation of David Copperfield. No-shows on dinner dates, even broken appointments to tighten me up at home. Damn, it was bad enough tolerating this behavior from insecure, intimidated brothers. You know damn well the margin of error was minimal for a chemically erected man from the lighter side.

Little Boy Blue had my birthday weekend to make up for all his transgressions. Yet while on Interstate 4 to Oakland to pick him up, my cell phone rang.

"Hey, boo."

I hated when he called me that. He didn't even say it right. I felt like it was cruel for white men to call sisters that, but as usual, I held my tongue and endured. I quickly learned that his use of the word was the forbearing of bad things, for every time he addressed me as such, I never liked the news that followed. I braced myself for the anvil that was about to be dropped on my head.

"Yeah, what is it?"

"Simone, I hate to tell you this, but something came up in Phoenix that I must tend to, so I won't be able to go to the Napa Valley with you. I'm sorry."

Though this rejection left me feeling crushed, I remained calm while on the road.

"It's okay," I lied. My response was cool and calculating, something on which he picked up.

"Listen, darling, can I take you to dinner when I get back in town on Tuesday?"

"No, Granville, that's okay," My blood began to boil. I hated when he called me darling too.

"Well, can I at least make it up to you, sweetheart?"

"Sure, Granville. I know a way you can do that."

"How's that?"

"Try fucking the next bitch you get involved with without Viagra. Or better yet, why don't you try a penile implant."

I wanted to throw the cell phone from my blue convertible, but my head hurt so bad that all I could do was put my lead foot on the pedal, fly up the freeway doing eighty-five, and hope that my cousin was home.

Fortunately, Ira was there, and we immediately launched phase one of Salvage Simone's Weekend plan. Thursday night was the kick-the white-man-to-the-curb pity party, complete with the tears of letting go, as well as champagne and weed to numb the pain of being stood up.

Friday was get-numbers-for-kicks night at Kimball's nightclub in Jack London Square, and I put on my sexiest red spaghetti-strapped dress. Once there, I danced the night away, seducing and securing the digits of many men.

Ira and I even took time out to shoot pool in the back of the spacious place. So many eyes were on my ass when I reached across the green table to knock the eight ball in the far pocket. As a matter of fact, one dude had the audacity to lean over as if instructing me. Feeling his hot air against my earlobe was annoying enough, but his hard-on rubbing against my backside was downright offensive.

Knowing I had to make my "See with your eyes, not with your dick" position clear, my response to his rudeness sent reverberations throughout the nightclub.

"You mean, I'm supposed to do it like this?" I said innocently.

I jabbed my elbow into his stomach, and the follow-through of my shot caused the butt of the pool stick to land in his rib. In one fell swoop, I made the shot, won the game, and delivered a message to all the perverts in the place. Minnesota Fats had better look out for Sensational Simone Hunter from the Left Side.

Though Ira and I laughed about it all the way to her house, as my head hit her bedroom pillows early that dawn, the reality of my weekend hit home, causing crystal droplets of hurt to roll down sad cheeks of despair. Little did I know, those tears would be kissed away by a master of seduction.

Instead of going to The Fifth Note, a cramped, crowded rowdy spot in Central Oakland, Ira and I adopted on Saturday nights, we returned to Kimball's to hear a live band play. Immediately, I thought we had erred, for as we checked our jackets, an intoxicated playa stumbled into me and almost landed on the seat of his pants.

"Are you okay?" I asked.

"Don't mind me, baby. I'm just falling for you."

Sharing a look of disgust, Ira and I shook our heads and kept it moving. Nearing our seats, corny night at Kimball's continued as another knucklehead came over to us.

"Do you take karate, boo, because your body is kicking," the man said to Ira. It was bad enough that his sad, sorry pick-up line was yelled just as the band wrapped up a Stevie Wonder selection, and the people nearby overheard his stupidity. There was something else kicking, and Ira, always the comedienne as well as fan of hip-hop, made it known to all, imitating her favorite Busta Rhymes song.

"When I came into the club and I smelled your breath, WOO-HAH, you need some Winterfresh." The whole place erupted in laughter, and Howard with Halitosis slinked away. Not even twenty minutes in the place and halfway through my first drink, I was wondering if we made a mistake. The noisy watering hole cross-town looked awfully good.

That thought vanished quickly when I felt the heat of someone looking at me. As if hypnotized, my heart started pounding fast as I looked straight ahead and saw a handsome, baldheaded chocolate figure peering in my direction. Dressed in a gray micro-suede casual suit complete with perfectly coordinated black sweater, he just sat there, staring and smiling. Then, just as he began to affect my senses, he turned his gaze toward the band on the onset of the Gap Band's "Outstanding," and began dancing in his seat.

Sipping from a white zinfandel as I admired his enjoyment of song, the natural rhythmic fluidity of his head bob had my mind racing. *Does he move his hips as loosely on the dance floor? Does he move like that in bed? Can the crazy critter in his mouth strum my moist guitar below? Mmm, I would sure love to find out.* Momentarily mesmerized and fascinatingly fixated in fantasy, the seated sex appeal oozing from him had me transfixed on his every twitch. I was having difficulty sitting still, and the thought of satisfying my curiosity left me hazy in heat.

The trip of imagination that left me sensuously soaked in sexual long-ing came to an abrupt end at the conclusion of the song. The band had wrapped up its evening, and the club deejay's night began. Barely skip-ping a beat, Kenny Lattimore's "Weekend" filled the air, and the object of my desire answered the tame portion of my nocturnal daydream when he rose and began dancing alone. Tall—about six-one, I guessed—sexy as hell, and mahogany brown, his fancy footwork was flawless. Not only was he moving to the time of the heavy bass line, but the swivel at his waistline seemed so effortless.

"Why don't you ask him to dance?" Ira said.

"I'm way ahead of you, girl."

He was still on the floor, grooving as the deejay spun Jaheim's "Just In Case," when I tapped him. Smoothly facing to me with a 180-degree turn, he grabbed my hand as if he read my desires from afar and led me into his world. Moving seductively into his tall, athletic grace, I gyrated my hips slowly, then did a sensuous body ripple.

He smiled.

"I see I got a live one here, huh?"

"I guess so," I responded, blushing.

"Okay, then I'll follow your lead, honey."

Most men describe my presence as sirenlike. I have bedroom eyes; a deep, seductive voice; broad shoulders; a small waist; long, sculpted legs; and D-cup breasts with erect nipples that protrude almost an inch from my mounds. When adorning a silk blouse, a chemise is mandatory, though sometimes the nipples of my girls are visible to all. There have been countless times I've had to pull the eyes of taller men from my cleavage to my face.

This night, however, I didn't mind if this full-blooded, able-bodied chocolate cutie enjoyed my monuments. In fact, at that moment, I wished Mommy had milk, so she could feed her handsome baby with her bottle-cap jewels. The freak in me ran roughshod in my mind as we danced.

To his credit, he remained a gentleman, even as I pressed my body against his chiseled frame and felt his arousal against my stomach. He tried to play it off by returning me to a polite space, but while doing this, he inhaled quickly, a clear indication that he liked what he saw. Another sign that boosted my self-confidence was when his gorgeous brown pupils dilated, a signal of interest for which Ira always told me to look.

"I enjoy the way you move," he commented as he eased me close once more. When the music went from Jaheim to Beyonce, I let him know I appreciated his compliment by emulating Beyonce's hip thrusts, then doing a hip grind to the floor. Returning to his chest, I continued placing sensual innuendoes into my movements by backing my thing up against his torso—nothing sluttish or hoochielike, but enough to hint at a mutual attraction.

Soon, Beyonce left us, and we finished dancing. Thinking he would meander back to his seat, what next left those sexy lips surprised me.

"Can I join you at your table after buying you a drink?"

Just hearing those words from this incredible incarnation of testosterone sent a heated chill through me. My response came after a ragged breath.

"Sure."

"What is your girlfriend drinking?" A shudder went through me like a lightning bolt when I heard the huskiness of his tone. My panties were soaked with intense wont as I wondered if his voice was as commanding when giving orders in bed. Mmm, I sure wanted to find out. Too bad I couldn't say it.

"My cousin and I are drinking white zinfandel."

"Sounds good. Be right back." Returning to Ira and myself in record time with drinks in hand, we finally exchanged introductions. The full-blooded god before us was Mitchell Morrison from New York City, on the coast for a business conference.

"Where are you staying?" Ira asked, rendering me invisible.

"At The Jack London Inn, up the street."

"That's a pretty expensive hotel," Ira commented.

"Tell me about it. I'm paying for the locale, I guess. It's within walking distance from the Bay Area night life, so I guess I can't complain."

"Oakland's night life is nothing compared to San Francisco," Ira announced. "We're going to a jazz restaurant tomorrow night to celebrate Simone's birthday."

Mitchell's eyebrows arched in delight. Seeing that made me blush.

"Why didn't you tell me it was your birthday weekend?" With that bulletin, he ordered us a bottle of champagne. This action finally rid the mute I had become.

"Mitchell, you don't have to do this. You barely know us."

My announcement was met with mock disgust.

"Trust me, Simone, I'm not Big Willie like that. But it is your birthday, and I would like to do something." As if on cue, our Moet arrived, and we proceeded to close the place down with jokes and merriment. Mitchell mentioned that he was dying when Ira did her Busta impersonation, but kept his hysterics inside because he was a foreigner in a strange land.

"Well, let us give you some left-coast hospitality," I responded with a twinge of flirtation in my tone. I guess the libations had given me courage because I can't remember being so forward. I guess his presence also had something to do with it. Oozing sex appeal, every word this chocolate Adonis spoke, every blink of those gorgeous brown eyes had me wanting him to feel the warmth of my center. I had never been the type for one-night stands, but I would have given the thought of being his love slave some serious consideration.

When we were leaving the club, Mitchell asked what we were doing thereafter, and once we told him we were going to Lake Merritt Bakery for breakfast, he asked if he could tag along.

"Don't you have to get up early in the morning?" Ira asked.

"Are y'all trying to get rid of me?" he countered with an adorable expression.

I just wanted to hug him.

"You can come along, if you want to," I said sheepishly.

You should have seen the sparkle that came from his eyes.

Over breakfast, our guest was both informative and funny as he described the Big Apple and its eclectic personalities. I actually got a feel of the city that never sleeps from his everyone-is-in-a-hurry-to-go-nowhere tales of impatience.

"It's like that in downtown Frisco," Ira responded.

"I wish I could be around to see for myself," he said.

"When are you leaving?" I asked.

"Monday afternoon," he announced. "JetBlue-ing it out of here so I can make it to work on Tuesday."

Just enough time for me to jump your bones, baby, my mind said. When the dirty thought left my mouth, however, it came out as, "What line of work are you in?"

"I'm a computer technician at a law firm," he announced.

"We both work in payroll at an advertising firm," Ira said. "By the way, I love your accent."

"My accent? Y'all are the ones with the accents," he said, smiling. "Listen to the way you pronounce water. WAH-TUR."

"So what, you say it like this: WHU-TUH," I countered.

"Don't hate on the left coast," Ira defended, bringing goodhearted laughter from us all.

The hilarity dissolved with his inquiry about our relationship situations.

"How come two attractive women are alone on a beautiful weekend like this? Where are your men?"

Ira and I lowered our heads briefly.

"You've got to be kiddin' me," Mitchell continued. "Don't tell me both of you ladies are available."

"Well, I have a Monday dinner date with a guy who seems like a keeper," Ira responded optimistically.

"Good luck with that," Mitchell said.

My reply was flat and unemotional.

"I just came out of something," I said.

Ira suddenly became my unofficial spokesperson. "Yeah, her asshole fiancé stood her up. They were supposed to go away this weekend, and he canceled at the last minute."

Mitchell nodded in sympathy. "I'm sorry, Simone."

"To make matters worse," Ira continued, "the motherfucker was taking Viagra just to—"

"Ira, that's a little too much information to be revealing to a total stranger," I interrupted. "Forgive my cousin, Mitchell. She never liked him."

Remarkably, Mitchell's expression remained unchanged during the revelation, though he did elicit a smile from us, whistling the theme from one of those Enzyte commercials.

"What about you?" Ira asked. "I know you must have them beating down your door back home."

What I saw next was both touching and revealing, and it just broke my heart. That smile that lit up Mitchell's handsome countenance and filled his face with joy disappeared when he replied, "She didn't want me. Twice." The look of complete pain when he said this had me aching inside for him, yet I liked the fact that he was not one of these men who hid his emotions.

"Damn, that's messed up," Ira said.

"She told me that our destiny was as friends. This came after returning to my life after a previous breakup. Seven months of wasted time."

"I'm sorry" was all I could say.

"It's cool, though. If I was spoken for, I probably wouldn't have let you dance so close, Simone." His energy returned, producing a smile with more wattage than before. That my name adjoined the tribute made me blush, as he continued. "Listen, if you ladies don't mind, I would love to accompany you two to San Francisco tomorrow evening."

Ira and I responded as one. "Sure."

We dropped him back at the hotel, and he wanted us to call him once we got in. Silly me, still in a trance from his early-morning aura, forgot to take his number; thank goodness Ira exchanged digits with him.

Sunday afternoon quickly turned to evening twilight, and as I sat in Ira's bathtub, my mind could not escape the fantasy of Mitchell inside of my pleasure chest. Pervading and perverting my brain once more, the thought of him swirling his tongue within the watery well of my core had my fingers dancing at the entrance to my garden. Probing and pleasing me with an active, oral apparatus, my chocolate fantasy made my labia tingle and turned my clit into a hot zone in this dream world. I slowly slipped a finger within myself as I imagined his slithering object trickling against then invading my femininity.

"I bet he can eat pussy well," I mumbled. Envisioning the combination of those full lips and fluttering butterfly between them munching on me had my clit thick and sensitive to both touches—Mitchell in fantasy with that lovely lizard darting from my pussy to anus, and mine in this soapy resting place. I squealed and struggled against the orgasm, from which I would try to flee, but of course, the inevitable tackled me, and a familiar sensation of release overwhelmed me.

Suddenly, my trip to Fantasy Island was disrupted by a concerned voice.

"Are you okay in there?" Ira yelled.

Too embarrassed to respond, the naughty girl in me needed to be punished, so I obliged by sliding underwater to a sudsy grave.

After drying off, I put on a sexy black leather miniskirt, and accompanied that by pouring into a silk red button down blouse and black pumps. Making my way to the mirror, I surveyed my attire and beamed proudly.

"Not bad for forty-two years old," I announced. Though I didn't have the courage to say it, I hoped that Mitchell would like what he saw.

Arriving at the hotel in Ira's black Altima, I placed a call to Mitchell's room and received no answer. Turning right toward the elevator, my heart stopped as the object of my desire approached me. He was immaculately attired in a rust-colored suede suit tailored to fit his streamlined body perfectly and complemented with a chocolate sweater with rust designs and matching boots. The smile on his face illuminated the lobby as he approached me with his hands behind his back, concealing something.

"Happy Birthday, Simone," he purred sexily, then presented me with a bouquet of red roses. Adding a soft kiss to my left cheek melted me further.

"Thank you, Mitchell," I said, blushing.

"Where are my roses?" Ira asked as we approached the car.

"Hold on," Mitchell said. Suddenly returning to the lobby area, he reached behind the registration counter and began walking back to the vehicle, again obscuring an object. The concierge gave it away with his cheesy grin.

"Of course, I couldn't forget about you," Mitchell announced, presenting my cuz with an ensemble of pink and red carnations.

"That's so sweet, Mitchell," I stated. "I can't believe you thought of her as well."

He blushed. "It's nothing. Really."

I loved his modesty.

"Don't think you're getting any from me because you gave me some flowers," Ira announced, bringing a howl from us as we drove off.

Though our conversation started with us speaking in general terms, I couldn't help but notice that Mitchell was a man of few chosen words, yet articulately verbal enough to confirm my theory that his brain was as sexy as the rest of him. As we crossed the Bay Bridge, the state of excitement in our suitor's voice increased, like a little kid.

"How far are we from Pac Bell Ballpark?" he asked.

"Not far," Ira and I responded in unison.

"Can we drive by?"

Ira the navigator and her front seat tour guide met our guest's request by motoring past Fisherman's Wharf, then by the home of Barry Bonds and the San Francisco Giants. Though nightfall surrounded us, it did nothing to diminish the spectacular iridescence of the stadium.

Mitchell loved it.

"Thanks, ladies. So, what's the name of this jazz club?"

"We'll show you in a little bit. In the meantime, why don't you just sit back and enjoy the Bay Area scenery?" I suggested. He did just that, commenting occasionally on the maze of hills that embodied the streets of San Francisco.

"It's like a series of rollercoasters," he added.

Somehow, that word left me wet and wanting, for I wondered if making love to him would be like riding the highest rollercoaster. Would his caress leave me fearful, excited, and anticipatory at the same time, much like a great ride does while ascending that first climb? Would his strokes leave me breathless and gulping for air? Would I get the same intense rush I receive when I climb higher and higher into physical bliss? Would my scales of ecstasy teeter out of control with each deep thrust inside me? Once at my sexual apex, would the orgasmic drop leave my head spinning in pleasure as I shuddered and twitched then begged for more? Would Mitchell excite me so much so that I would become an insatiable queen in heat, not getting enough of him, always wanting more and more of the thrill of the great rollercoaster between his legs? Mmm, I would sure love to find out. I hoped my face didn't betray these thoughts and reveal my attraction to him. But if he had to do a thong check, I would have been done for.

Anyway, we arrived at Rasselas', a quaint little jazz bar in the heart of the city. It was there that my fantasy entered into that strange dimension where orgasms in mind came to life, and truth met fiction.

Once seated, the band broke into "I Like The Way You Move" by Outkast, which surprised us because Ira and I thought it only played jazz.

Mitchell immediately grabbed Ira's hand and led her to the circular, carpeted center where the band jammed and danced. My God, I enjoyed my voyeuristic view. Placing my cousin's hands on his waist, they launched into a gyration that would have put a male stripper to shame. I never saw a man move his hips so loosely, except for those calypso dancers at West Indian carnivals. I couldn't help but imagine what his horizontal tango was like. The thought of me finding out left me in a tizzy, warm all over.

Cold water splashed on that vision, however, when I saw him whisper something in Ira's ear, which brought a laugh. Without delay, my thoughts shifted from me feeling him to being happy for Ira, which saddened me slightly. The sentiment was a tolerable disappointment, however, because I knew if something jumped off, I would get the juicy details later.

After the music stopped, my cousin and former desire returned to the table at which we were perched, with Mitchell facing me.

"Damn, you can move," Ira said.

He blushed. "I've been told that before."

It was at that point I got up to answer nature's calling.

Suddenly, Mitchell rose and grabbed my hand. "Simone, could you do me a favor?"

Intrigue and curiosity etched my face as I responded, "Sure."

"Take off one of your shoes."

Following his orders, I obliged, and was met with this intense stare, like I was being sized up. *What's going on?* I thought. *What made me do that?* That steamy gaze was followed with an unnoticeable nod to everyone except me. I saw it—no, check that, I felt it. And it scared me.

Returning from the bathroom, I noticed that Mitchell and my cousin had switched seats, placing me next to this undeniably attractive man. That he got up to let me in instead of sliding over made the moment all the more intriguing.

"So, Simone," he asked with an impish grin, "is there anything else you want for your birthday?"

"I couldn't ask for anything else," I replied. "I made a new friend from New York City, and I'm having a wonderful time." Considering the way it started and the occurrences thereafter, I didn't know how it could be topped. Up to this point it had been my best birthday ever. In hindsight, I couldn't believe how daft I was.

"Oh, I see," Mitchell responded. My thoughts were all over the place during this exchange. I looked to my cousin with one of those *I'm still trying to figure out what's going on* looks, and my nervous gaze was met with a taunting glance, as if she knew exactly where Mitchell's inquisition was headed.

The quartet broke into some jazz, and at that point Ira made the comment that they sounded awful. After we finished our drinks, we ended up at Mel's Diner, near the Marina in Pacific Heights. That's when things got a little clearer, thanks to my ever-observant cousin.

After having our meals, I again excused myself to the ladies' room, only to find that with my return, Mitchell was again seated next to me and reached for my hand, peered into my eyes, and started smiling.

"Simone, is there anything I could give you for your birthday?"

"Mitchell, your presence is sufficient enough. I'm really enjoying your company." I became fearful and nervous, and for the life of me, I couldn't imagine why. My heart was pounding in my chest, and I started to clench and unclench my free hand. But I didn't pull my other hand away.

"I see," he said once more, this time with a look of disappointment creasing his face. Then he placed his hands on the table. I longed to reach out and stroke them. Tormenting myself with the observation of his long, thick digits, the torture continued as I thought of how desperately I wanted to prove that the size of a man's penis matches the shape and size of his fingers. But I restrained that notion because I still had no clue.

Suddenly, the waitress came and disrupted my vision by bringing me a slice of chocolate cake and balloons.

"Happy Birthday, Simone," Mitchell said while kissing me full frontal; not a French kiss, but a seductive peck that left my lips and pussy afire with desire.

My response came after a blush. "Thank you, Mitchell."

"Simone, is there anything else you desire on this special day?"

By that point, I was in a tizzy, trying to figure out why he kept asking me about a birthday present.

"Mitchell, meeting you was one of the best presents of my life, and I can't see how anything can surpass that."

Ira, sitting across from me, just shook her head in disgust.

"I understand," Mitchell said once more then excused himself to the bathroom. At that point, Ira clued me in completely.

"Girl, you had better let this man make you feel good, or I'll slap you silly. Simone, *he* wants to be your birthday present."

It took a second for me to come to grips with this, but when I did, I was floored.

"Ira, you know how I am," I responded, reminding her that I wasn't into one-night stands. You see, I have always been the one who preferred monogamous relationships. Growing up, guys knew who to call for the quick fix, and they knew I didn't swing that way. Some had the audacity to call me looking for other women, and I would ask why. They would laugh, and say that I wasn't that type of girl. I always thought of myself as special, and when I shared myself completely, that was real special, even at forty-two years of age. That's why I was torn. Would it be special for Mitchell, even if it were for a night?

"Girl, I know that, but your time is about due. Besides, he's polite, cute, and I think he really likes you. Cuz, I got a real good feeling about him."

"But he was talking to you on the dance floor at Rasselas'," I argued.

"He was talking to me about you, Simone."

"I have to think about this." That's what I told her, but hearing her words made a feeling come over me, one that shook my soul. It wasn't a lustful one, but something much deeper, like an aching desire for a romantic connection of mind and spirit. I wanted to enfold Mitchell in my body and reciprocate the special feeling with which he left me. My sugar walls tingled as I envisioned him kissing me all over, then parting me and penetrating me with strokes that seemed familiar. My muscles would clamp around his erection and milk the warm seed of pleasure right into the protection he wore. Then I would remove it and nibble on his swollen tip, because I wanted him to feel as good as he made me feel. My mind wanted it, my body craved it, and my soul yearned for it, but would my mouth say it?

Mitchell came from the bathroom and felt the need to add fuel to my indecision by kissing me once more, this time with tongue. The way he fluttered it in my mouth let me know he was a master at eating pussy. I didn't retreat from his boldness or from what came next from his luscious brim.

"I want to be your birthday present, Simone. Can I make love to you this evening?" he finally uttered.

What could I say? This man had me feeling like I'd known him a lifetime. My inflamed tunnel simmered as it yearned for some serious plunging from his bold, brazen erection. I wanted my lips, then moist throat and saliva to encompass his phallus and pleasure him. Just as he had done with his presence this weekend, I wanted to give to him the joy he returned to my flagging spirits.

And I will, I decided privately.

Verbally and physically, my actions would not and could not indicate such. So, as we left the restaurant and drove back to Oakland, I remained coy. You see, Momma wanted Daddy to think about what he was asking to be unleashed upon him—that is, if I chose him to satisfy me. I had to control my love slave, even though I knew my birthday present would probably turn me out once between those hotel sheets. We drove to Ira's house, and upon our arrival, the risqué seductress began to emerge.

"Ira, I'll drive Mitchell back to his hotel," I announced boldly.

Hearing that nervous gulp from the backseat made me wet. After getting out, Ira and I shared sisterly hugs and a look that men never realize; the one knowing exchange we make when we can take all of a man sexually and leave him whimpering like a little boy wanting more of his favorite candy.

"Let him take care of you, cuz," she whispered in my ear.

"I will," I responded. I flipped the script on my birthday present by opening the door for him to my convertible. Sharing a quick glance, I think he noticed my sexual aggression, but I didn't care. After all, it was my birthday.

Arriving at the hotel, then his room, I was ready to give myself to him. But ever the gentleman Mitchell was. He fixed me a cordial from his bar, and as our glasses clinked, my heartbeat screamed, "Take him, girl."

"Here's to birthdays," he said.

"Yes, my birthday," I replied.

"I'm so glad you're here. I thought you might think of me as a dog for desiring you so much."

"No, I don't, Mitchell," I assured as Ira's voice reminded me to "…let this man make you feel good." Fighting off a self-depreciating moment, I thought about the pain Granville administered to me, and a single tear rolled down my cheek.

Somehow, Mitchell felt my thoughts. "He really hurt you, didn't he?" he inquired.

"Yes, he did." As I said this, that one droplet had morphed into a waterfall, and as I reached into my purse for a tissue, I felt steamy lips kissing each side of my face, wiping away the pain.

"Simone, after tonight, no man will ever hurt you again."

Did he know something I didn't? To this point, I couldn't explain my actions, which were causing me to feel a slight twinge of guilt. I was giving myself to a stranger who was passing through on a business trip, and he was telling me that no man would ever hurt me again. What could he mean by that?

Yet somehow, my instincts told me to trust him, that everything would be okay. The serious look in Mitchell's eyes melted me as he made it known in words that I was in a soothing haven.

"Let me be your comfort zone tonight, Simone," he said. And with those words, I let go of all inhibitions. Mitchell's tender kisses found my face, landing on my forehead, grazing my eyes, my cheeks and chin. Soon, he found my brim, and I welcomed him in hungrily. Those soft, full lips of his tasted good as we began a kissing marathon that lasted moments yet seemed like hours. Tongues and teeth dancing together, we stood and pressed our bodies together as we did a clothed dance of passion. His hungry hardness pressed against my belly, but it wasn't enough for me. Rising on my toes, I felt his dick at my warm, wet core and breathed heavily. *Yes, Daddy,* my mind screamed as our mouths maddeningly mingled. *Take Mommy on this fantasy she so desperately needs.* My hands probed him and felt the arch in his back that told me he had movement in those hips. I loved the feel of him in my arms.

Before long, my birthday present did some of his own exploring. With light, pleasurable touches, he caressed my frame, and a fire ran through me, causing a tremor. I wanted the hard needle at his groin to inject me as soon as possible, but I could tell he had a slow hand, which I appreciated so much. Grasping, then gently groping my abundant orbs, his hands made their way to my large nipples, and through my blouse and bra, he made them stand at attention by pinching them. After kissing them through the clothes, he slid his hands to my round backside. As he squeezed each buttock with his large mitts, I struggled to contain the twitching waves of pleasure that came from my vagina. Teasing my neck and torturing the soft curvature of my shoulder with his titillating, tantalizing, tireless creature, every movement of his lips on my frame had me groaning with a mixture of anticipation and arousal. Chile, what he was doing with that tongue had me wanting him to eat my pussy as if he were famished. Wanting to fuck his brains out, I had to have more and more of him.

"Hands up," I ordered, and he complied. Removing his sweater, I sucked on his cute nipples as I massaged his baldhead. Using swirling, wet circular motions with my mouth, I heard his approval through a deep baritone groan.

"Do that shit, Simone," he uttered. Then, just as suddenly, he came to.

"What's wrong?" I asked, circumventing the momentum of our foreplay.

"I'm supposed be pleasing you, right? Lay down, Simone," he commanded.

With that, I flopped back on the king-size bed. I could tell that my beauty impaled his heart with need because he ripped open my blouse. It was an expensive one, but for some strange reason, I didn't care that buttons flew all over the place. I wanted him to touch me, tease me, and torture me in every way imaginable, then tame me. I needed more and more of him.

I felt his hands as he slowly yet seductively undressed me. Cupping my breasts with care and pushing them together, he placed both of my long, luscious nipples in his mouth. The way his head tilted to the side as he hungrily lapped my bosom drove me crazy.

Propelled upward with his tender, yet animalistic touch, I thought I would have cardiac arrest the way he played with my frame, and I wore a helpless, hopeless expression, as if I had no control of my body. This man was good.

Soon, after he undressed my bottom, he made his presence known in my womanhood by tickling the sensitive exterior with his fingers, then sensuously sliding a digit in. Screaming out in ecstasy, my torso synchronized with the movements of his finger, and I damn near lost my mind.

The best was yet to come, for my birthday present lowered himself to the entrance of my pussy and probed me with that tongue for which I had been waiting. Wiggling and writhing in excitement, he locked his brim to my furnace and sucked my saucy, succulent sweet spot as if trying to retrieve the secret ingredients of a powerful pussy potion. That paintbrush of a tongue fluttered like an escaped moth, and he made hungry munching sounds with his mouth like my shaved snatch was his favorite meal. Matching his fingers and jaws with eager hip thrusts, my cunt was sopping from his oral pleasure. Giving off heat and scent, I was ready for that full, shivering orgasm that I hadn't experienced in some time.

But he wasn't ready for me to come. Unhurried and unrushed, his mouth left the insides of my walls and sucked my clit between his teeth. Humming against me like a vibrator, he licked the folds of my femininity like it was his favorite ice cream cone. I almost died for that orgasm to leave me, but I fought it with every muscle in my thick frame.

But not for long, because a singular order came from below that released the pleasurable tension that built within.

"Come," he said. "Come now, Simone."

How could I not when I heard his husky demand? My body tensed as a spiral of uncontrollable delight rippled through me. That infernolike feeling swallowed my frame inch by inch and brought a throaty release from a voice unfamiliar to me.

"Shit, yes," I bellowed as my body twitched. The voice left me fearful, for its foreign growl was accompanied by extended alien shudders of my legs. As I convulsed, he sucked my toes while massaging my feet.

This man had me climbing walls, and as he unwrapped my real present from its clothed packaging, I wanted to please him as much as he did me. But when I saw the aroused equipment at his groin, I had my doubts. Mitchell Morrison was an awesome specimen, about nine thick inches worth.

"Mmm, that's a nice birthday present," I said, panting as he lay on the bed. Damn, that tool looked so good standing at attention. I loved his huge, violet, precum glistening tip, and it had a hook that drenched my pussy even more. The wild, wet animal between my legs needed that huge tranquilizer.

Not yet, however. The need for Mommy to suck that chocolate nightstick was even more urgent. Lowering my lips to his engorged flesh, I employed my teeth, my saliva, and the strength of my jaw and throat so that he would feel a mouth around his member like he never had before. Squeezing his scrotum, the look on his face had a mixture of disbelief and bliss as my oral cavity widened and widened, then took all of him and a small portion of his testicles in. But not for long because he was so hard that I gagged and almost messed up our moment. Lifting my mouth off his erection, I noticed it was stiffer, as I had to pry this tool off his stomach to resume my oral stimulation of him.

His expression of lust when my tongue ran down the sensitive underside of his shaft brought a wicked grin to my face. The challenge of deep-throating him had me wanting to suck all his juices from him, so I resubmerged him into my oral cavity. Dazed and dizzy in delight, I knew he loved my talent, for his breath became ragged and choppy. Grunting and panting, every muscle in his body was tense, as if he needed that salty release to leave him. As he neared his climax, I fingered myself so that we could experience simultaneous pleasure. I felt his balls tighten as I stroked them with my free hand while bobbing my head up and down on him.

"Take it all, Simone," he ordered as his hips arched off the bed. Then, came the warm spurts of satisfaction I had been dying to taste since I laid eyes on his magic wand. Mmm, that shit was good too. So good that the spasms I experienced from another orgasm had me shaking all over.

I licked the spillage of his semen off my hand and nibbled on his sensitive, still swollen bulb, then he pulled me to his face and we kissed leisurely. Pausing ever so slightly, we both smiled as we both knew what was next.

It was such a turn-on to see him barely fit into that Magnum Trojan. That alone sent shivers coursing through me. Repositioning ourselves, juices of anticipation trickled down my thighs as I anticipated his massive tool entering me. As soaked as I was, at first it hurt a little, as he was so thick. Soon, his slow strokes eased the pain, and my body began accommodating him. My tunnel of passion surrounded his stiffness like an Isotoner glove to a hand, and I loved it.

Pretty soon, the tempo of my birthday present's strokes increased as my cavern became more accommodating. Not only did his dick feel good along my walls, but that hook hit places that destroyed my senses, making me forget everything wonderful that culminated with the moment. I could only concentrate on the present, the now, the sensation of his skin slapping against mine. He sent jolts through me that left me gasping for air.

Soon, our bodies moved together as if we could have been doing a tribal dance. My cunny was making squishing sounds like never before. It flowed so much juice that I thought water was coming from a faucet.

"Mitchell," I said, moaning, "you see what you're doing to me? Do you hear my pussy talking to you? Do you…Do you?"

"Yes, baby, I hear it. Happy Birthday, Simoooooonnneee," he responded.

Over and over, he pounded me in a good way. He owned that kitty that evening, making me shimmer, squirm, shudder, squeal, and shake as tidal wave after tidal wave of hot orgasms crashed through me.

But my gift needed relief as well, so after being satisfied with his staying power for an hour or so, I squeezed hard as the pulsing of his member sent a stream of his liquid love into the condom. Feeling his release reach the top of me, I wish I had known him better because I would have let him go inside me bare so the heated caramel could have cooled off my tunnel as it oozed down my walls. That's a good feeling. But the one with which he left me was sufficient for the moment, for his orgasm ignited every nerve in my body, from temple to toes. The sensation I felt next was indescribable, and all I can remember is that I couldn't stop shaking.

Moments later, we collapsed in each other's arms, like mated insects, breathing heavily in unison. I could not have even more satisfied with my birthday present. I couldn't think of anything that could surpass this moment in time.

Except...of... course...what's... gooiinng...onn between...my legss... assss I... fiinnishh... thiiss... storrryy... "Damnn, M-Mitchell, please...come...up...for... air...."

"Baby, you taste so good. I'm surprised I didn't mess up your flow sooner."

Between the sheets
with the authors...

Goldie Banks is a newcomer on the erotic scene. At present, she is working on several writing projects and plans to hit the literary scene by storm. Banks resides in Baltimore, Maryland.

E. Geoffrey Depp was born on 1965 in Toledo, Ohio. He was raised by his mother in Dayton, Ohio, where he graduated from high school in 1983. In 1986, he joined the United States Army and received an honorable discharge after eight years of service. Depp has received numerous awards from the International Society of Poets and has been published in four of their compilations.

His favorite authors are Maya Angelou, Paul Lawrence Dunbar, and Langston Hughes. He enjoys gospel, jazz, blues, and reggae music. His background taught him that there is a fine line between racism and pride in your race. Above all, he believes never forget God and who you are.

One day Depp aspires to change someone's way of thinking and improve their life through his poetic works.

Nancey Flowers paid tribute to her parents by using their native Jamaica, West Indies, as the setting for her first novel *A Fool's Paradise*. Flowers attended Morgan State University in Baltimore, Maryland, where she received her bachelor's degree in mass communications with a minor in journalism.

Flowers is also the author of *No Strings Attached* and the #1 Essence Bestselling novel *Shattered Vessels*. She is a contributing author in the erotica sensation *Twilight Moods* and the anthology *Proverbs for the People*.

Flowers served as program director for The Harlem Book Fair, is a contributor to *Black Issues Book Review*, and is former managing editor of *QBR The Black Book Review*. She is also editor-in-chief of *Game Sports* magazine.

Penelope Flynn, though a newcomer to the erotic genre, is no newcomer to writing. An avid reader and writer from childhood, Flynn's love for myth, legend, and fairytales, as well as traditional, classical, and modern works has resulted in the creation of a sophisticated, original, and accessible writing style that draws in readers, rendering them willing captives of Flynn's fantasy and modern erotic romances.

Humorously self-described as the Coco Chanel of erotica, Flynn illustrates in visually exquisite detail the tremendous depths and dizzying heights of human erotic and emotional entanglement. With several short stories to her credit and two novel-length works in progress, Flynn is dedicated to exploring the subtleties and intricacies of adult interpersonal encounters in contemporary and whimsical settings.

Born and raised on the east coast, Flynn has enjoyed significant travel in Europe and the Mediterranean and currently makes her home in the southwest.

William Fredrick Cooper is the author of *Six Days In January* (Strebor Books, 2004), a trailblazing novel that explores the issues and insecurities of black men concerning love. The Bronx resident has received rave reviews in periodicals in England (*Pride Magazine*, November 2004), Canada, and the United States.

Affectionately known as "Mr. Romance," Cooper is a contributing author to several anthologies: Zane's *SISTERGIRLS.COM* (Strebor Books, August 2003), *Twilight Moods* (Flowers In Bloom Publishing, August 2002), and Zane's *Caramel Flava* (Summer 2006). The secretary of Brother 2 Brother Symposium Inc., a creative initiative that encourages Black men and teens to read, he has served as host, conference facilitator, and moderator to many literary events throughout the United States and Canada.

Anna J is an erotica writer who also walks the runway in her spare time as a full-figured model. Coauthor of *Stories to Excite You: Menage Quad,* Anna put her writing skills to the test in this hot collaboration that was released during the fall 2004.

Her debut novel, *My Woman His Wife*, is high on the charts and a good read for those who enjoy a steamy love affair with a little bit of drama to boot. And if your Anna J cravings still aren't satisfied, you can also find another hot story of hers in *Fetish: A Compilation of Erotic Stories* in bookstores nationwide. Anna J was born and raised in Philly, where she still resides and is currently working on her sophomore novel, *Aftermath*, which is the sequel to *My Woman His Wife*.

Kenji Jasper is a native of Washington, DC. He was first paid for his writing at the age of thirteen. Since then, his work has appeared in *The Village Voice, VIBE, Essence, Atlanta Magazine, The Chicago Sun-Times, The Charlotte Observer,* and on National Public Radio. He is the author of three novels: *Dark, Dakota Grand,* and *Seeking Salamanca Mitchell,* all published by Random House books. *The House on Childress Street,* his first work of nonfiction, will be published in January 2006. For more information on Jasper visit his website at www.kenjijasper.com.

Natosha Gale Lewis is a native of Philadelphia. She is the bestselling author of two adult novels, *Only Fools Gamble Twice* and *Men Cheat Women Experiment*. Lewis recently released her first children's story, *The Adventures of Squally the Squirrel,* a book about stranger-danger issues. Lewis attended Rosemont College where she received a bachelor of arts in business communication and Webster University where she received her masters of arts in communication management.

Currently, Lewis is hard at work on several literary works. She presently resides in New Castle, Delaware, and is the proud mother of one daughter.

Scottie Lowe is the founder, CEO, and the creative driving force behind www.AfroerotiK.com, the most unique website dedicated to showing the true beauty of Black sexuality in all its many facets. AfroerotiK creates customized and personalized erotic stories written from a decidedly Afrocentric perspective and embraces diversity in sexual expression. Tired of erotica that portrayed Black women as man-stealing gold diggers and brainless nymphos, and Black men as thugs, players, and emotionally immature dick slingers, she decided it was time to write erotica that represented the complexity and full spectrum of African Americans. Look for her highly controversial upcoming book, *In Loving Color,* to create quite a stir with literary works of art that are dripping with sensuality and explore groundbreaking, socially relevant topics. It will include breathtaking photography that will be sure to arouse and stimulate intense passion and establish *In Loving Color* as the standard for Black erotica.

Marissa Monteilh (Mon-tay), a former model, television news reporter, and commercial actress, originally self-published her first book, *May December Souls,* in November 2000. By the following January, Monteilh signed a two-book deal with Harper Collins, who rereleased *May December Souls* in March 2002, then released her second book, *The Chocolate Ship,* in January 2003.

In June 2003, Monteilh inked another deal with HarperCollins for her third title, *Hot Boyz,* which was released to rave reviews in May 2004. In July 2004, Marissa signed a two-book deal with Kensington Books. *Make Me Hot,* the story of how desiring beauty can get ugly, will be released in January 2006 through Kensington's Dafina imprint.

Monteilh is cowriting two books, one on fateful love called *Never Say Never,* and the, a other book of nonfiction, called *The Crown Prince,* explores the life of her father, a well-known saxophone player.

Maryann Reid, a graduate of Fordham University, recently received her masters of fine arts degree from the University of Miami. She is the author of *Use Me or Lose Me, Sex and the Single Sister,* and *Marry Your Baby Daddy,* published by St. Martin's Press. Reid is known for her witty, sexually charged stories of single career women determined to balance it all in their lives and control their own destinies. Currently working on her fourth novel, Reid is a relationship advisor and a frequent guest on radio and television talk shows. She lives in Brooklyn, New York.

Dara Tariq a native of Detroit, resides in the North Carolina Smoky Mountains where she is pursuing a graduate degree in psychology. In addition to writing erotic fiction, Tariq hosts enlightening sex workshops. She is working on a how-to guide for exciting sex as well as an anthology of her short stories. You can contact Tariq at daratariq@aol.com, and she welcomes your visit to www.daratariq.com.

Jamez Williams is a writer from Brooklyn, New York. He launched his literary career when he contributed his first short story entitled "The Question" for the acclaimed book *Souls of My Brothers*. A consummate movie buff, Williams loves to paint his stories and characters with a cinematic tone matched with a strong emphasis on dialogue. He is currently working on several titles for launch in 2007.

Winslow Wong has been a persona on the internet as an erotica writer with his website, loveworks4all.com, which highlights up-and-coming African American erotic fiction writers. This is his first time being published in print form. Wong lives in New York City and intends to move from the web to print completely over the next two years.

Twilight Moods

Available in stores

"An explosive collection of some of the most sensual erotica from today's hottest up-and-coming authors."

–E. Lynn Harris, *A Love of My Own*

"Playful, erotic, sensual, seductive…*Twilight Moods* touches the pleasure dome."

–QBR, The Black Book Review

Twilight Moods brings you stories from a dazzling array of today's hottest authors. Prepare yourself because your temperature will rise as Timmothy B. McCann gives it to you "Fuller, Deeper, Smoother" while Courtney Parker is "Holdin' It Down" on her end. Joylynn M. Jossel wants to know if you've been "Daydreaming at Night" and Sandra A. Ottey helps you start your workday with her "Blue-Collar Lover." Lolita Files spices up lunch with a little "Bobby Q's Sauce." Rochelle Alers steams up the evening with a hot and seductive "Anniversary."

These sensual narratives will make you "Twist" like Tracy Grant's story and bring you back to read them over and over. Whether you're in the mood day or night, whenever the time is right, pick up *Twilight Moods* and as Eric E. Pete says, "Please Come Again."

No Strings Attached

Available in stores

By #1 Essence bestselling author Nancey Flowers

Please accept this invitation to:

Reason: Misplaced dick in another woman
Time: 3:40 P.M.
Date: May 20, 1999

Felice Jackson is sexy, single, and satisfied—or so she claims. She is an affluent, thirty-something entrepreneur who is partial owner of the successful firm Jackson and Jackson Financial Consultants. The only problem is her very active sexual relationship with her ex-husband and business partner, Bedford Jackson.

Felice is disgusted with men, but not enough to shut them out of her life physically. She enjoys the touch, smell, and taste of men too much to deprive herself. Instead she decides to stand at the helm of life and call the shots in relationships. If a man can do it, Felice can too. She isn't going to shed another tear for these tired-ass men.

Felice enjoys her no-strings-attached creed—until her secret past collides with her present.

More titles to whet your palette...

Make Me Hot – Marissa Monteilh
The Chocolate Ship – Marissa Monteilh
Hot Boyz – Marissa Monteilh
May December Souls – Marissa Monteilh
Dr. Feelgood (January 2007) – Marissa Monteilh
Sex and the Single Sister – Maryann Reid
Use Me or Lose Me – Maryann Reid
Chocolate Kisses – Maryann Reid
Marry Your Baby Daddy – Maryann Reid
Mr. Satisfaction – Maryann Reid
My Woman His Wife – Anna J
Aftermath – Anna J
Fetish – Erotica (Anna J)
Men Cheat, Women Experiment – Natosha Gale Lewis
Only Fool's Gamble Twice – Natosha Gale Lewis
Twilight Moods – Erotica
Six Days In January – William Fredrick Cooper
There's Always a Reason – William Fredrick Cooper
Sistergirls.com – Erotica (William Fredrick Cooper)
Caramel Flava – Erotica (William Fredrick Cooper)
Seeking Salamanca – Kenji Jasper
No Strings Attached – Nancey Flowers
Shattered Vessels – Nancey Flowers
The Criss Cross – Crystal Lacey Winslow
Life, Love & Loneliness – Crystal Lacey Winslow
Four Degrees of Heat – Anthology (Crystal Lacey Winslow)
All You Can Eat: A Sensualist's Buffet – Penelope Flynn
Crave, Throes, Bliss – Penelope Flynn
Blackfunk I – Michael Presley
Blackfunk II – Michael Presley
Blackfunk III – Michael Presley
An All Night Man – Erotica
Making Love In the Rain – Marlon Green